a brand-new

The Wallflower Academy

Miss Pike's Wallflower Academy is a finishing school designed to find even the most unconventional of debutantes a husband. And this latest cohort of young women aren't your *typical* wallflowers. Follow the girls—abandoned by their families, jilted by ex-lovers and running from their scandalous pasts—as they shed their "wallflower" status and find love!

In *Least Likely to Win a Duke*

Gwen's hopes of making an advantageous match are slim until she *literally* bumps into a duke. But Gwen knows nothing can come of their attraction... not with the secret she's keeping!

And look out for Rilla and Finlay's story coming soon!

Author Note

This book wouldn't exist without a great number of people. Anyone missed from the list is entirely my error, as are any mistakes that you find (please don't look).

Mary and Gordon Murdoch

My wonderful husband

Stephanie Booth

Amy Rose Bennett

Kathryn Le Veque

Awo Ibrahim

Carly Byrne

Hannah Rossiter

Carolyn Smalley

Krista Oliver

Ruth Machanda

The Harlequin typesetting and proofreading teams

EMILY E K MURDOCH

Least Likely to Win a Duke

Recycling programs for this product may not exist in your area.

ISBN-13: 978-1-335-59593-5

Least Likely to Win a Duke

For questions and comments about the quality of this book, please contact us at CustomerService@Harlequin.com.

Harlequin Enterprises ULC
22 Adelaide St. West, 41st Floor
Toronto, Ontario M5H 4E3, Canada
www.Harlequin.com

Printed in U.S.A.

USA TODAY bestselling author **Emily E K Murdoch** is read in multiple languages around the world. Enjoy sweet romances as Emily Murdoch and steamy romances as Emily E K Murdoch. Emily's had a varied career to date: from examining medieval manuscripts to designing museum exhibitions to working as a researcher for the BBC to working for the National Trust. Her books range from England in 1050 to Texas in 1848, and she can't wait for you to fall in love with her heroes and heroines!

Books by Emily E K Murdoch

The Wallflower Academy

Least Likely to Win a Duke

is Emily E K Murdoch's debut for Harlequin Historical.

Look out for more books from Emily E K Murdoch coming soon!

For my parents,

Who encouraged me to write when I couldn't.

For my husband,

Who emboldened me to write when I wasn't.

And for my wonderful readers,

Who told me to write even more.

Lastly, to PB, PB, BB and BB.

Chapter One

This was absolutely the last place Miss Gwendoline Knox wanted to be—not that she had any choice in the matter.

Murderess wallflowers were rarely wanted at home.

'There y'are,' muttered the coach driver, rather unceremoniously dropping her trunk to the ground. It rolled, mud splattering up one side of the leather case. 'Academy.'

Gwen swallowed and looked up at the large manor house, its beautiful Tudor bricks glowing in the afternoon sun. Imposing chimneys pumped out smoke and the large front door had a highly polished bronze knocker.

'But where am I supposed to—?'

The whip cracked and the horses stepped forward, pulling the coach away and leaving Gwen alone on the drive. Silence quickly spilled into the gardens.

If only her mother had agreed to accompany her, Gwen thought wistfully as she picked up her trunk, leaning slightly thanks to its weight. But that would have meant talking about…the incident. Perhaps this was best.

Besides, this was why she had been sent to the Academy. To get out from under her mother's feet, prevent any hint of scandal and find a husband. Gwen tried to push the unkind thoughts from her mind, but they intruded, nonetheless.

If Mother had been kind enough to come with me, she would not have been so unkind as to send me here.

It was an unpleasant thought, and it was getting her nowhere. The bright autumnal sun was drawing long shadows across the gardens, and a chill in the air hinted at an icy evening.

Stepping forward timidly, Gwen knocked on the door, which was immediately opened by a footman in blue livery.

'Miss Knox,' he said smoothly. 'Miss Pike is expecting you.'

Gwen was certainly not expecting the hall she stepped into, conscious of the mud she was spreading into the magnificent space. High ceilings, a beautiful red carpet, and landscape paintings along the walls: the very picture of elegance.

'Ah, Miss Knox!'

A smiling older woman, perhaps nearing fifty, was approaching rather like a battleship. Gwen took a step backwards.

'How pleasant to make your acquaintance,' said the woman, who could only be Miss Pike. 'The Wallflower Academy welcomes you.'

'And no one will miss you there!'

Her mother's parting words rang through her mind.

'It's not as if women like you deserve happy endings, do you? Not after what you've done...'

Gwen winced. It was bad enough to be labelled a wallflower by one's own mother, but to be sent to such a place! It was scandalously embarrassing.

'I do not want to be here,' she said, the words slipping out before she could stop them.

They did not appear to offend Miss Pike. 'Of course you don't,' she said with a broad smile, waving her hand as though opinions mattered little. 'And you won't be alone.

Matthews, please show Miss Knox to her bedchamber. The end room.'

A flurry of corridors passed Gwen by until she was standing in a small yet genteelly furnished bedchamber. A large bed, a writing desk, a toilette table and a wardrobe were the only items within it, but a large bay window looked out onto the south of the house, towards the rear gardens. She could see kitchen gardens, what appeared to be a walled rose garden, and an abundance of carefully manicured lawn.

She turned. The footman had gone. She had not even noticed his departure.

Breathing out slowly as her heart rate started to slow, Gwen sank onto the end of the bed and closed her eyes. This was not the end of the world. She would manage.

'Goodness, you look terrible,' said a cheerful voice.

Breath caught in her throat, Gwen was unable to say anything as her bedchamber door opened, and a pair of ladies entered.

'Sylvia,' said a woman with black skin and a broad smile.

She had on her arm the hands of another lady, a little older, with milky white eyes.

The door shut and flickers of panic tingled up Gwen's spine. To be so enclosed with unknown people…

'My word, your bedchamber has the most outstanding view,' said Sylvia, leaning towards the window. 'We're all jealous, you know.'

'Oh, I don't know,' said the one with milky eyes, who had been helped to the window seat. 'I don't think I would mind. I'm Marilla. You can call me Rilla.'

Gwen nodded weakly. She was always terrible with names, but she wasn't about to forget Rilla in a hurry. When had she lost her sight? How could she speak of it so calmly?

'I don't hear the new one laughing,' said Rilla mildly. 'Don't you worry about it, whoever you are. I don't—you shouldn't.'

'Gwendoline Knox,' Gwen said weakly, head spinning and in desperate need of solitude. She had risen early for that day's journey. 'You can call me—'

'Do you have any beaus?'

'N-No!' Gwen spluttered, startled into speech by Sylvia's blunt question.

She was still grinning as she leaned against the window. 'I only asked.'

'Don't hound her, Sylvia,' said Rilla.

'I'll hound whoever I want,' said Sylvia brightly. 'I've got to find entertainment somewhere in this place.'

They laughed, and Gwen smiled nervously. As long as she didn't draw attention to herself…

They were not as dull as she had expected. An Academy for Wallflowers…well, her mother had considered it perfect. The perfect place to hide someone. Gwen had tried to imagine the sorts of ladies who were sent to such a place—women no longer wanted by their families, who had tried, and failed, to make a match.

The beginning of the Season had been only a few weeks ago, and Gwen knew precisely what her mother expected of her: to keep her head down and make a good match.

But how was she expected to do so in an Academy full of ladies who could conceive of nothing worse than making light conversation with a handsome gentleman?

'Are we it?' Gwen flushed as laughter resounded around her bedchamber at her question.

'It?' repeated Sylvia with a giggle. 'Were you expecting something far more impressive?'

'Don't tease her, Sylvia,' Rilla said with mock severity. 'You forget, you've been here an entire Season! You can no longer remember how frightened you were when you first arrived.'

A slight pink tinge came to Sylvia's cheeks. 'I suppose not. Yes, Gwen—can I call you Gwen?'

Gwen would have permitted her to call her anything she liked if it meant the focus of the conversation moved on quickly. 'Yes.'

'Yes, Gwen, we are "it"—at least some of it,' said Sylvia with a grin. 'There are—what...? Five of us here now? You make six. I am least likely to be wed—'

'I think I'd agree with you on that one,' muttered Rilla.

'Daphne is least likely to say boo to a mouse—'

'She does this,' Rilla said to a bemused Gwen. 'It's her way of keeping track of us, apparently. Some ladies come and go rather quickly.'

'They...they find husbands?'

Gwen could hardly believe it. For all the wonderful references Miss Pike had sent her mother, it had been hard to fathom how the Academy could marry off so many wallflowers in such a short time.

'Oh, Miss Pike has her ways,' said Rilla dryly.

'She does know what she is doing most of the time,' said Sylvia, glancing at Gwen with a knowing look. 'So, you are here for a husband, are you?'

Gwen wished heat would not immediately flush up her décolletage, wished it would not pinken her cheeks and make her words incomprehensible.

What would she be? Least likely to form a coherent sentence?

'I—I... That is...my mother wants—'

'Oh, mothers,' said Sylvia dismissively. 'I was sent here by my mother.'

'Me by my father,' Rilla said curtly. 'Such as he is. But not for marriage. No, the blackguard believes—'

'Miss Knox does not need to hear our sob stories,' interrupted Sylvia firmly.

Gwen swallowed, curling her fingers around the blanket on the bed. The tension taut in her shoulders and neck was starting to give her a headache, and Sylvia was right. She certainly did not need the histories of the ladies who had invaded her bedchamber.

What she needed was quiet and solitude—a chance to think over all she had heard, all she had seen. All that she might now expect.

She was a prisoner here, sent by her mother after her own scandalous marriage, after the…the incident had become a fact. What she, Gwen, was going to do about it… Well, that was quite another matter. A matter that required due consideration—and she was not going to be able to think with all the noise in here.

But first, Gwen had questions which needed answering. 'What…what happens here? At the Wallflower Academy, I mean? How does she—Miss Pike—how does she… marry us off?'

Rilla chuckled. 'It's all very simple, Miss Knox. You have no need to be concerned. Miss Pike gives us lessons—'

'Lessons in how to be more interesting and charming young ladies,' Sylvia interrupted, rolling her eyes.

'Lessons on attracting a gentleman,' Rilla continued, a smile curling her lips. 'And then eligible gentlemen are invited to come and meet us.'

'View us,' said Sylvia wryly. 'Like specimens. Like animals in a zoo.'

Gwen swallowed. It did not sound particularly appealing. She had never been one to enjoy being looked at—which was all to the good, for her mother had pronounced her plain when she had first started curling her hair and pinning it up.

No, to be invisible. That was the thing. To go through life without being noticed, without attention, was all she desired.

The thought of gentlemen arriving at the Academy to look at them all, as though through a catalogue…

'I will hate it,' she whispered. 'I just want to be left alone.'

'Plenty of opportunities for that,' said Sylvia, and there was little laughter in her tone this time. 'Some of us have been here for years. 'Tis not a given that you will ever be chosen.'

Was that bitterness in her voice? Gwen could hardly tell. There had been such mischief in everything Sylvia had said since barrelling into her bedchamber.

'You will get accustomed to it,' said Rilla quietly. 'We all do.'

Gwen nodded mutely. It sounded awful. So, gentlemen would come to…to examine them.

'We have lessons on how to speak with confidence, how to stand tall, how to select topics of conversation,' Rilla explained, her hands folded in her lap. 'Music, art, languages…the normal things.'

Sylvia rolled her eyes. 'It's completely ridiculous. As though being shy, being a wallflower, is something needing to be cured.'

Only then did a natural smile creep across Gwen's face. Until now, her fears of being forced to change, to be a different person, to lose so much of who she was had overwhelmed her.

'You are not at all the wallflowers I had expected,' Gwen admitted with an awkward laugh.

Rilla grinned, her pale eyes turning in Gwen's direction. 'I am not here as a wallflower, you understand. 'Tis my father's intention—'

'And I'm not a wallflower at all, but a prisoner,' declared Sylvia with a wink. 'My father wants to marry me off without having to bring me out into Society. So here I am, stuck amid all these quiet ones. I manage to gain sufficient conversation at the official dinners, of course. You have missed the first one.'

Official dinners? Gwen's cheeks blazed with heat at the idea she had missed something important. Miss Pike's letter had said that any time was perfect for her arrival, that she should not rush her goodbyes with her family.

It had not prevented her mother from bundling her off as soon as possible…

'Official dinners?' she repeated.

Rilla smiled wearily. 'Miss Pike hosts six dinners throughout the Season. Only the very best and most eligible gentlemen are invited—though of course, they must all be accepting of a wallflower as their bride.'

As their bride.

Gwen's stomach twisted most painfully and her grip on the blanket increased.

Because that was what she was here for, wasn't it? To make a match. To be married off, cast away from her family to make her own way in the world. To be hidden amongst the most unlikely of ladies.

'And I have missed the first?'

A rather wicked smile spread across Sylvia's face. 'You did not miss much—it was a complete disaster! Oh, Gwen, it was awful. The gentlemen Miss Pike had procured were so immensely dull they did not ask us anything, nor start any conversation—and of course this lot said nothing either!'

There was a peal of laughter from Rilla. 'Speak for yourself! I tried to ask Mr Whatshisname something about the meat course, and he said—'

'"I don't speak to wallflowers!"'

Both chorused this, and then fell into peals of giggles, the loudest snort coming from Sylvia.

Gwen looked at the laughing women and tried to smile. It was all too much: too much noise, too much expectation, too much going on. Her mind clouded, her head spun. She tried to make sense of all the information she was being given, but her bones ached from the long carriage ride, and the very last thing she wished to do at this moment was have dinner with what Miss Pike considered to be eligible—

'Don't worry,' said Rilla, a smile still dancing on her lips. 'The second official dinner is this week.'

Gwen's stomach turned horribly, threatening to return the meat pie she had hesitantly accepted at the inn just a few hours ago.

The second official dinner—so soon? She would barely have enough time to settle into the Academy!

The room closed in, as if the air was running out, and Gwen gasped for breath. 'I… I need…'

'Goodness, you sound awful, Gwen,' said Rilla, a slight crease of concern appearing between her eyes. 'Are you quite well?'

Gwen shook her head, unable to speak. Then, remembering Rilla, she said, 'Y-Yes.'

'She needs some air,' said Sylvia firmly. 'A walk in the garden. I will go with you…show you the way—'

But Gwen had already risen and waved a hand. 'Oh, no, I can easily—I—I would like to be alone, if you do not mind.'

Fear seared her heart at the thought of giving offence, but Sylvia only sighed. 'You wallflowers are all the same.'

Gwen swallowed, shame flooding her veins, but a second glance at the beautiful woman showed her Sylvia had meant no harm.

It was just too much. Too many opportunities to reveal the truth.

'I have to...' Gwen tried to speak, but made no effort to continue as she half walked, half stumbled out of the bedchamber.

It was not difficult to find her way outside. Once she had descended the staircase into the hall, she opened the front door and stepped out into the cold yet welcoming air. There were sufficient borders and hedges here, along the drive, in which to lose herself.

Her skin prickled with the cold, but at least it was cooling. Gwen paced, hardly looking where she was going, entering into one of the portions of the garden lined with hedges.

The Wallflower Academy. It was like a bad jest someone had made in their cups, and yet it was real. She was here. The tall redbrick building loomed above her. She had no home, no friends—although that might soon change—and no idea what she was going to do with herself at these awful dinners.

If only I was not guilty of something so terrible, Gwen thought bitterly as she turned a corner, her skirts whipping because she was walking so fast.

Then she could have asked her mother to allow her to remain at home.

But it was not to be. She had to live with the consequences of her actions, and this was far more pleasant than a prison—even if the punishment included being paraded before gentlemen for their enjoyment!

Gwen's eyes filled with tears as she turned hurriedly around the next corner, the hedge brushing against the sleeve of her gown. How could she bear it? What could possibly make the Wallflower Academy endurable?

She turned another corner and walked straight into the most handsome gentleman she had ever seen.

Chapter Two

Percy Devereux, Duke of Knaresby, sighed heavily as his footsteps thudded down the front steps of the dratted Wallflower Academy.

Academy. The cheek of Miss Pike to call it such a thing, when places like Oxford and Cambridge existed in the world. Why, a finishing school concerned with dancing and decorum was hardly an 'academy', in his view.

Besides, Miss Pike was dreadfully dull. If she was any indication of the poor women sent to such a place, it was no wonder the so-called 'wallflowers' found themselves left on the side-lines of every ball and conversation of note.

The bright autumnal air shimmered with the afternoon sun, and Percy watched the merest hint of his breath billowing on the breeze. The Season had begun, and it brought with it little pleasure and less excitement.

It was only down to Staromchor's mother that he had even come at all, cornered at Almack's just days ago. A 'charitable duty'—that was what the Dowager Countess had called it.

A damned nuisance, more like.

That dinner he'd been forced to attend had been outrageously dull, and he had firmly vowed he would only drop by a few times for the look of the thing.

Still, the Academy was only a twenty-minute drive from Town, and it was not so very arduous to make the trip—as long as it was infrequent.

But when there were far more interesting diversions to be had in London—concerts and card parties and riding in the parks—it was impossible to see how he would be dragged out here more than twice in the whole Season.

Percy squared his shoulders and thanked his stars he had performed his duty without having to see a single blushing wallflower. In, five minutes with the dreaded Miss Pike, and out. Not bad.

Striding down the driveway, gravel crunching under his riding boots, Percy pulled on his gloves and tried to calculate what time he would arrive back at the Knaresby townhouse. Almost four o'clock, by his reckoning. Just in time for—

A heavy weight halted his path, so dense and immovable Percy was almost rocked off his feet. But the weight itself was not so fortunate. Down it fell, in a tumble of skirts and ribbons, and to his horror Percy realised he had toppled not some statue unexpectedly in his path…but a woman.

'Dear God,' Percy muttered, shaking his head at the irritating distraction now preventing him from reaching the stables. 'Apologies, I am sure.'

His gruff remark was ignored, however, as was the hand he offered the young lady who had so unceremoniously been toppled to the ground.

A fierce glare came from bright eyes, and unfathomably Percy's breath caught in his throat.

Then his hand was pushed aside and the young lady, dark-haired and apparently furious, rose to her feet, brushing at her skirts.

Ah. One of Pike's wallflowers.

A lazy grin slid onto Percy's face as he waited for the stammering apology he was doubtless about to receive. After all, he was a duke. And though they had not been introduced, it would be clear from his elegantly tailored coat and graceful top hat that he was—

'Why cannot you look where you are going, oaf?'

Percy blinked. The woman before him had just picked a leaf from her skirt and flicked it to the ground, not looking at him as she spoke—but she was looking at him now.

Those bright eyes he had noticed before were now shining with irritation, and a frown creased the otherwise pretty face. Lips were pressed in a rather furious expression, and the lady did not stop there.

'Do us both a favour, Mr Whoever-You-Are, and consider a little when you walk with no thought to your surroundings, for there are others in the world beyond yourself!'

After a ringing silence, the woman clapped her hands to her mouth, eyes wide, cheeks a flaming pink which was, although Percy tried not to notice, most becoming.

Her horror at her own words could not have been more evident, and Percy did the only thing he could: he laughed.

By Jove, he had not expected that! No woman had ever spoken so to him in his life. Admittedly, there must have been a few who had done it behind his back, but still... They all respected the name and the title, never speaking abruptly or disrespectfully.

This was no wallflower—she could not be. What was she doing here, at the Wallflower Academy, with such an unrestrained and violent temper?

'I—I... I do beg...' the woman stammered, her hands not leaving her mouth so her words were muffled.

If only the pink in her cheeks did not make her so alluring, Percy mused, taking a proper look at her as a woman for the first time. An elegant figure, a gown that might have seen many Seasons but was still relatively fashionable, and a large muddy patch on her behind.

A behind that was well formed, even if it was difficult to tell through the fabric…

A lurch in Percy's stomach pulled him to his senses. Now was not the time to be measuring a young lady's assets, impressive though they might be.

Still, his curiosity must be sated. 'What is your name?'

'Nothing,' the woman said hastily, turning away. 'Good day.'

For a moment Percy could hardly believe she had done so. What? No elegant curtsey? No apology for leaving his presence? No flirtatious grin, moreover, and no teasing hint at her name? No invitation for him to call again? No manners at all?

Hardly aware of what his feet were doing, Percy found himself following the woman up the gravel path towards the Academy. Which was foolishness. He was a duke! Ladies were meant to run after him, not the other way around! It was most unaccountable, this need he had to know her name…

'You must have a name,' he said reasonably, his lungs inexplicably tight. 'Everyone does.'

'It is no concern of yours,' came the swift reply over the lady's shoulder.

Remarkable… Since rising to his title Percy had been inundated with ladies, all simpering and smiling, ready to be delighted—something he hardly regretted—but this was the first to actively avoid his presence.

Perhaps it was because she was unaware of his station, his title. That must be it.

Drawing himself up as best he could, while still pacing

after her, Percy said, impressively, 'I am Percy Devereux, Duke of Knaresby.'

A strange noise emitted from the woman before him. It might have been a laugh, or a cough—he could not tell.

'My name is definitely no concern of yours, then,' came the reply.

There was nothing for it. Percy's curiosity was aroused, and despite his better judgment, and all sense of decorum, he reached out.

No woman walked away from him.

'Wait.'

His hand was on her arm, which was covered by her sleeve. There was no reason for the sudden rush of heat, the tingle in his fingers, the sense that it was he who had been knocked over this time.

Everything swayed a little. The world stayed the same, of course, so perhaps it was he who swayed. Perhaps they both did.

The woman had halted, as if unable to walk forward, and was staring as though she had been cornered by a wild dog.

Percy swallowed. He was acting strangely…far out of character. He had not come here to accost young ladies; he had not even wanted to come here at all.

What was such a woman doing at the Wallflower Academy?

'Did you come here to find a husband?'

The words had slipped from his mouth before he could halt them, and Percy found, to his distraction, that they had a rather pleasing effect. Once again the woman's face was tinged with pink, but she looked defiant.

A most intriguing look.

'I do hope, Your Grace, you do not believe I bumped into you merely to gain your notice!'

In truth, Percy had half wondered that very thing—but now she had spoken, now he heard the tremor in her voice, he could not believe it.

'If…if you could release me?' she said softly.

Percy was still holding on to her and had no desire to release her. His curiosity was still piqued, and he was certain she would run off as soon as she was unrestrained. But the connection between them… There was something there. Something he could not explain.

'Unhand me, sir.'

Sir! The audacity!

Very slowly, one finger after another, he released her.

It was like a small bereavement. The connection was cut, the world stopped swaying, and Percy found he had rather enjoyed the dizziness his touching her had produced.

Yet things were not entirely back to normal. The woman had not fled, as he had expected, but was standing before him with wary eyes and hands clasped before her.

Percy examined her. She was no wallflower. He was certain.

The first of Miss Pike's 'official dinners', as she called them, had been one of the most dull affairs of his life. Never before had he been presented with such a quiet bunch of ladies, and although the bolder one, a Miss Sylvia, had attempted conversation, it had been so stilted Percy had left before dessert, his promise to Miss Pike be damned. There was only so much a gentleman should have to do as a favour to his old governess.

He had never met anyone at the Academy like the woman before him now.

Fire lay under that shyness, Percy was sure. He had felt it when she had berated him so heartily for his inattention.

Though the sparks had disappeared, there was something still smouldering under those dark eyes of hers. Something he wanted to fan back into flames.

'Look,' said Percy imperiously, and irritation flushed through his voice, 'I merely wish to know the name of the person I knocked to the ground, that is all. Your name please, miss?'

Unless she was a servant? Surely not. Percy knew enough of good breeding and the clothes of a maid to know one when he saw one.

A tutor, perhaps, at the Academy? He had heard Miss Pike complain that she needed additional help. Was this it?

'I just wish to know you,' Percy said, trying to inject a little of the Knaresby force into his words.

The woman's gaze dropped. 'No, you do not.'

'Are you always this contrary?'

A mere hint of a smile curled across her lips. 'No.'

He chuckled as a cold breeze blew past them. The sun was setting in earnest now, and he would certainly not be back in Town as expected. His mother would have to wait.

'And when people chastise you for that stubborn streak of yours,' he said, 'what do they call you?'

The smile on her face broadened, and Percy's stomach lurched as her beauty blossomed.

Dear God. She was a marvel.

'They…they call me Miss Gwendoline Knox. But mostly they call me Gwen.'

Gwen.

A shiver went down Percy's spine—which he allotted, of course, to the cooling of the afternoon. It had nothing to do with the wallflower before him. It couldn't.

Oh, don't bother lying to yourself, he thought.

It was natural to be attracted to such a woman. She had all the features and form Society expected in a woman to be called pretty, and yet she had…more.

Putting his finger on it would be difficult. And Percy wanted to put more than a finger on her.

Miss Gwendoline Knox. Gwen.

How he dearly wished to call her Gwen. Such an intimacy, of course, would be insupportable. No noble-born gentleman would consider it. No well-bred lady would allow it.

'And now you can be on your way.'

Percy's gaze snapped back. 'Why would I want to?'

Gwen frowned, and glanced back at the manor before saying, 'Well, you cannot wish to stay here in the cold, talking to me.'

Heavens, how little she knew. Percy could see it in her now he came to look closely. The fear of the wallflower… the expectation that she would never be enough. Not entertaining enough, pretty enough, clever enough. The assumption that she would be passed by. The knowledge, deep within her, that no one would wish to know her, that any conversation would be borne of pity, not interest.

What was it like to go through the world in such a way?

'Because you are a wallflower?' he said, with a wry grin.

A flash of sharpness in her eyes, an inclination towards rebellion, then it was gone.

'Yes.'

'At this awful Academy?' Percy said, looking up at the building before him.

A stricken look overcame Gwen's face. 'Is it truly that bad? Is its reputation unfavourable? I only arrived an hour ago.'

Ah.

Percy found it a challenge to consider his words carefully before he spoke again in this woman's presence. He was, after all, a duke. Well, he had been for the last few months. More, he was a Devereux. His family had been bred for careful and considered conversation, for every word to mean something, to convey the very best feelings and hide the rest.

And here, with her, this woman who had berated him just as swiftly as she'd blushed before him, his feelings betrayed him. They offered him nothing but plain truth—something rather dangerous when a duke.

'I did not mean… Not awful,' he said. 'I merely meant… Well, what is the word?'

Gwen looked at him silently. A prickle of discomfort, not unpleasant, crept up his neck. How did she do that? Look at him as though he was merely a servant himself? As though he was not eminently superior to her?

It was uncanny. It was delightful.

'Intense,' Percy landed on, unable to think of anything better. 'Intense, I suppose, for everyone involved. Just a marriage market under a different name.'

'And you are not married?'

It appeared he was not the only one whose tongue was eager to betray its owner. Percy saw a flush cover Gwen's cheeks, but she continued to hold his gaze defiantly.

Interesting… A wallflower with a dash of curiosity as well as a temper. Most interesting… And she found him just as interesting, did she not? Only a woman interested in a gentleman would ask said gentleman about his potential wife, would she not?

Percy found to his surprise that a flicker of pleasure was curling around his heart at the very thought. It appeared Miss Knox was just as intrigued by him as he was her.

Yet it was not possible, of course, for this conversation to go further. Percy straightened his shoulders as the thought, though unwelcome, hit him with its truth.

He was a duke. She was a wallflower. Probably of little family and no real reputation, if her parents had been forced to send her here to find a match.

And Percy Devereux, Duke of Knaresby, was hardly free himself to make a choice in the matter of his own marriage. He had a duty, a responsibility, to marry a woman of excellent breeding, impressive dowry and, most importantly, respectability in Society. He needed someone far more impressive than a mere wallflower.

A shame. This Gwendoline Knox was rather starting to grow on him.

But he had a far more important focus at the moment, and he was late for old Mr Moore. His mother and the solicitor would not wait for ever. James's will had to be read.

Not that he wanted to dwell on such matters, but he was left with little choice after the way he had arrived at his title.

'No,' Percy said with a wry smile. 'No, I am not married. Not for the lack of my mother's efforts, however.'

'Good,' said Gwen. 'I mean—not good! Just…fine. Fine.'

Fine. A mediocre word from a rather extraordinary woman.

Percy saw the interest in her eyes, the desire flushing her cheeks. He watched the way she leaned ever so slightly closer, all thoughts of escaping him clearly gone from her mind.

It was flattering, of course. And it was a relief, in a way, to see the effect he had on women—even those he had rather unceremoniously accosted by way of greeting.

But that did not explain why his body was responding. Why he wished to take a step, bridge the gap between them. Why, when she shivered in the cold of the afternoon, he wished to place an arm around her and pull her near, to share his heat. Wanted to tip her head back and capture those lips and—

Percy cleared his throat.

No, that would not do.

Still, he could not help himself. A little further teasing would do no harm. 'Just "fine"?' he said.

Gwen hesitated, her gaze moving from his eyes to his lips before it fell to her hands. 'Your Grace, you must realise there is a reason I am here. At the Wallflower Academy, I mean.'

'I have no idea,' said Percy honestly. This was no wallflower, he was sure.

'I am not particularly eloquent,' said Gwen to her boots. 'In talking with gentlemen, I mean.'

'We are talking,' he pointed out.

'No,' said Gwen, glancing up with a smile she was evidently trying to hide. 'You are badgering me.'

'Probably.' Percy grinned. 'Rather fun, don't you think?'

He needed to step away. A small part of him knew that, even if it was shrinking at an alarming rate. Step away from the wallflower and return to Town.

'So, you are not here to find a husband?'

Gwen glanced back at the manor house for a moment before saying, 'No. At least, I don't... I am not desperate.'

She said the last word rather too firmly, if Percy was any judge, although he could not understand why. Surely a woman like this would have no trouble in attracting a nice gentleman? A country squire, perhaps? Someone who could keep her comfortable.

A vision of another man touching Gwen rushed through Percy's mind and his heart rebelled. In an instant the image was gone, though his hand was still clenched in a fist.

'Least likely to win a duke, though,' said Gwen quietly. 'Not after what happened at home, I mean.'

'At home?' Percy asked, his curiosity piqued once more. 'What do you mean by—?'

'I must go inside. They will be wondering where I have got to,' said Gwen in a rush. 'Good day, Your Grace. It was…'

Words failing her, Gwen turned and half walked, half ran up the drive to the steps of the Wallflower Academy. Within a moment, she was gone.

Percy stood, unable to move. As swiftly as she had entered his life she had disappeared.

'Least likely to win a duke.'

So she had said. And yet he was intrigued.

Forcing aside the desire which had so quickly blossomed in Gwen's presence, Percy shook his head, as though that would rid him of the confusion miring his mind.

Miss Gwendoline Knox. A wallflower unlike any he had ever met.

Percy smiled. Well, it was only a week until Pike's second official dinner. His invitation had so far gone unanswered. Perhaps it was time to reply and reward himself with more of Gwen. Demonstrate to her just what calibre of man she had been so quick to run from.

Chapter Three

'This dinner,' said Gwen with an awkward smile. 'We truly have to attend?'

Rilla grinned. 'It is not that bad.'

Night had fallen a few hours before, and Gwen's bedchamber had once again become a gathering place for the two wallflowers who had first welcomed her to the Academy.

If anyone had thought to ask Gwen—and no one had—she would have requested they use Sylvia's bedchamber. It was not as well-proportioned as her own, and neither did it have such an impressive view. Nonetheless, Sylvia herself was no wallflower, and revelled in the company of others.

And Gwen...

Sitting in the window seat by the bay window, Gwen looked out at the flickering torches that Miss Pike—or 'the Pike', as she was affectionately yet fearfully known by the other wallflowers—had ordered to be placed along the drive.

In mere moments carriages would be rattling along that driveway, bringing gentlemen of eligible suitability from London to dine at the Wallflower Academy. There would be conversation. There would be attention. There would be expectations.

There might even, Sylvia had teased, be some sort of recital required, when the gentlemen returned to the ladies after their port and cigars.

Gwen's stomach lurched painfully at the mere thought.

Entertainment. Diversion. Singing. God forbid.

She had been blessed neither with musical talent nor an ear for a tune, and if she was forced to step up to the pianoforte…

Well, there would be no chance of a match for her then. And if Percy should decide to attend—

But Gwen forced that particular thought from her mind. There was no possibility that the Duke of Knaresby—which was how she should consider him—would be attending the second official Wallflower Academy dinner this evening.

Firstly, she told herself sternly, he was a duke, and had no need to hightail it to a house of wallflowers to find a bride. Goodness knew what sort of gentlemen did resort to such a thing.

Secondly, he had no interest in her. A certain curiosity, true—she had seen it in his eyes. A thirst for knowledge, however, did not translate into a hunger for…

And thirdly, Gwen thought hastily, as she tried not to recollect just how delectable the Duke's lips had looked, she was in no rush to be married. Her mother might consider her a problem unless she was darkening someone else's doorway, but she was not eager to be a wife.

'So, you are not here to find a husband?'

'No. At least, I don't... I am not desperate.'

Her cheeks flamed with heat.

'I can *feel* you worrying.'

Startled, Gwen looked over at the blind woman, who was smiling. 'You can?'

Rilla laughed. 'They really aren't that bad, these dinners of the Pike's.'

'They're not?' said Gwen hopefully.

It was only a dinner. A few hours of good food and polite if a little stilted conversation. A chance for Sylvia, the only one among them who truly wished to shine, to play the pianoforte and sing and dazzle.

And then bed.

The comfort and the sanctuary of her own bedchamber. Gwen swallowed as she looked at its current inhabitants. All she wanted was a bedchamber empty of all others, where she could rest alone and try not to think of the shocked, wide eyes haunting her dreams…

It had been a relief to discover the food was good and the beds comfortable at the Wallflower Academy. Gwen had not been sure that would be the case when she had first entered the Tudor manor, with visions of gruel and slops clouding her mind.

'You're brooding again.'

''Tis all very well for you Rilla,' said Gwen darkly. 'You cannot see all the gentlemen staring at you, wondering why your family was so desperate as to place you here, wondering why you are so unmarriageable.'

'Well,' said Rilla with a dry laugh, 'with me I suppose they can see without needing to wonder.'

Gwen laughed. She could not help herself. Rilla had been encouraging her all week to laugh when she felt like it, rather than censor herself around her merely because she was blind.

'Ah, a laugh!' Rilla grinned, her pearly eyes moving in Gwen's direction. 'You are finally becoming one of us, then, if you are able to laugh at me and with me. Took you long enough.'

'I have been here only a week!' protested Gwen with a laugh of her own, some of the tension in her stomach dissipating. 'And besides, I have never met a blind lady before.'

'Well, we're not special,' said Rilla with a shrug, placing a bracelet on her wrist. 'Which reminds me—do you have a moment?'

She was proffering a letter she had taken from the pocket of her gown.

Gwen took it. 'And this is…?'

'A letter from my father,' said Rilla, with a coldness Gwen had not expected. 'Summarise it for me, would you?'

Blinking down at it, Gwen's gaze took in a medley of affectionate words.

My darling child...hope to hear from you soon...worried for you...think of you daily...

She swallowed. Not phrases *she* had ever received in a letter from a parent. 'You don't want me to read it?'

Rilla shrugged. 'It's always the same. Never mind, give it here.'

Gwen handed it back wordlessly. Oh, to have a father alive! Or a mother who cared enough to write with such warmth, such love…

'Right, then. Are you adorned and ready to descend?'

Gwen's heart skipped a beat. Her first presentation to the eligible bachelors Miss Pike believed would be suitable for her wallflowers. Would she meet their expectations? Would she disappoint them all? Worse, would it be a repeat of the first official dinner, which Sylvia and the others had told her was such a disaster?

'I suppose we have to go?' The question was rhetorical, really, but Gwen had to ask it. 'We cannot… I don't know… Plead a cold, or a headache, or something?'

'Not if you don't want the Pike swimming up here to discover whether you are feigning,' said Rilla wryly. 'Trust me, once you have been subjected to her battery of enquiries you really do have a headache.'

What had occurred in these walls between these wallflowers before she had arrived?

But she'd had no opportunity to ask questions—not that she would have had the boldness to do so and draw attention to herself. There were plenty of secrets in her own past, after all, that she would rather keep hidden.

She would do anything but have the other wallflowers discover what she had done.

Gwen rose. She had not bothered with jewellery or adornment. This was not the time to hope for pleasant conversation. Her mind was still ringing with the words of the Duke who had knocked her to the ground and then taken her breath away in quite another manner.

The thought of conversation with other gentlemen was quite out of the question.

Chatter in the Academy rose as the wallflowers left their bedchambers and descended the stairs. Gwen's foot almost slipped on the next step. She could hear them. The gentlemen.

Gentlemen. Men.

Men she did not know and who would look at her as a piece of meat. What was it Percy—the Duke—had called it?

'Just a marriage market under a different name.'

A smile drifted across Gwen's face, although she tried not to think about Percy.

He was not wrong.

'There must be a better way for us to meet eligible bachelors,' she breathed.

Rilla laughed. 'Come on, Gwen. Spend more than one minute thinking about that. Can you imagine us at a ball? Some of us can barely talk to gentlemen, and I am hardly a suitable dance partner.'

Gwen's stomach twisted as she missed the last step and almost pulled Rilla down with her. 'I do apologise!'

'You do remember I am the blind one, don't you?' Rilla said with a laugh, straightening her skirts as she stood at the bottom of the staircase.

Gwen smiled weakly and nodded. Then, remembering Rilla would not see her expression, she said, 'Yes, I will try to remember.'

They had halted in the hall, with its impressive landscape paintings oppressive in the dim, candlelit evening. The door to the drawing room was about ten feet away. Laughter. Chatter. Men's voices. Low, deep, and utterly confident.

Something painful tightened across her chest. If only there was anywhere else Gwen could be in this moment… But no, home was not an option. No longer home, no longer a place she was welcome. She would have to resign herself to the corridors and rooms of the Wallflower Academy.

This was now her home, but Gwen knew not for how long.

'There they are,' one of the wallflowers whispered—rather unnecessarily, in Gwen's opinion.

They all stood there, as if unable to step back and unwilling to go forward. Gwen could guess what they were feeling. If it was anything akin to her own feelings it was a painful mixture of embarrassment, fury at being subjected to such a thing, and fear that the reality would be even worse than her imaginings.

'You will be married!'

Gwen's mother's words echoed painfully in her mind—the last thing she had hurled at her daughter before she had stepped into the coach taking her to the Wallflower Academy.

'You are unlikely to win anyone's affections here, Gwen-

doline, and it is time for you to find your own place in the world. Without me, without scandal following you, and without whispers of what you've done. Any misstep, and I warn you...'

I warn you.

Gwen swallowed, tasting the fear on her tongue. It was infuriating to force down all thoughts and her temper—the part of her that seemed most natural. But then, she had seen what that temper could do. She must never let it out again. Not after shouting at the Duke, anyway.

Even if she would be sorely tempted when certain irritating dukes knocked her to the ground.

'It's just a dinner,' Gwen said aloud into the silence of the hall. 'Just food.'

'If that helps you,' said Rilla with a dry laugh. 'Come on. Let's get this over with.'

The drawing room was brilliant with light, compared to the dull hall. Inside, the room Gwen had seen in the comfort of quiet evenings, with silent reading and gentle conversation between the wallflowers, had been transformed.

Miss Pike truly knew what she was doing, Gwen had to admit. The faded furnishings had been improved dramatically with silk hangings, and there were velvet cushions on every sofa and armchair. Elegant books had been placed carefully around the place, as though to emphasise the wallflowers' reading habits, and someone had—surely on purpose—left a half-finished painting of exquisite beauty near the curtains by the bay window.

A bureau had been opened up to reveal a drinks cabinet for the gentlemen, and the pianoforte had been uncovered. A fire was roaring in the grate, and there were more candles in one room than Gwen had ever seen.

They illuminated...right in the centre, surrounded by a

gaggle of chortling gentlemen… Percy Devereux, Duke of Knaresby.

If it had not been for Rilla on her left, Gwen was fairly certain she would have stopped dead in her tracks. Her heart certainly did, and a painful squeeze followed as it tried desperately to return to its rhythm.

But it couldn't. It pattered painfully in her body. And Gwen could do nothing but stare at the tall, dark and grinning gentleman who was watching her with a possessive expression.

Not, not *possessive.* That was surely her imagination.

Nothing could have prepared her for this moment. It was unthinkable—incomprehensible. Had the Duke not had enough of her foolish conversation that afternoon when she had so thoughtlessly walked into him?

Gwen could not take her eyes from him, and after managing a few steps more came to a halt in the drawing room. Rilla halted too, evidently unwilling for quite different reasons to approach the group of gentlemen.

A roaring rushed through her ears and Gwen blinked, just to ensure she was not seeing things.

But she was not. In fact, it was getting worse the longer she stood here. Percy—*the Duke of Knaresby, she must remember that*—was walking over to her, with that same smile on his lips and an imperious look in his eyes.

'Wh-What are you doing here?' Gwen stammered, hating the hesitancy in her voice but unable to do anything about it, trying desperately to forget how she had yearned to see him.

It was ridiculous. What would a duke need the Wallflower Academy for? Surely he had far more interesting evening entertainments to attend?

Percy raised a quizzical eyebrow. 'Why, I am here to see you, of course.'

Heat blossomed up Gwen's décolletage and she hoped beyond hope he had not noticed. But of course he had. Or did she imagine that twinkle in his eye…a little too knowing?

'Who is it?' asked Rilla, her unseeing eyes staring at the gentleman before her. 'At least have the good manners to introduce yourself, man.'

Gwen swallowed. The situation was going from bad to worse, but there was nothing she could do to stop it.

Conversation continued around them in the drawing room…mumbled words Gwen was sure were questions being asked about her.

How did a wallflower on speaking terms with a duke arrive at the Academy?

But she could not do anything about the gossip surely circulating at this very moment. Gwen might appear to be a wallflower, but she had a good enough understanding of decorum to know her duty.

'Your Grace, may I have the honour of presenting to you Miss Marilla Newell?' said Gwen, hardly aware of each word that came out of her mouth.

Percy bowed low and Rilla dipped into a curtsey.

'Miss Newell,' said Gwen, swallowing in an attempt to moisten her mouth. 'May I introduce H-His Grace, Percy Devereux, Duke of Knaresby.'

'Duke of—? Well… Very pleased to make your acquaintance, I'm sure,' said Rilla. 'Very pleased.'

Try as she might, Gwen was unable to keep her eyes from the Duke as he bowed. She wished to goodness she had managed to resist the temptation, for the instant their gazes met he winked.

It was not heat this time, but something rather akin to it that rushed through Gwen's body. A warmth…a prickle of interest—something that drew her to him, pulling a smile across her face against her better judgment.

'Goodness, a duke,' said Rilla conversationally. 'Gwen, why did you bother coming here if you have such a striking circle of acquaintances?'

'I think we are needed over here,' said Sylvia, stepping forward hastily. 'Come on, Rilla. Your servant, Your Grace.'

After dipping the fastest curtesy Gwen had ever seen, Sylvia shepherded Rilla away and left Gwen alone with the handsome Duke.

Not that she thought him handsome. Obviously.

That would be foolish, Gwen told herself, *for he certainly does not consider you any such thing.*

But after convincing herself over the last six days that she had seen the last of the Duke, it was rather discomforting to find him not only at an evening dinner which she would be forced to sit through, but to be accosted by him the moment she entered the room…

'Well, you have made your point, turned up and surprised me,' she said quietly, so only Percy could hear. 'You can go now—back to your companions or back to Town, which is where I suppose you will go.'

'Nonsense,' said Percy briskly. 'I came for dinner, and I am very much looking forward to the conversation of my dinner companion.'

A little of the tension in Gwen's shoulders seeped away at these words. With five wallflowers, and seemingly double the number of gentlemen—the Pike had outdone herself—there was little chance she would be seated beside this particular gentleman, who made her whole body shiver whenever he came close.

A knowing smile teased across Percy's lips. 'I have, of course, applied to Pike to ensure you are seated beside me.'

Gwen's mouth fell open, and she saw with some surprise that the Duke's gaze followed her lower lip. 'You—you haven't?'

His eyes glittered. 'She's my old governess—you didn't know? She thinks my conversation would be good for you.'

Governess? It was rather difficult to picture the Pike anywhere but here. 'Your governess?'

The Duke was prevented from replying by the resounding gong echoing from the hall. Instead, he moved to her side and put out his arm without speaking, a haughty look on his face.

Speaking was not necessary; his meaning was clear. He intended to accompany her into the dining room and she was supposed to be grateful for the honour.

Entering the second official dinner of the Wallflower Academy that Season on the arm of a duke!

Gwen could never have dreamed of such a thing—would never have expected such attentions from any gentleman, let alone one with a title!

But there was something strange about this man. The pomposity was to be expected, she thought dryly, because he was a duke. There was the arrogance she'd always thought dukes would have, the expectation that anyone in his presence should be thanking him on bended knee for paying them any attention whatsoever.

Could there be any more to him than superciliousness?

Percy cleared his throat. Gwen's heart tightened for a moment, but the warmth created by his presence was spreading through her body and she could do nothing but take his arm.

'Thank you,' she said in a small voice.

He nodded.

As they stepped forward together Gwen was conscious of every eye in the room upon her, wallflowers and gentlemen alike. That must account for the strange tingling in her stomach and just below. There could be no other explanation.

And then he hesitated.

She glanced up at Percy. His eyes were roving the table. He was evidently unsure where he should sit.

Unsure? A duke? Did they not always have the greatest precedence?

His hand tightened on hers. 'I… Uh…'

'Over here, Your Grace!' The angelic tones of Miss Pike. She was gesturing to the head of the table. 'Only the best seat for our most esteemed, our most…'

Her words washed in and out of Gwen's ears unheard as Percy resumed his pace and helped her to the seat beside his.

As he did so, the wallflower opposite her picked up a spoon, immediately dropped it with a clatter onto her wine glass, and flushed crimson.

Sylvia leaned past two of the gentlemen without offering either a glance. 'All these wallflowers!'

'Hush!' Miss Pike frowned.

Gwen's stomach turned, but Sylvia merely flashed a grin. 'Rilla and I rather hoped you wouldn't be a true wallflower, Gwen, but I can see by your flush that you're just like them!'

It was all Gwen could do to smile and say nothing. Well, she had managed it, then. In just one week she had put aside her temper and faded into the background. As her mother had always wished.

They sat in silence until the first course was brought out—some sort of soup. Pea soup? Normally Gwen would not care for such a thing, but she eagerly picked up her spoon and began to eat.

If she was eating, she could not be expected to maintain conversation.

'You look very…nice.'

Gwen choked, spewing green soup across the crisp white linen tablecloth. *Nice?*

'Do not tease me,' she said in a low tone.

She was fortunate tonight. Miss Pike had evidently endeavoured to find a few talkative gentlemen, for a pair of them were having a spirited conversation about the latest horse racing at one end of the table, and Sylvia was engaged in a debate on poetry with a man three seats along.

No one seemed to have noticed her shameful soup spurt…although a footman was looking at her rather despairingly.

Surrounded by the noise of the conversation, Gwen glared at the Duke beside her.

'I am not teasing,' said Percy amiably. 'If I was teasing you…'

He put down his spoon and twisted in his seat to face her. Gwen tried to ignore him, to take another mouthful of soup, but her hands did not obey her. Quite contrary to her desire, she also twisted, the better to face the Duke.

His face was a picture of solemnity, and when he spoke it was in a low voice—so low only Gwen could hear him. 'If I was teasing you, I would say you are the most…the most beautiful woman I have ever seen.'

Scalding heat seared Gwen's face.

The cheek! Did he wish to offend her, then? Was this all some game? Some trick to entertain him?

'So that's not true, then?' she asked fiercely. The arrogance of the man!

'Oh, no, it's all true,' said Percy lightly. His eyes did not waver. 'A duke never lies. I just wanted to tease you.'

Gwen swallowed, soup entirely forgotten. How was it possible for a gentleman to make her feel like this? As though…as though her skin was waking up for the first time, tingling, aching for something she did not understand?

She glanced across the table and saw Miss Pike nodding encouragingly at the pair of them. 'You do know what the Pike will think, don't you? Now you've insisted on sitting next to me at dinner, I mean.'

Percy shrugged nonchalantly. Evidently to him the opinions of a woman like Miss Pike were inconsequential. 'Let her think what she wants. I certainly know what *I* want.'

This was ridiculous!

Gwen tried to turn away, but for some reason her body did not wish to comply. On the contrary, it wished to be nearer. Gwen found herself leaning closer, and to her great surprise Percy did not move back.

'This is ridiculous,' she said in an undertone. 'You are a duke and I am—'

'Nothing,' Percy said quietly, all laughter gone from his voice. 'I remember what you said, Gwen. And, despite my turning up here in my best cravat and most elegantly embroidered waistcoat, you are not impressed by me, are you?'

How easily they did it, Gwen thought with a shot of pain through her heart.

The way gentlemen flirted, responded so quickly, with such wit. Just like they did in novels. It was most unfair. She had no knowledge of the world, no knowledge of men or their ways. How was she supposed to spar with him?

'Impressed? No,' Gwen said quietly.

Was that a flash of anger she saw in those commanding eyes? 'Why the devil not?'

'Because you have done nothing impressive, Your Grace, save bearing a title you inherited and did not earn.'

Not for the first time in his presence Gwen raised her hands to her mouth in horror at what she had said. When would she learn that her temper had to be hidden away, never permitted to surface?

Percy did not look offended, but he hardly looked delighted. 'I see.'

'And besides, if…if my father was alive, he would ask you…' Gwen licked her lips as she hesitated, and saw with wonder the flash of desire in Percy's eyes. 'He d-died just a few months ago. Suddenly. He would wonder, as I am, why you, a duke, are noticing a mere commoner like myself?'

'I am asking myself the same question.'

'And he would ask you what your intentions are.'

It was a bold statement, and Gwen could hardly believe she had spoken it. But Percy did not look away. And even though a shiver rushed up Gwen's spine, she did not break the connection either.

'Well,' said Percy, 'if your father was alive, I would tell him.'

She laughed—and immediately clapped her hands over her mouth as most of those at the table looked at her.

It took a moment—it seemed an age—but eventually they all returned either to their soup or their conversations.

Except one.

Percy was chuckling under his breath. 'You are not really a wallflower, are you?'

Well, perhaps this is rather enjoyable, Gwen thought as she took in the handsome, strong jaw of this man who seemed unable to leave her alone.

Why not flirt with a duke? It would certainly not lead anywhere. She could consider it practice. A distraction.

'And you?' she said lightly. 'Are you really a duke? I only have your word for it, after all.'

Gwen had thought her remark rather witty, but it had a most unexpected effect on the gentleman. A shadow swept over his face, and a flash of anger, of fury, and for the first time since they had been seated at the table he looked away.

'I apologise,' Gwen said quickly. Whatever she had said, she had clearly offended him.

Percy laughed dryly. 'You do not know what you are apologising for. Do you?'

It was too much. Gwen was all at sea in their conversation—which always seemed to be the case whenever she was in the company of the Duke of Knaresby. Percy did something to her—something she could not understand but could only guess at:

She liked him. She was attracted to him. She found him most irresistible, even if his manners were incorrigible and his conversation haughty. Was this why she was acting so strangely…as though drawn like a moth to a flame?

'No,' Gwen said helplessly. 'I do not. I am sorry.'

Somehow that was the right answer. A teasing smile on his lips, Percy reached towards her and took her hand in his.

Gwen almost gasped aloud as he raised it to his lips and kissed the very tips of her fingers. Oh, to feel those lips, to feel the warmth of them… The pooling desire in her body was crying out for it. Such a simple movement, yet one so heightened with promise of more.

'Gwendoline Knox,' said Percy quietly, her hand still in his, 'when I make you do something that requires an apology, you will really need to mean it.'

Chapter Four

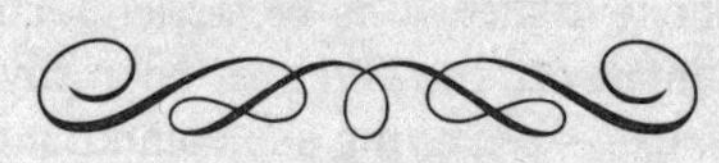

'Then I realised it was in my pocket the entire time! Reminds me of the time I went hunting with Buxhill and Lindham—you know them, of course? Fine gentlemen, but not so good with a horse. Did I ever tell you where I got my filly from? Lovely ride, really pleasant manner—though when I first purchased her naturally…'

Percy's chin almost touched his chest and he jerked up, sleep swiftly pushed back. Never mind that the impending slumber would have been appreciated, it would not do to be seen napping while Westerleigh chatted away at White's.

That was the trouble with the gentlemen's club, Percy thought, as he nodded vaguely at whatever the old boy was saying and leaned forward to pick up his cup of tea. It was cold.

White's was all very well—a sterling establishment, and he wouldn't hear a word against it—and yet… There was just something rather old-fashioned about it. Percy glanced about the Blue Drawing Room, where he had settled himself not an hour ago. Decorated in the finest furnishings the seventeen-seventies could lavishly permit, there was a rather tired air about the place. The leather was worn to skin in some places on the armchairs, and each of the little tables upon which the gentlemen rested their cups—tea, whisky, or other—were chipped.

In truth, Percy thought, stretching in an attempt not to show Westerleigh that he was bored by his monologue, there was nothing interesting at White's. When it boiled down to it—and the meat here was dreadfully boiled—it was all about the people one interacted with.

And when one of them was Westerleigh…

A yawn threatened to reveal his boredom, but Percy managed to stifle it just as a gap appeared in the conversation. 'Yes, indeed,' he said.

The Earl of Westerleigh nodded pompously, evidently unaware that his dull monologue was putting his companion to sleep. 'And, of course, there was nothing for it but to continue! When I spoke to the man in question, he told me…'

Percy could not have recounted precisely what this anecdote was about for love nor money, having totally lost the train of the conversation, but that was rather an advantage. It left him free to think about a more pleasant topic.

Like Miss Gwendoline Knox, for example, and the way candlelight illuminated her face when she was embarrassed—or aroused.

Percy swallowed, but saw that old Westerleigh hadn't a clue. No one in the place was listening to a word he said, and he had not noticed that his young companion had quite another thing on his mind.

A young lady with dark, almost black hair curling around her bright, expressive eyes. Eyes that had danced with confusion and mischief as they had conversed at that Wallflower Academy dinner.

And to think he nearly hadn't attended.

Percy dreaded to think how he might have spent that evening talking to some of his mother's dull friends, listening to dull tales like Westerleigh's, eating dull food…

Instead he had been treated to the most delightful display of restrained irritation he had ever seen. Why, if they had been alone, Percy was willing to bet Gwen would have walloped him for the things he had said—and quite rightly, too, in some cases.

'Gwendoline Knox, when I make you do something that requires an apology, you will really need to mean it.'

He shivered at the very thought. Oh, the things he would like to do to Gwendoline Knox… It was almost criminal, how delectable she was. Far more interesting than old Westerleigh, though Percy was not so unpolitic as to say so.

It was strange, though. Any other Thursday in Town, Percy would have expected some of his acquaintances to be here—rather than this old friend of his father who was boring him at present, his moustache bristling in the almost continuous speech.

'I thought to meself, *This is it, young chap!* Of course in those days gentlemen had far more opportunities for adventure—none of this Grand Tour nonsense you chaps dally with. No, it was to war for me, and I discovered to my surprise…'

Percy nodded. On any other day Westerleigh's new topic might have lifted him out of his listlessness, but not today.

No, unless a certain lady walked into White's, with a delicate air and a fierce temper…

Percy was smiling—a most uncommon occurrence in White's. One did not come here to be entertained. One came to escape the world. The trouble was, he did not particularly wish to escape the world today. At least, not one particular part of it.

Not that he should.

He folded his hands firmly in his lap, as though that would prevent him from being rash. It wasn't *his* reputation, after all, that would be harmed. It would be Gwen's.

Their unequal stations, her innocence, his lack of honourable intentions…

Gwen would take a great risk in just being seen speaking to him, Percy knew. The censure of Society… But then, he would risk the wrath of his mother. It was almost the same thing.

'And then I—Knaresby, old thing. Where are you going?' Westerleigh blinked in surprise.

Percy pulled his coat straight and nodded politely to the older man. 'Duty calls, my dear chap.'

'Ah… Well, duty and all that,' said the older gentleman comfortably, reaching for the glass of brandy which had been refilled subtly, without request, by a footman as soon as it had been emptied. 'Quite understand.'

Percy was impressed—because he certainly didn't understand. He could not comprehend why he was walking out of White's at this early hour, why he was instructing his man to ready his horse, and why he was directing that horse out of Town.

'Your Grace?'

In fact, he—

'Your Grace? Devereux?'

Percy halted. Of course. *He* was 'Your Grace'. It was still taking a bit of getting used to.

The demure words had been spoken by a footman in White's colours, his hands clasped together before him almost as a supplicant.

What on earth did he want?

'Yes?' Percy prompted.

The footman smiled awkwardly. 'It is only… I need to speak to your steward, Your Grace.'

Percy blinked. 'My steward?'

What on earth for? There had never been any need for his steward to be involved in his White's membership.

The footman inclined his head. 'To organise your bill, Your Grace. 'Tis a small matter…'

'Oh, that's easy enough,' said Percy, his shoulders relaxing. 'You had me worried there! Here, how much is my tab?'

He pulled his pocketbook from inside his jacket, and saw with surprise that the footman looked genuinely flummoxed.

'I… You… Your steward,' muttered the man. He cleared his throat. 'Dukes do not carry money!'

Heat flushed Percy's cheeks. 'They…they don't?'

No one had told him that. But then, there were so many hidden rules, weren't there? So many things others just seemed to do without thinking, as easily as breathing.

Whereas every breath he took was a determined gasp.

'I must speak with your steward,' the footman said firmly, carefully avoiding looking at the pound notes in Percy's hands. 'That is the proper way of doing things.'

Proper way of doing things? *Well, that's as may be,* Percy thought, as he gave his steward's name to the clearly embarrassed footman.

James wouldn't have allowed a mere servant to talk to him like that—make him feel the fool. Besides, he had never been one to enjoy 'the proper way' of doing things. Not before the title, not after.

Why else, he thought as the autumnal air whipped past him, chilling his ears and giving him a greater desire to arrive, *would I be so intrigued by Gwen?*

Why else would he be arriving unannounced at the Wallflower Academy?

It was not so far out of London that a visit was unwarranted or surprising, but as far as he knew there were no planned events this afternoon. No teas, no music recitals, no card games, no dinner—and certainly no ball.

A wry smile slipped across Percy's face as he surveyed

the old manor house as it appeared around a corner. That was a thought… Gwen at a ball.

Miss Knox.

He really needed to remember the bounds of propriety, Percy reminded himself as he slipped off his horse and handed over the reins to a stableboy who had rushed forward.

He might have called Gwen by her first name at the dinner, and he might have looked as though he wished to slowly unwrap each and every piece of her clothing, wanted to kiss every inch of her skin…

But that didn't mean he was going to do anything foolish. Except turn up here unannounced, of course.

His knock on the front door of the Wallflower Academy was therefore accidental. He had not meant to do it. His feet had just meandered to the door, and now he was there it seemed ridiculous not to knock.

Precisely what he intended to do, Percy was not sure. His thoughts were not forming properly. For some reason his heart was thumping loudly. He could hear it in his ears, feel the tight pressure in his chest.

When a footman finally answered the door, Percy astonished himself and the servant by barking, 'Gwen!'

The footman blinked. 'I beg your pardon, Your Grace?'

Percy shifted on his feet, as though that might help him remember both his manners and his senses.

You are not falling in love with a mere wallflower, he told himself sternly. *After everything you have been through to get here, you do not need any complication. You know the sort of woman you must marry. You know the criteria. You are just being polite. You are visiting the Academy. You could be visiting any of them.*

The array of wallflowers currently in residence at the Academy rushed through his mind.

Perhaps not. None of them attracted him as Gwen did. None of them drove a need in him…a want that was starting to affect his judgment.

Percy jutted out his jaw imperiously—or at least as imperiously as he could muster. 'I thought I would visit the wallflowers.'

This was evidently an unusual statement. The footman looked a little concerned, and swallowed hard before saying, 'Is…is there an invitation upon your person, Your Grace, that I could see?'

'Invitation?' repeated Percy, completely bemused. 'What would I need an invitation for?'

'Well, you see, it's a matter of…of delicacy,' muttered the footman, his boldness deserting him. 'Having gentlemen in the house unaccompanied…'tis not right…'

Percy cleared his throat, but said nothing.

The man had a point.

Miss Pike had probably created the rule after a difficult situation. One that should certainly not have occurred. A scandalous one. Involving a wallflower and a rake, no doubt.

Someone entirely different from him.

'I think, in the circumstances, you can make an exception,' Percy said, smiling and taking a step forward.

It was a step he had to immediately retract, as the footman did not budge.

'Circumstances, Your Grace?'

The man knew him and yet was determined to refuse him access! The blackguard!

'I am a duke,' Percy said pointedly.

'And I am a footman,' said the footman stoutly, not looking Percy in the eye, but rather gazing at something just beyond his left shoulder. 'I know my place, and I am sorry to say, Your Grace, my place is in here and yours is out there. Unless you have an invitation…'

Percy stared at the man helplessly. Foiled—and by a footman. no less! It was most infuriating. Just beyond this man was a woman who was bold and brash and a wallflower. She was also shy, and a multitude of complexities Percy had still to understand.

And once he understood her he could leave her alone and get back to his primary goal this Season: finding a wife.

It was simple as that.

Understand Gwen, then leave her.

The twist in his stomach told Percy he was attempting to fool himself, but he ignored it and instead directed all his ire towards the unfortunate footman before him.

'Miss Pike,' Percy said in a cold tone, 'will hear about this.'

The servant drew himself up. 'I hope so, Your Grace.'

Muttering curses under his breath against servants in general and footmen in particular, Percy turned away from the man and walked down the steps.

It was galling to be so close to Gwen and yet be unable to see her…

A slow smile crept over Percy's face as he stepped towards the stables and he halted in his tracks. If he skirted around the other side of the house—not towards the stables but towards the orangery—there was a very real chance he would be able to see her.

But that would be a foolish thing to do. Something only a lovesick mule would do. Percy knew better. He would get his horse and ride straight home. That would be the sensible thing to do.

Stepping lightly across the gravel, and hoping the dratted footman was not watching, Percy crept away from the stables and towards the westerly side of the house where the large orangery stood. A little dilapidated now, it nonetheless offered a perfect view into the dining room and the drawing room of the house.

Surely Gwen would be in one of those at this time of day…?

Highly conscious that he had no idea whatsoever what the wallflowers imprisoned inside the Academy found to fill their time, Percy crept through a rather cumbersome hedge and across a border, ruffling a rose.

Soon he found himself at one end of the orangery.

And was rewarded.

Looking through the orangery and into the room beyond, Percy could make out Gwen and the other wallflowers, evidently having a lesson in dinner etiquette.

They were all seated at the dining room table with places set and a plethora of knives and forks before them. An irate-looking Miss Pike was striding up and down, delivering a monologue perhaps not unlike the one he had been subjected to by Westerleigh.

The reactions of the wallflowers, at least, looked the same as his. From where Percy was standing, it appeared that the black wallflower—Sylvia, wasn't it?—was trying to stifle giggles.

Percy smiled as he watched Gwen attempting to pay attention despite the obvious tedium.

How had a woman like Gwen ended up in a place like this?

True, she was shy—but there was a real temper under that hesitancy. Her beauty, her conversation… It did not seem possible that Gwen could not find a match. Percy was certainly finding her far more interesting than he should be…

He gasped. Gwen had looked up, right into his eyes, her gaze fierce, sharp, as though she had heard his thought. As though she had not approved of it.

Taking a hurried step backwards, Percy felt his foot slip on some mud, toppling him to the ground. The wind knocked out of him, he gazed up at the gloomy grey sky and wondered what it was about this woman she managed to cause someone to be tipped to the ground every time they came near to each other.

When he'd managed to right himself, brushing off as much mud as possible, Percy looked up to see Gwen red-faced and the other wallflowers giggling around the table.

Blast. He had obviously embarrassed not only himself, but Gwen too.

What had overcome him? Bringing him to the Wallflower Academy without an invitation, skulking around like a common cad, slipping over with shock when a mere glance met his eye?

He was a damned duke! He had responsibilities—duties in Town unable to be ignored. So why was he here, pulled towards this woman?

It was a question Percy could not answer, but he would soon need to.

After exchanging a few words with Miss Pike, Gwen rose, curtsied, then started towards him.

Oh, hell. What was he supposed to say? How was he supposed to explain why a duke was hiding in hedges and falling beside orangeries, all to see a wallflower he must not pursue?

'Well,' said Gwen quietly, opening the door of the orangery and leaning against the doorframe. 'You seem to have made your acquaintance with the ground.'

Percy glared. How did she do it? There was no malice in her tone, no coquettish teasing as he had learned to expect from eligible young ladies. Instead, Gwen appeared to be…earnest. Honest. It was a strange thing to see in a lady of marriageable age, and Percy found himself rather undone by the entire experience.

'I… I fell,' he snapped.

By Jove, he needed to gather his thoughts and tame his tongue, or he would be making even more of a fool of himself than he already had!

The damp from his fall had started to seep through his breeches.

'Yes, I saw,' said Gwen, still quietly.

There was mischief in her eyes, but it was held back by a reticence Percy did not quite understand.

'There is a front door, you know. I've walked through it myself. 'Tis not too arduous.'

Percy forced himself to speak. 'I wasn't permitted entry.'

Gwen stared. 'Goodness, why on earth not?'

He shrugged, as though that explained the situation. When it became apparent from Gwen's waiting expression that it did not, Percy tried to make the entire thing far more impressive than it actually was.

'I was forbidden entry because…because it was believed the place would not be safe with me in it,' he said, waving an arm expressively. 'That you wallflowers would not be safe with me. Have to fight me off with a stick, I suppose.'

Gwen's cheeks flushed scarlet and she glanced behind her, presumably at someone carefully listening in. Decorum had to be upheld. They could not be alone.

It was instantaneous. He'd crossed a line—some line Percy had had no idea was there—and she'd closed herself off.

The mischievous air was gone, replaced only by the demeanour of a quiet, uninterested wallflower.

'Well, I will say good day, then,' said Gwen, and moved to shut the door.

'Wait!' Percy acted on instinct, his desire to impress disappearing, subsumed by the need to keep her with him.

He looked down. He had placed his hand on hers, and even through his riding glove he could once again sense that strange, yet enjoyable tingling that typically preceded one of his beddings.

Percy was no innocent. He did not have to wonder what this meant. He wanted her—badly. Needed to know every inch of her…to tease pleasure from those lips now parting in wonder at his presumption in touching her. Then he'd leave her behind.

But Gwen did not know that—and it was best she never knew. Percy might take the pleasures of courtesans, but he was not one to take the innocence of a wallflower—not one under the protection of a lady as fearsome as Miss Pike, anyway.

Carefully, and slowly, as though any sudden movement might break the connection between them, Percy removed his hand and moved back.

'Your Grace, I do not understand why—'

'Come with me.'

Gwen's eyes widened, her breath catching in her throat, and Percy stepped towards her, his desire to dominate her will forcing him forward. He wanted to see the change in her as she spoke. Not just hear her words, but sense the change in her breath, feel the heat of her skin.

'I… I beg your pardon?' Gwen whispered.

'On a ride,' Percy said high-handedly. 'I have my mare here, and I am sure there are horses in the Academy's stables. Come with me. On a ride.'

For a heady moment he thought he had convinced her. Gwen examined him, her eyes appraising, and Percy felt scrutinised as never before. What was she looking for? Trustworthiness? A sense of his being a rake?

She would find both—and more besides, Percy thought with a wry smile. But what he was far more interested in was what *he* would find when spending more time with her.

Gwen Knox. There was something about her…something he could not put his finger on though he very much wished to. Something she was hiding. Something more than was natural for a wallflower.

Something that one day he would uncover.

'No,' she said firmly, though her lips curled into a smile. 'You are jesting with me.'

'I am not jesting with you,' said Percy, piqued at her immediate refusal. 'Come riding with me.'

'You came all this way from Town to ask me to go on a ride?'

'I came all this way to see you.'

Percy could think of no better way to put it. It was the truth. She had drawn him here inexorably, against his better judgement and seemingly against the wishes of the footman who guarded the door.

But he was here, and so was she.

Gwen had had no need to leave her lesson to speak with him—she had chosen to do that of her own volition. She wanted him. Percy could sense it.

The fact was it was absolutely impossible—foolish, even—for a duke and a wallflower to be conversing like this…

Well, Percy would deal with his conscience later.

'Do you not need to marry a woman of—of good fortune and connections?'

Percy blanched. The bold question from Gwen had come from nowhere, her words clear and without malice.

And she was right.

Percy wished to contradict her immediately, tell her that

his choices were his own, and he could wed—or bed—whomever he wished.

But it would be a lie. A boldfaced lie and one she would discover soon enough. Gwen had seen the need in him. For Percy certainly did need to find a wife with a dowry and a good reputation.

Needed to far more than she could ever realise.

'I see the truth in your eyes, you know. You cannot hide it.'

'I…' Percy said, but words failed him.

This was ridiculous—words never failed him. He was a master at wit and at wooing, but when it came to Gwen… she undid him. It was most unfair, for he had never wished to impress anyone more.

'Well, when you work out the answer,' said Gwen gently, 'come and tell me. I cannot help but feel, Your Grace, you are teasing yourself far more than you are teasing me. Good day.'

And with that she closed the door of the orangery and returned not merely to her seat in the dining room, but further into the Academy and out of sight.

Percy leaned heavily against the glass of the orangery—then hastily stood as it made an awful creaking sound.

This woman was going to be the death of him.

How had Gwen put it?

'Least likely to win a duke.'

Percy shook his head with a smile. *Least likely?* That was not precisely how he would have put it.

Chapter Five

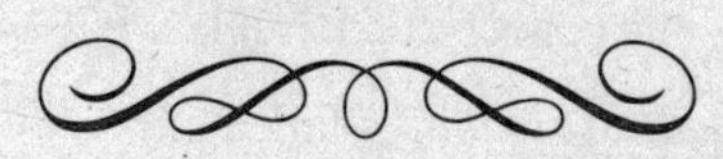

Monday slid into Tuesday, which was very much like Wednesday, and before Gwen knew it she had been at the Wallflower Academy almost two weeks.

Days repeated each other in the same tired, dull routine she was already accustomed to, and it was difficult to see how some of the other wallflowers, who had been resident in the place for months, if not years, suffered such boredom.

Breakfast, and then a little light reading was expected from all the wallflowers—but not too much. Gwen had been subjected to a lecture one day from Miss Pike, on how too much reading was wont to make a woman a bluestocking.

'And if there is one thing worse than a wallflower,' the indefatigable Miss Pike had said sternly, 'it is a bluestocking.'

Gwen had spotted out of the corner of her eye a particularly irritated scowl, but no one had been bold enough to contradict the owner of the Wallflower Academy.

Which was probably all to the good. Gwen had no desire to bring attention to herself, or to challenge the fearsome Pike and have even a hint of a suggestion of returning home to her mother.

Not after the chaos she had endured at home. She had left that behind. She would never face that again.

After breakfast and light reading came lessons—something Gwen was resigned to.

Lessons. The Academy made her feel as if she was back in the schoolroom, learning her alphabet and practising her handwriting, but these lessons were irritatingly childish.

Small talk and conversation. Napkin folding. Disagreeing with one's conversational partner. Using forks and spoons. Walking with one's head at the correct angle. The appropriate way to speak of the weather. Identifying a person's rank at a distance. Music appreciation.

If Gwen had had anywhere else to go, she would have packed her things and been off within three days of arriving at the austere Academy.

By Thursday afternoon, several days after Percy—the Duke of Knaresby…she really must remember to give him his correct title—had arrived so strangely at the Wallflower Academy and played some sort of jest upon her at the orangery, Gwen could not remove his words from her mind.

'Come riding with me.'

If she was truly so desirous of leaving, Gwen thought painfully, as she sat in silence in the quiet of the afternoon with the other wallflowers, some reading, some embroidering, Rilla just gazing sightlessly into space, then why had she not accepted Percy's invitation?

A ride… Something she had forgone since she had left home. An opportunity to see some of the countryside about the place. More, a chance to leave the confines of the Wallflower Academy for more than five minutes in the garden.

It would have been heavenly.

It would have been glorious.

It would have been far too much of a temptation to bear.

Which was why Gwen was rather surprised to find herself bundled into a dog cart at this awful time in the morning.

It was all Sylvia's fault, of course.

'Sylvia, what on earth is this about?' Gwen had asked, yawning, after being dragged out of bed by Sylvia, who had already been dressed. She had got into her own gown and been pulled down the servants' staircase to this dog cart waiting by the side of the Academy. 'Have you lost your senses?'

She certainly had.

The morning air was freezing, and Gwen's mind had whirled at such an unexpected turn of events.

What was Sylvia thinking?

Sylvia's expression was sharp and determined. 'I'm not staying here to rot for ever. I don't care what the Pike says. I'm not going to be married off, and my parents won't take me back—not my father, at any rate.'

Gwen tried to follow her rapid words. 'But that doesn't explain—'

'I'm running away,' Sylvia pronounced proudly. 'On!'

The dog cart jerked forward as Gwen attempted to take in the words just spoken. Running away?

'So what am I doing here with you?' It was all she could manage.

The day was so early, her breath blossomed before them.

Sylvia grinned. 'You're no wallflower.'

Gwen swallowed. 'Y-yes, I am.'

The lie tasted bitter, but she had no choice. She could not be found out. She had to fade into the background and—

'No, you're not,' Sylvia said, quite calmly, leaning back in the dog cart as if she frequently drove such a conveyance. 'And though that place is no prison, let's be honest. Our families don't want us. They can call it an academy as much as they want, but it's just a place where unwanted daughters are left and abandoned.'

Gwen tried to think of words to counter Sylvia's argument, but she could not. Was she herself not a perfect example of this?

'No, the whole world is out there, and I am tired of being treated like a child, ordered about by the Pike as though I have no idea what I'm doing,' Sylvia said firmly.

'And so…a dog cart?' asked Gwen helplessly. 'And abducting me, I suppose? Is that the plan?'

Sylvia's grin was bold. 'All part of the plan. You can get out, if you prefer, but I thought you'd be interested in getting out of this place.'

Gwen's gaze flickered up to the tall manor house slowly disappearing into the distance.

She had no wish to be there, it was true. But where else could she go?

And Sylvia was no fool. Though she had not shared the information, she must have a plan. They must be meeting someone, wherever they were going. She must have some family who would take her.

Gwen sighed. 'This is ridiculous.'

'This is an adventure!' beamed Sylvia. 'Finally!'

It did not feel like much of an adventure when the dog cart brought them to a loud, noisy and most definitely stench-filled street. There were countless people meandering up and down, carts, dogs, a man on a horse, a woman leaning out of a window shouting something…

It was overwhelming. Intoxicating.

And the dog cart had disappeared into the melee.

'Is…is this London?' Gwen asked in wonder.

Sylvia snorted. 'This place? No, just a small town where I thought I could find…'

Her voice trailed away and Gwen narrowed her eyes. 'I thought you had a plan.'

'I did,' Sylvia said, though her defiance was lacking now. 'I planned to leave the Wallflower Academy. Now I have—'

'Sylvia Bryant, you have no idea what to do next, do you?' Gwen said, with dawning comprehension and panic rising in her chest.

She was in a strange town she'd never heard of, with a woman with no plan at all, no luggage, no money—what on earth were they going to do?

The panic started to solidify into shame. Her mother had ordered her to be obedient and not to draw any attention to herself! And here she was, bound to get into trouble with the Pike when they got back.

If they could get back…

Sylvia looked wretched. 'I… Well, I didn't expect it to be so—'

'No one wants us, Sylvia,' Gwen found herself saying, the shame and panic mingling to bring her temper out. 'We're at the Academy because we have nowhere else to go! It's not a prison if you have no alternative!'

Sylvia's cheeks were reddening. 'I never said—'

'Gwen? Sylvia?'

Against all the odds, a voice was calling their names—a voice that came from a coach.

Gwen's stomach twisted as a face appeared in the window of that coach. Of all the people—

'What are you doing here?' asked Percy brightly.

Her heart skipped a beat. This was most untoward—what on earth was *he* doing here? And how was she supposed to explain?

'It's your duke, Gwen!' Sylvia said eagerly. 'My word, do you think he could take us—?'

'He'll take us straight back to the Academy, and you

must pray the Pike hasn't noticed our absence,' Gwen said, far more firmly than she felt.

If they were lucky, they could slip back in and pretend the whole thing had never happened.

As long as Percy could be trusted to keep his mouth shut…

A lopsided lazy grin slipped over the Duke's face as he clambered out of his carriage. 'I didn't think to see you here!'

His words were directed at Gwen, who refused to meet his eye. It was going to be painful, asking him this, but—

'Can we have a lift?' Sylvia asked cheerfully.

Gwen blinked. How did she do it? Speak so boldly, without any care, to a duke?

'Sylvia,' she hissed under her breath. 'I think—'

'Oh, I'm more than happy to take you back to the Academy,' said Percy, though his gaze was firmly fixed not on Sylvia, but on Gwen. She could feel the intensity of his gaze even without looking up. 'Come on. I'll—'

'I don't think so, Y'Grace.'

Gwen looked up. A man's voice had spoken—one she did not recognise. Now she had looked up, she could see it was Percy's driver.

He looked a little embarrassed, but it was nothing to the surprise on Percy's face. 'Why in heaven's not?' he asked.

'Well, because…because dukes don't pick women up off the street,' said the shamefaced driver. 'Not in daylight, anyway.'

Heat blossomed across Gwen's chest. Was the man insinuating—?

'This duke does,' Percy said firmly, offering a hand to Sylvia. 'A gentleman always rescues a lady, my man, and in this case there are two. Gwen?'

She had no choice but to accept his hand into the coach.

Settling beside Sylvia, Gwen gave her a stern look that received nothing but a grin in reply—and then Percy himself seated himself in the carriage.

'You're running away, aren't you?' he asked conversationally.

Before Gwen could do anything, Sylvia nodded blithely. 'Gwen tried to stop me, but I was determined.'

'Yes, I can see that,' said Percy softly.

Gwen looked at her hands, clasped together in her lap, as the carriage jerked forward.

This was outrageous! It was all Sylvia's fault—running away, indeed—and Percy would never let her hear the end of it, she was sure. Why, he would—

'I think it's best,' came Percy's quiet voice, 'if we say no more about it. We'll be at the Academy in less than twenty minutes, and you can slip back in. It's still early.'

Gwen swallowed, and managed to force herself to look up in gratitude.

Her breath caught in her throat. How did he look like… like *that*?

As though it was his greatest pleasure to rescue her.

As though he had hoped for nothing more when he awoke that morning.

As though spending just a few stolen minutes with her, even in the company of Sylvia, was a gift she could have bestowed upon no more grateful recipient.

Gwen forced herself to breathe. She was seeing far more in that look than existed, she was sure.

And he was right. In an inordinately swift amount of time the Academy could be seen through the carriage window, and Sylvia's shoulders had slumped.

'Not a word,' Gwen said firmly as the carriage came to a halt.

And, most surprisingly, Sylvia obeyed.

The two of them said nothing to Percy as they descended from his carriage, nothing to each other as they slipped through a side door and walked the familiar route to the drawing room, and nothing to the wallflowers who looked up curiously as they entered.

Gwen stepped over to an empty seat after retrieving her embroidery from the box. Her heart was thundering as she pulled out her needle and examined her progress.

What a disaster the morning might have been!

'Miss Knox?'

Besides, Gwen told herself firmly, her gaze drifting over the crimson thread slowly forming a rose on the embroidery hoop between her fingers, *a carriage ride with a duke is not simple. And it was Sylvia's fault, entirely.*

And it meant something. She was sure it did. If not to her, then to Percy. Certainly to the Pike, if she ever found out.

'Miss Knox!'

Startled, Gwen dropped her embroidery hoop. It slipped to the floor with a low *thunk*, and after she'd leaned down to pick it up the mirage of the Pike before her did not disappear.

'Miss Knox, you do not attend!'

Gwen swallowed. It was one of the most common critiques she had to endure from the sharp eyes of Miss Pike: not attending.

As though it was that easy.

As though she could force from her mind the face of Percy Devereux.

As though she could forget the way he had spoken to her at the dinner, the way he had held her hand, skin to skin, something Gwen had never done with any gentleman before.

As though she could pretend she had not seen him that morning.

Their connection was something she longed for. A connection which drew something out of her she did not understand. Yet she knew where it led…

Oh, she knew.

'Yes, Miss Pike,' Gwen said hastily, conscious that the owner of the Wallflower Academy was waiting for a response. 'I do apologise, Miss Pike. I was thinking about… about the next rose.'

'Rose?' Miss Pike raised an eyebrow.

Gwen lifted her embroidery. 'Yellow or white?'

For a moment Miss Pike glared, as though attempting to discover whether there was an impertinence somewhere in the wallflower's remark.

Eventually it appeared she could find none. She sniffed. 'White. There is a letter for you.'

Her hand shot out and Gwen stared at the letter within it. Cheap paper and no seal—just a dot of sealing wax. Her heart sank, all hopes that it might have been a note from a certain gentleman disappearing in an instant.

There was only one person that letter could be from.

'You know, Miss Knox, I believe you are doing well in your comportment classes,' said Miss Pike stiffly, as though it physically pained her to say something pleasant.

Sylvia was seated behind Miss Pike, and Gwen saw her grin, and then make a silly face behind the older woman's back. Gwen stifled a laugh. She would not permit Sylvia to get her into trouble, no matter the inducement. Not even when she had dragged Gwen into a dog cart to run away from the Academy.

'But I wish you would try harder in your dining etiquette,' continued Miss Pike, a creasing frown appearing between her grey eyes. 'Really…disappearing off in the last fork lesson… I was most displeased.'

Gwen swallowed. Percy's face swam into view—that

teasing smile, that shamed expression when he'd been caught slipping over in the mud by the orangery.

He was a delight.

He was a torment.

He was a duke. Certainly not someone she should be thinking of.

'Yes,' said Gwen quietly, taking the letter from Miss Pike's hand and choosing not to comment on the negative remark. 'Thank you for your kind words, Miss Pike.'

If possible, the Pike's frown deepened as she examined her, and Gwen did not attempt to hold her gaze. It would be a fruitless task. Not only because her natural shyness did not permit it, but because Miss Pike clearly had decades of practice in fearsome gazes.

Gwen's gaze slipped instead to the roses in the embroidery in her hands, one complete, one half finished, the other a mere outline. She swallowed hard, forcing down the remembrance of that strange encounter.

What had Percy been thinking? Sneaking around the side of the Academy, looking in at them from the orangery, and then saying such strange things to her—almost flirting with her. As though she was a prize to be won, a lady to be courted, a prospective bride…

The thought was unconscionable. No gentleman would consider her a worthy match, Gwen was sure. No dowry, no real family name, no spirit or conversation to recommend her.

Only a temper which, once unleashed, could be deadly.

Her throat was dry, and no matter how many times she swallowed Gwen could not regain her composure.

She was being ridiculous.

Likely as not, dukes flirted with anything that moved. She was not special. She had not attracted him for any particular reason.

She was here because it had been impossible for her to remain at home after the scandal.

But that did not explain why he had come here, all the way from London, a full twenty-minute ride. Gwen could not comprehend it. Surely he would be inundated with invitations for parties and concerts, opportunities to visit Court, to see old friends and make new acquaintances…

What did it all mean?

'I see you have made quite an impression on the Duke of Knaresby.'

Gwen's eyes snapped back to Miss Pike, whose frown had disappeared and been replaced by an expression she could not place for a moment.

Then it became clear. Greed. Of course.

Miss Pike would be well rewarded by my Mother, Gwen thought darkly, *if she marries me off to a duke.*

It would be quite a coup for the Wallflower Academy. She doubted whether anything so wild had ever occurred in the place.

'I think you have done well with him so far, Miss Knox,' said Miss Pike calmly, utterly unable to see the flush on her charge's face—or simply ignoring it. 'I would have had you pegged as the least likely to win a duke. But I believe more conversation is required to hook him. You will need to put in more effort.'

Gwen could hardly believe those words were being spoken—and in the drawing room before all the other wallflowers, too! She could only see Sylvia and Rilla's expressions, to be sure, but if they were indicative of the others' she would soon be under a most direct interrogation.

'I cannot… I will not… I do not believe the Duke will be returning,' Gwen managed.

At least she was almost certain those words had come out of her mouth. She had intended them to do so.

'Nonsense,' said Miss Pike cheerfully. 'I will ensure he receives every invitation.'

If only she had a little bravery, a little determination—anything to force her mouth to move and her thoughts to pour into the conversation. If only she could make it clear to Miss Pike that she had no desire whatsoever to see Percy—the Duke—again.

Except she did.

Gwen could not lie to herself, even if she wished to lie to others. Seeing Percy was the only potential event of interest on her horizon—a horizon that stretched out seemingly for ever, littered with boring lessons, dull afternoon teas, insipid conversations at dinner and nothing else.

Nothing until she found a husband.

But she never would.

Gwen could confide in no one at the Academy—not yet. But she did not need the opinion of others to know that her secret would be ruinous to any potential husband, let alone a duke.

She would not put Percy and his family name through such scandal.

Not, Gwen thought hastily, her cheeks searing with heat, *that Percy was even considering her in such a manner.*

This was all Miss Pike's fantasy. She wished to see something that was not there, Gwen told herself firmly. It was not. At least, not from his side.

Miss Pike sighed. 'Why do you not go outside, Miss Knox, and read your letter there? I believe you are in great need of fresh air…you look most flushed.'

It was all she could do to nod mutely, rise, place her embroidery on her seat, and leave the room without falling over. As she stepped away the room spun, which to Gwen's mind was most unhelpful. And each step was a leaden beat against the drum of her own heart, which did not appear to be beating properly.

'You look most flushed.'

Well, it was no wonder she looked flushed. As Gwen opened the front door and stepped into the blessed cool of the afternoon's autumnal air, she tried not to think of Miss Pike's critique, her words of encouragement in Percy's direction, the gaze of all the other wallflowers and, worst of all, the letter in her hand.

The letter she knew she would have to read.

Gwen walked around the house, past the orangery, the sight of which at least tugged her lips into a wry smile, and continued across the lawn towards the ornamental gardens. The one just before the kitchen garden had a nook she had made her own, between a corner of the redbrick walls and a growing evergreen tree which gave her protection from the wind.

It was there, on a small bench which must have been placed there at least a decade ago, if the growing moss upon it was anything to go by, that Gwen seated herself and slowly cracked open the sealing wax to unfold the letter.

It was, as she had expected, from her mother. It was short, cruel, and to the point. Just like every one of the almost daily letters she was receiving.

Gwendoline,

Goodness, I have never been so entertained in all my life as when the Crawfords come to visit. Their company is most welcome now that I have removed you from the house, and their son pays me such flattering compliments—nothing, of course, my dear Walter could complain at, and in fairness it appears there is little gentlemen of real taste can do in my presence but praise it.

Why, I had to be quite forceful with the Major just last week when he kissed my hand, and in public too! I soon put him to rights, but I am sorry to say it only seems to have increased his passion.

That is the benefit of marrying a man like Walter. He recognises that my beauty cannot be diminished by his affections. I really was the most fortunate of ladies to have snared him.

The inn is doing well, though you did not ask. We are thinking of renaming it. Naturally we simply cannot let it be known as the Golden Hind any longer.

I receive very few reports of your conduct at the Wallflower Academy, so I must presume it is bad. I am disappointed, Gwendoline, but not surprised. You always were a most contrary thing.

While I have made not one, but two impressive marriages, you are lagging behind in your duty to me. When will you find a gentleman prepared to have you? I am sure Miss Pike does all she can, so it must be your deficiencies, your faults prevent it.

Remember, this secret of yours is one I could spill at a moment's notice, and if I am led to believe by Miss Pike's reports that you have been disobliging, I am willing to share it.

Even if it leads to the ruin of us both.

Keep me informed of any gentlemen you believe worthy of your attentions, if you are able to find any. I hope you enjoy your long sojourn at the Wallflower Academy.

Your Mother

PS I have redecorated your bedchamber and made it my sewing room. Why did you never say the light was so delightful? You cruel thing, keeping such a pleasant place from me.

Gwen leaned against the crumbling brick wall and exhaled slowly, but it did nothing to relieve the tension in her shoulders, which was creeping across her skin like a wire, prickling painfully, tightening her chest, making every breath more difficult.

She should not have read the letter. She probably shouldn't read any of them. She had known before the seal had been broken that it would contain words such as this. Words that hurt. Words that pained deeper than any cut.

Despite her better judgment, Gwen looked again at the letter. Each capital had been elegantly curled. Her mother's handwriting was so like her own. It was as though her own words were biting back at her.

'Gwen—I mean, Miss Knox?'

Gwen stared at the approaching figure of Percy Devereux, who was stepping around the borders with purpose towards her.

No. It could not be.

She had dreamed him up…his appearance was only a figment of her imagination. She had been thinking about him too much over the last few days, that was all. She had not expected to see him, had assumed he had returned to whatever business had taken him from London. She had dwelt too much on his face, on the way his lips curled when he looked at her, that tantalising scent that was his and his alone.

But she was not dreaming him. She could not be—not with the few other wallflowers taking a walk around the gardens staring so curiously at him.

Percy stopped before her, his gaze dancing to the letter in her hands and then back to her face.

Gwen swallowed, the tension in her shoulders spreading to her throat, making it difficult to speak. What could she say? Her mind was swimming with the harsh words of her mother, preventing her from breathing calmly, from even thinking clearly.

Keep me informed of any gentlemen you believe worthy of your attentions, if you are able to find any.

Well, she had certainly found one.

'A letter, I see,' said Percy. 'From your mother?'

Gwen's heart skipped a painful beat. 'How did you know?'

She had spoken too quickly—an accusation, not a question.

Percy shrugged, as though he had not noticed the fear within her. 'Well, you mentioned that your father had died just recently, and you have not spoken of any sibling. *Is* it from your mother?'

Frantic thoughts did Gwen no service, offering her no possible reply save, 'Yes.'

She had to get rid of it. Even the smallest chance that Percy might catch a glimpse of some of her mother's words… It did not bear thinking about. But she had brought no reticule.

'I did not expect to see you here,' she said as calmly as she could manage, quickly folding the letter and placing it in the one place she could be certain no one would touch: down the front of her corset. 'I would have thought you'd return to London.'

Only then did Gwen realise that Percy's cheeks had pinkened and his gaze was most inexplicably focused on her breasts.

Ah.

The action of placing something in one's corset did not raise any comment in an Academy designed for wallflowers. They were all ladies there, and often without a reticule… Before a gentleman, however, it was rather a scandalous thing to do.

Gwen rose, her only thought to distract the Duke from the rather hussy-like thing she had just done. 'Will you walk with me?'

'Walk?' repeated Percy in a dazed voice, as though he had been hit over the head with a mallet. He blinked, then his eyes focused. 'Walk. Yes, as you wish. Walk…'

It was all Gwen could do to keep her breathing calm as she stood at Percy's side and started to walk slowly through the gardens. He was so close; if she was not careful her fingers would graze his own.

She could feel the heat of him, the intensity of his presence—or was that merely her imagination? Whatever it was, it was overpowering. Intoxicating. Painful. Thank goodness they were not technically alone, what with the other wallflowers gawping at them across the flowerbeds.

To be so close and yet not to touch…to feel the incompleteness of her desire… Gwen knew it was scandalous even to think such things, but she was sorely tempted. Just to know…

'I am beginning to think,' she said quietly, 'that you never leave the Academy.'

Percy chuckled, and picked at the dead head of a seed pod as they passed a border. 'Not with you stuck here. I prefer to be here.'

It was mere politeness, that was all, Gwen told herself. It was foolish to think Percy would not say such a thing to any lady he was walking with.

Still. It was pleasant to hear such things.

'Ensure Miss Pike does not hear you say that,' Gwen tried to say lightly. 'She will consider you a gentleman wallflower and may seek to imprison you here alongside us.'

'I can see compensations in that,' came the quick reply.

Gwen looked aside. How was he able to do it? Was Percy an unusual gentleman, able to return any flattery with a quip of his own? Or were all gentlemen, and dukes in particular, trained in such fawning?

'It was from your mother, wasn't it?' asked Percy quietly as they turned a corner to walk in the rose garden, where a few splendid white blooms were still fragrant on the air. 'The letter? I saw the way you flushed, Gwen, I hope you do not mind me saying so.'

Gwen swallowed. 'And what if it was?'

She had not intended to be so combative, but it was difficult not to be. What did he want with her, this duke who surely had offers of far more interesting conversation elsewhere?

'Nothing. I just…' Percy's voice trailed away, and Gwen was astonished to see in his face what appeared to be genuine curiosity. 'I am interested. In the letter. In you. In—Damn.'

Gwen waited for further clarification, but it did not appear to be forthcoming.

It did not make sense—*he* did not make sense. A duke would hardly interest himself in the affairs of a wallflower—particularly one with no name and little prestige.

Yet there was something about him. Something that drew words from her Gwen could not imagine revealing to any other. Something that made her trust him more than anyone else she had ever met.

'It was from my mother,' she admitted. She paused at a rose bush, reaching out to cup a blossom. It would make an excellent model for her embroidery. 'She…she has remarried, and is rather pleased to have me removed from under her feet.'

That was putting it politely.

Gwen had to congratulate herself on her restraint, especially when Percy asked a most interesting question.

'I suppose she is encouraging you to be wed yourself, then?'

The tightness that had emerged in her shoulders the moment she had started to read the letter started to lessen. Though she could not explain it, there was relief in speaking the words aloud, even to someone like Percy. Someone who looked at her with such… Well… In anyone else, Gwen would have called it longing.

'No one wants to marry me.'

The words had been spoken before Gwen could call them back, and highly conscious that she was discussing her marriage prospects with a duke, she forced herself to laugh and continue walking through the gardens.

'I mean to say, all wallflowers are a rather difficult prospect,' she said swiftly, babbling, 'and I do not believe myself any different from any other wallflower. I merely speak the truth of the situation in which we all find—'

'Gwen.'

She halted. The single syllable from the Duke was sufficient to stem both the tide of her words and the movement of her feet.

Percy was smiling. That roguish grin she was starting to depend on more than anything was dancing across his lips. 'I would not be so sure that no one wishes to marry you, you know. I mean, not myself, obviously. I have a reputation to—Certain criteria must be met before I—'

Her hands were in his. Gwen was unsure how it had happened—she had certainly not stepped forward and reached for him. But that left only the possibility that he had stepped towards her and claimed her hands with his own.

And that could not be.

As Gwen's heart pattered most painfully in her chest, her breath short and her mind spiralling, she knew she must be mistaken.

Percy was right beside her, inches away. Why, if she just stepped forward she would close the gap between them… feel not only the strength of his hands around hers but the movement of his chest with each breath, the power of his body…

And that was when Gwen knew she was in trouble.

As she gazed, speechless, into the dark eyes of this Duke who so easily bewitched her, a desire rose within her that she could not and would not contain.

A desire she had never felt before.

A desire to be kissed, and to kiss in return.

To be held close, closer than was acceptable for a gentleman and a lady…a duke and a wallflower.

'I wondered…' breathed Percy, and Gwen shivered at the warmth of his breath on her skin. 'I wondered whether you would permit…'

His voice trailed away and Gwen unconsciously leaned closer, desperate for him to continue. In this moment she would have given him anything.

'Yes?' she whispered.

And there it was—the same desire that rushed through her veins was in his eyes. He wanted something she could not give.

'Permit me to take you on a carriage ride next week?'

Gwen blinked. There did not appear to be any teasing in his eyes, but he could not be serious.

A carriage ride with a duke?

He had said himself, just moments ago, that she was most unsuitable for him. *Certain criteria,* or something.

What would Miss Pike say? What would Society say,

seeing a wallflower from the Academy out with a duke in the intimacy of a carriage?

'How can I refuse?' said Gwen with a wry smile. 'What day suits you best?'

Chapter Six

It was not the incorrect day. Percy knew this to be impossible. He had been counting down the hours, not merely the days, since Gwen had agreed to come with him for a carriage ride.

Sunday after church, that had been the day agreed, at two o'clock. Plenty of time for Gwen to finish her luncheon, Percy had theorised, although his own stomach had incomprehensibly rebelled at the thought of food when it came to his own meal.

'And where are you going?' asked his mother sharply, as Percy pulled on his greatcoat and hunted for his favourite top hat.

Percy missed only a beat before he replied lightly, 'Oh, taking a lady out in the barouche. You know how it is...'

He smiled at his mother, a finely dressed, impressive-looking lady. She had been pretty as a young girl. Percy knew that from the portrait on the landing upstairs in their London townhouse, but she had become a far more handsome woman.

A woman who was now frowning. 'I see.'

Was it the fluttering of discomfort he felt at his mother's look, or something else curling within his stomach? Perhaps it was hunger. Percy had been unable to eat anything, despite his mother's glares at the dining table.

'I must be off, Mother,' Percy said, a little too brightly, opening the front door. 'I know you would hate for me to be late!'

'Hmph…'

That was the only sound he heard before the door closed behind him.

Percy grinned. And the grin did not fade as he grew closer to the Wallflower Academy, or when its redbrick frontage appeared at the end of the drive. Yet below the smile was something else…something that worried him.

It was a strange sort of gnawing at his stomach that recalled the sensation of hunger yet could not be the sole reason.

It was only when Percy drew back the reins and slowed his barouche to a stop outside the Wallflower Academy that he was able put his finger on precisely what it was.

Still. It was so unlike him.

Nerves?

He had never been nervous with a lady before in his life.

No, as Percy jumped down from the barouche, and admired the coat of arms so recently painted on its doors, he knew it was foolish to be nervous.

What did he have to be afraid of?

It was only a drive with the most beautiful woman he had ever met.

Only a wallflower with a temper like a tiger.

Only a suggestion to the world at large and Society in particular that he was courting said woman…a woman he could never marry.

Percy cleared his throat and attempted to push aside his rebellious thoughts. It was madness. If his mother knew he had not called upon Miss Middlesborough, or Lady Rose, or the Honourable Miss Maynard…well, there would be trouble.

Trouble for another time. For now, his thoughts and heart were filled with one woman, and as Percy strode forward to knock smartly on the front door of the Academy he was filled with the foolish hope that it would be Gwen herself who would open it.

Of course that was not the case.

'Hmm…' said the footman, in a remarkably similar tone to Percy's mother not half an hour ago. 'Miss Knox, I presume?'

'The Duke of Knaresby, actually,' said Percy, with what he hoped was a winning smile.

Neither the smile nor the jest appeared to have much impact on the footman. Indeed, it had rather the reverse effect from the one Percy had intended: the footman glowered, then slammed the door.

Taken aback, Percy turned and looked at his barouche.

He could not have mistaken the day.

He had even gone so far as to pencil the date into his diary—a most unusual event.

No other lady required such attention.

No other lady, Percy could not help but think, *was Miss Gwendoline Knox.*

The knot in his stomach had risen and was now in his throat. He should get back inside the barouche and leave. It was a ridiculous proposition to have made to a wallflower with no name and no dowry.

Percy knew what was due to him as a duke, to be sure, but he was equally cognisant of what he owed to the Dukedom.

Heirs.

The next generation did not spring out of nowhere. One had to create it, and with a woman who had the breeding and elegance one expected in a duchess.

Gwen was not that woman.

Percy hated the thought, but could not deny its veracity. Gwen was a wallflower, far below his station, with no family to recommend her nor any position in Society to protect and elevate his own.

She was, in short, precisely the sort of woman his mother would not be impressed by.

A prickle of excitement seared his heart. Perhaps, if Percy was honest with himself, that was part of the attraction. Gwen was beautiful, yes, with a temper that only flashed when she allowed herself to be provoked, and she made Percy wish to bed her immediately, if only to remove this all-consuming desire from his body.

But that could not be. His… Well, his rather unusual rise to the Dukedom of Knaresby required him to avoid all potential for scandal and find a wife with enough prestige in Society to paper over the cracks of his own respectability.

Oh, he hadn't caused any true scandals. Not really. But as a man he had been reckless, thoughtless of consequences, easy to befriend and easy to egg on… It was a miracle, really, that he hadn't got into more trouble.

And he certainly couldn't bed Gwen just to get her out of his system, no matter how much he might wish to.

Gwen was no courtesan, happy to exchange her body for coin or the protection of his name. She was different. Precious. He'd seen that in the flush of her cheeks whenever he looked at her, whenever his growing desire slipped into his words.

Percy's jaw tightened. Besides, she was protected by the iron fist of the Pike, as he had started calling her in the privacy of his mind—ever since Gwen had mentioned the nickname.

The Pike would certainly not permit any of her ladies to be taken in such a way.

No, Percy was a fool and he knew it.

As the wind rustled in the trees around him, their leaves starting to fall and their golden colouring splashing the drive with their red and yellow hues, he turned to the barouche.

This had been a mistake. He should leave before he made even more of a fool of himself.

He therefore had to perform a rather uncomfortable twist to face the Academy once again, when the sound of the front door opening and the swishing of skirts met his ears.

'Gwen—Miss Knox,' Percy corrected hastily as he almost fell over in his haste.

The smile which had already started to creep across his lips disappeared in an instant. There was Gwen, beautiful as ever, with a simple yet elegant pelisse around her shoulders. The painful lurch in Percy's stomach informed him, with very little potential for misunderstanding, that although he could neither wed nor bed the pretty wallflower, that fact did not prevent desire.

And there was Miss Pike. She stood beside her charge, a frown deep across her forehead and a glower on her face.

Percy smiled weakly. 'Ah… Hello, Pike—Miss Pike.'

Blast. If only he could maintain some sort of decorum. Percy tried not to notice Gwen stifling a giggle, nor the additional creases appearing on Miss Pike's forehead.

'Indeed,' she said, with a deference he knew her wallflowers did not often see in the woman. 'Your Grace. I have to say I am surprised—a barouche?'

Percy waited for more information, but there did not appear to be any. 'I assure you it is in most excellent repair, and will provide a smooth and gentle ride for Miss Knox.'

Damn his searing cheeks and the unexpected twist in his stomach! It was hardly Percy's fault, was it, that the innuendo was right there for anyone to see?

Gwen had certainly seen it—that, or there was another reason why her cheeks had darkened and her gaze dropped.

He really could not make her out. Sometimes wall-flower…sometimes impassioned woman, Gwen was a medley of things Percy found rather intoxicating.

'I am sure it is a most impressive barouche,' said Miss Pike with a fawning laugh, 'but I was given to understand that this would be a carriage ride of a different nature.'

Percy stared. *Different nature?* Surely she did not believe him to be so much a cad as all that? If he'd had nefarious intentions, he would not have collected Gwen from the front of the Academy!

'Different nature?' he repeated, as an awkward silence crept between the three of them.

Gwen cleared her throat and spoke to the ground. 'I believe what Miss Pike intends to say is that a barouche can only carry two.'

Once again Percy waited for the rest of the explanation, but it was not forthcoming. 'I invited you, Miss Knox, and no other. Was I supposed to provide a second barouche for your companions?'

Miss Pike rolled her eyes with a smile. 'Really, Your Grace, I thought I had taught you better! I should have thought it obvious that your carriage requires sufficient room for a chaperone!'

Ah... Too late, Percy realised what the two ladies had assumed about this journey, and why Miss Pike was wearing a rather severe pelisse of her own, with no adornment of any kind.

Yes, it should have been obvious—and to any gentleman of real merit it would have been clear. Taking Gwen out on her own would be a recipe for scandal if they were spotted, and Percy could expect that someone would inform his mother immediately of the unknown woman in his company.

Alone with him. In his barouche.

But it was rarely a concern for a man of low rank, and it had never been of concern to Mr Percy Devereux, when he had been that man. It seemed a long time ago now. No woman had ever attempted to compromise him into matrimony then. There had been no point.

But now…

'Such an honour…such a pleasure to have you gracing us with your presence,' Miss Pike was saying, with an ingratiating smile on her face as she curtseyed again. 'So wonderful to…'

Percy allowed her to continue. It was nothing he hadn't heard before; the woman had been fond of him for years. Although admittedly the Pike's reverence had dramatically increased upon his ascension to the title. It was astonishing, really, just how welcome his presence was wherever he went now that he was a duke. No one had been much interested in his company before.

'Ah, there you are,' said Miss Pike, turning back to the door which had just reopened.

Percy glanced at it too, and was astonished to see Miss Marilla Newell appear, guided by a footman. Another wallflower?

'Miss Pike,' said Miss Newell firmly. 'I think you must admit, once and for all, that I hardly meet the requirements to be a chaperone. It might have escaped your notice, but I am blind.'

A shot of embarrassment flooded through Percy's bones and he looked away, even though he knew the lady could not see his gaze—but Gwen laughed and stepped forward towards him.

'Do not mind Rilla,' she said in an undertone as the

blind wallflower and Miss Pike began a heated argument in murmured whispers. 'She rather enjoys teasing people, and she is not shy at all about her blindness. It is…it is most agreeable to see you.'

Percy smiled weakly. 'Right. Yes. Good.'

'And furthermore, Miss Newell, you must consider your future here at the Academy!' Miss Pike's words had risen in volume, only increasing Percy's embarrassment at the whole situation. 'Why, you have been here three years and…'

'We could just…go…' said Gwen quietly.

Percy blinked. The wallflower had a rather scandalous look about her—a mischievous twinkle in her eye he had only glimpsed once before, when she had attempted to flirt with him at the dining table.

It did something rather strange to him. Not unpleasant—no, Percy would not describe this sensation as unpleasant. But it was…different. He had bedded ladies before…even dallied with the idea of having a mistress, before deciding it was probably more trouble than it was worth. Expensive things, mistresses.

He knew desire, knew passion.

Knew what it was to make love to someone.

But this was not that feeling.

True, it was similar—a rising stirring in his stomach that both dropped to his manhood and rose to his heart. But it was different. Warmer. Deeper. And a twinge of pain came with it…a bittersweet sort of knowledge that something was not quite right.

'We could,' said Percy with a smile. Raising his voice, he turned to the arguing ladies on the doorstep of the Academy. 'Miss Pike, Miss Newell—I promise not to kiss Miss Knox, if that is what it takes for you to trust me. I shall bring her back within the hour and we shall keep to the country lanes. No visits to Town. Will that do?'

There were splotchy red patches across both Miss Pike's and Miss Newell's cheeks.

'Well, really!' said Miss Pike. 'Percy Devereux, I have never heard the—'

'Excellent,' said Percy cheerfully. 'Come on, Miss Knox.'

To his great disappointment, Gwen was wearing gloves. And after Percy had helped her into his barouche, though there was the pleasure of being close to her, of having been of some small service, there was no opportunity to touch her again. Not as he would like, anyway.

Leaving behind the astonished voice of Miss Pike and the laughter of Miss Newell, Percy tapped the horses with his whip and the barouche moved forward, crunching along the drive.

Only then was he able to lose himself in his delectable consciousness of Gwen seated beside him. That was the real benefit of a barouche, Percy thought gleefully, as the horses settled into a gentle trot and they reached the road, taking a left to meander along a country lane. It might not offer the most comfort, nor the most elegance—but, goodness, did it offer an opportunity for intimacy!

Gwen was seated beside him, her hips pressed against his own. With every movement of the carriage Percy could feel her. His arm, now dropped to his side, nestled against hers.

It was enough to stir something hungry within him, something Percy immediately forced down.

This was not that sort of carriage ride.

'I…' Gwen swallowed when Percy glanced at her. 'I have never been in a carriage before. With a gentleman, I mean. Alone.'

It was perhaps the most endearing thing he had ever

heard. Percy saw the hesitancy in her, the nervousness at being around him, and it spurred on his feelings of power.

How delightful to be around a woman who was so easily impressed, so easily won over.

'Well, I would not concern yourself,' Percy said brightly, in an attempt to put Gwen at ease. 'I have been in plenty.'

Only as the words left his mouth did Percy see his mistake—too late. Gwen's face fell, her gaze dropping to her hands, and he saw tension creeping around her mouth as her lips pressed together.

'I see,' she said quietly.

'No, you don't,' said Percy quickly, hating himself for speaking so thoughtlessly. 'I meant… Well, there is no trick to it— no brilliance one has to offer. You just have to enjoy yourself. The responsibility to entertain is upon myself.'

A smile crept over Gwen's face at this pronouncement. 'Something you are well practised in, I would think?'

'Yes. I mean, no.'

'Well? Which is it?'

The temptation to say nothing—to sweep this awkward moment away and focus instead on the beauty of the countryside and the woman beside him, anything except be honest—weighed heavily on Percy's heart.

Gentlemen were not honest. Dukes certainly weren't. Very few occasions in their life required them to be.

It was often easier to just ignore one's feelings, push aside all and any desires against Society's expectations, and instead laugh.

Percy sighed. 'My mother arranges carriage rides for me with eligible young ladies—but you cannot be surprised, surely? I am the Duke of Knaresby.'

By God, he would have to do better. Percy hated the twisting pathetic words he had used instead of the direct honest ones he wanted to. Words ringing in his heart as well as his mind.

This is different, Gwen, because you are different. You are special. You are becoming more special to me with every visit, and I don't know what to do with myself when I am without you.

Percy cleared his throat. Words he could not say.

'In a way, then,' said Gwen, 'we are under the same pressures, the same obligations. We both live in houses with older women who are determined to marry us off.'

He could not help but laugh at that characterisation of his mother. 'Something like that, yes—only in my case… Well… What do you know of the Duchy of Knaresby?'

Gwen stared, obviously surprised.

Percy was a little surprised himself. As he directed the barouche along another country lane, not meeting a single person along the way, he wondered what had possessed him to start on this topic.

He had never spoken openly about it before.

Why now?

'In truth, I had never heard of it until we met,' said Gwen. 'Why?'

Percy sighed. 'Many reasons… My father was not the Duke of Knaresby.'

For a moment he hesitated. There was no need to tell Gwen his sorry tale, was there? Only a woman who might have a permanent connection with him needed to hear it, and Gwen was certainly not that woman.

Marry Gwen? A woman with no connections, no name, and no opportunity to better Percy's position in Society? A woman who did not fit James's criteria?

Ridiculous.

Still, he continued. 'The Duke was my uncle—my father's brother. He died along with his two sons, in a terrible accident, and just months later my brother…'

His throat tightened and he found he could not continue.

When was the last time he had spoken about James?

Not since the funeral. Not since they had laid his brother in the cold, damp earth.

'I am sorry to hear of your loss.'

Gwen's voice was sweet, gentle, soothing to his soul.

Percy cleared his throat and found he had the strength to continue.

'I am the last Devereux—the last male in the line, anyway… I never thought I would… No man should face such a thing. My brother was the most…the best brother anyone could have…'

Percy cleared his throat once more, and blinked rather rapidly at the road ahead of them.

He was not about to permit himself to show something as uncivilised as emotion!

'He taught me almost everything I know about being a man, a gentleman,' he continued, in a rather more controlled tone. 'He was eleven years older than me, and our father died when I was very young. Indeed, my brother was the one who taught me what a gentleman should look for in a wife.'

The words hung in the air most uncomfortably, and Percy wondered what in the name of goodness had come over him.

A subtle glance at his companion showed him that Gwen had raised an eyebrow. 'Indeed?'

'Indeed,' said Percy, retreating into the haughtiness which was his fortress in difficult conversations. 'Elegance, of course, and beauty. Good manners, a good family—far more important now I have inherited the title.'

'Indeed,' repeated Gwen.

A prickle of discomfort seared across Percy's chest, but he refused to pay it any heed.

'Blonde, naturally,' Percy continued blithely. 'And a good singer, with only one sibling—'

'And here I am, an only child,' Gwen interrupted with a wry smile. 'And not blonde, to boot. Though I think I am unlikely to make a match for…for other reasons.'

Percy flushed. God above, it was not as though no other gentleman in Society had dissimilar requirements! He was just more honest about them. Did he not deserve such a wife?

'My brother taught me the criteria, and now he is gone,' Percy said stiffly. 'And the last time I saw him…'

His voice failed him. The last time he had seen James neither of them had known it would be. Just a hunting party… just an evening spent talking and laughing and drinking and smoking. As any father and son would. At times, it had been hard to recall that James wasn't Percy's father.

And what had his brother said?

'Now, you must promise me, Percival…'

Percy had grinned adoringly at his elder brother.

'Not to marry a woman who does not fit my requirements. I won't have just anyone joining this family!'

'I have no thoughts of matrimony—' Percy had tried to say.

But James had cut across him.

'Promise me, Percy. Promise me you will marry someone who fits these conditions exactly. Promise me!'

And Percy had swallowed. *'I promise.'*

'I promised him,' he said aloud to the waiting Gwen, his cheeks red. 'Promised I would marry someone he would have approved of. It was the last thing I ever said to him.'

Gwen looked at him curiously. 'Almost a deathbed promise, then?'

Percy's jaw tightened. He was not going to cry. 'I honour him by seeking out a woman of whom he would have approved.'

He tried not to glance once more at Gwen. *Blast.* A woman James certainly would *not* have approved of.

Grief threatened to overwhelm him, just for a moment, but Percy pushed it back. He would honour his brother's wishes. He would speak calmly and matter-of-factly with the wallflower, then he would take her home. This had been a mistake.

He cleared his throat. 'Neither James nor I expected that a title would be our fortune. Consequently, as you might imagine, I was not raised to be a duke, nor even a duke's brother.' Percy laughed bitterly. 'Many in Society do not consider me to have the upbringing—nor, in truth, the breeding—to be a duke. Least likely to distinguish myself, I suppose.'

'Well,' said Gwen, nudging him gently and making Percy's stomach lurch most uncomfortably, 'I certainly have not seen you display the decorum I would expect in a duke.'

Their laughter mingled in the cool autumnal air and Percy was enchanted despite himself. There was no denying it. She was beautiful, witty, kind, all wrapped up into one. But James would not have liked her because of her low breeding and lack of title, her dark hair and surely half a dozen other reasons…

His traitorous heart ached at the thought of disappointing his dead brother. Did Gwen know how rare a gift she was?

Percy pulled back on the reins and slowed the barouche to a stop. Enjoyable though the journey was, for this he wanted to be stationary. He wanted to look into Gwen's eyes…see her reaction to him.

He wanted to know whether what was sparking in his heart was sparking in hers.

'You know,' he said quietly, glancing at her, 'we are truly not that different.'

A mocking smile teased at Gwen's lips. 'Yes, I suppose so. I must marry someone—anyone who will have me. I am least likely to make a good match, let alone win a…a man's heart. Whereas you…you must wed a beautiful, wealthy, well-connected someone. Not so very different.'

Painfully conscious of her arm resting beside his own, Percy turned in the barouche towards her.

Gwen's gaze did not drop, meeting the fire of his own.

'Well, you meet one of the criteria, at least,' Percy whispered.

Something was happening. Something he could not explain and had no wish to halt.

He had to—

He shouldn't.

Drawn to her inexplicably, unable to stay away, Percy leaned slowly towards her, not moving his hands, bringing his head closer to hers. His lips closer to her lips.

He could not stop looking at them, could not understand why he was not already kissing her when this desire had grown inside him so passionately.

For a heart-stopping moment Percy was certain she'd permit the indelicacy…lift her lips to his own and claim him as he wished to claim her.

A few inches…not even an inch…and Percy stared at the delicately delicious lips which were now mere seconds away from touching his own.

Gwen pulled away.

'I don't think—W-We shouldn't…' she said breathlessly, looking away to the horses, her fingers tightly wound in her lap. 'You promised the Pike.'

Percy could hardly help himself. He wanted to ignore the world and its expectations, push aside all memories of James and what he would demand of his little brother, and instead…

He knew he should lean back, give her space, give her a moment to compose herself—but he didn't want her composed. He wanted her underneath him, begging for more, desperate for his touch.

He forced that image of Gwen away but the reality of Gwen remained before him.

Dear Lord, such a pretty temptation.

'Perhaps we shouldn't,' he murmured. 'But I want to.'

Gwen's laughter was gentle as she raised a hand to his cheek. Percy leaned into it, desperate for her touch—anything to quench the growing desires within him. But it did nothing but augment them.

'I think,' said Gwen quietly, 'that you should return me to the Wallflower Academy.'

Percy groaned. 'You're no wallflower…you're a torturer.'

'You chose your own method,' said Gwen lightly, removing her hand and clearing her throat. 'Well, Your Grace. I think it is best you take me home. Then you can return to London and seek out this perfect wife your brother prepared you for.'

Chapter Seven

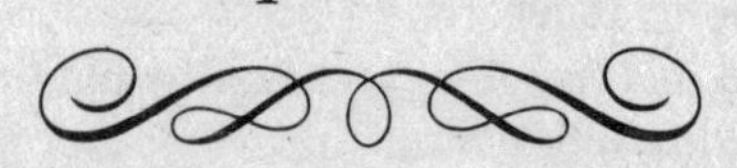

'And, of course, there are many elements that might make a conversation dry. The first thing that can make a conversation dry is the topic itself. The second thing that will make a conversation dull is the primary narrator. The third thing that makes a conversation boring…'

'This whole conversation is boring,' muttered Sylvia under her breath.

Gwen tried not to giggle, though it was a difficult task. After all, Miss Pike had been monologuing about the difficulties of entering, maintaining and refreshing a dull conversation for at least ten minutes—with, it appeared, little awareness that her own soliloquy was perhaps just as dull as the conversations she was encouraging them to avoid.

'So, when a gentleman chooses a topic you have little interest in, what should you do?' asked Miss Pike, rearranging her skirts in the pew, as the large church grew busy with people and noise. 'Miss Sylvia?'

'Leave him in the dust and—'

'Now, there is nothing worse,' said Miss Pike, turning to her wallflowers and speaking over the grinning young woman, 'than a lady who is unable to show interest in a gentleman's conversation—even, as I have said, if it is most dull. I assure you there will be topics gentlemen wish to discuss which border on the banal!'

'Nothing could be worse than this lecture,' Sylvia breathed to Gwen, who was seated beside her on the pew behind Miss Pike.

Gwen was forced to turn her giggle into a cough. At least this lecture could not go on for ever—the gentleman at the front of the nave had just risen, and the vicar was nodding approvingly.

Miss Pike turned swiftly. 'Another cough, Miss Knox? I would hate to think you had caught a chill on your carriage ride with His Grace. I should have forbidden it.'

'No, no, just a tickle in my throat,' Gwen said hastily.

She was still a little unclear just how much power Miss Pike had over them, but if it was anything like she feared, the older woman could send any of the wallflowers to bed without any supper if they so much as hinted at having a cold.

And then she would have no opportunity to see Percy.

The thought flashed through her mind unconsciously. Gwen half smiled as she noticed it. Not that she had any plans to see Percy. It would be ridiculous to expect to see him again so soon after yesterday's carriage ride.

So soon after yesterday's revelations about his marital expectations. And his brother's requirements. Requirements that were understandable, in Percy's position. And even more understandable after hearing about the loss of his brother.

After yesterday's almost-kiss…

'I think I will leave you,' said Miss Pike severely. 'This wedding is one of my greatest triumphs, and I should rightly be seated behind the bride. A gentleman with two thousand a year! Any of you should be grateful even for the idea of being so well married. Good afternoon, ladies.

Enjoy the wedding, and we will continue this conversation later.'

The wallflowers inclined their heads politely as the owner of the Wallflower Academy elegantly swept across the church. Only when the footsteps of the Pike halted, as she sat imperiously at the front of the church, did all the heads turn in one direction.

Heat seared Gwen's cheeks.

All were turning to her.

'Well?' Sylvia demanded.

Gwen blinked. She could not be asking what she thought she was, could she? She would not be so indecorous, and in a church—

'Tell us everything about this duke of yours!' Sylvia said eagerly. 'And when I say "everything", I mean *everything*! Quickly… Lizzie could be marching down the aisle at any moment!'

'Do not skimp on the details,' said Rilla. 'I can do without any description of the Duke, though.'

'Speak for yourself! I need to hear about every iota of conversation, every touch, every thought that flew through your head,' said Sylvia with a laugh. 'Come on, Gwen—we will live vicariously through you! Oh, that handsome duke!'

Her stomach stirring uncomfortably, Gwen groaned, dropping her face into her hands as raucous laughter filled the church, along with a cry from Rilla that no one had told her he was handsome.

'You didn't want a description!' Gwen said into her hands.

Rilla snorted. 'You know I did not mean it!'

Other clamours echoed around the church as all the wallflowers demanded the full story, though there were a few pink cheeks as other congregants glanced over at them and the Pike glared over her shoulder.

It was all too much. Gwen had known she was a woman who found no delight in the attention of others for most of her life. But she had a temper—a temper unbecoming in any woman, let alone a wallflower.

The idea that all her new friends—friends who really hardly knew her, and who saw her as naught but a fellow wallflower, like them, with no dark secrets—wanted to hear about each moment she had spent with Percy, those precious moments…so unexpected…

If she spoke of them aloud they would surely disappear into the ether like vapor, gone like mist on a winter's morning.

'There is really not much to tell,' Gwen said weakly as she lifted her face from her hands and saw, much to her disappointment, that the wallflowers had, if anything, grown closer.

Sylvia raised an eyebrow. 'So the Duke did not invite you on a carriage ride?'

Gwen's stomach twisted. 'Well—'

'And he did not force Miss Pike to permit you to go alone, despite the provision of a perfectly good chaperone?' asked Rilla dryly.

Gwen smiled weakly. If this had been happening to any other person—anyone other than her—she knew she would perhaps be barraging that wallflower with the very same questions she was being subjected to. She would want to know all the details. How it had felt to be so singled out, to be in the presence of a gentleman with such a grand title, to feel his hand on her own, to feel him move closer and closer, inch by inch, his fierce gaze softening as it focused on her lips…

Gwen swallowed.

Her heart was not fluttering, she told herself firmly. She was merely tired.

And not tired because she had been unable to sleep last night, desperately trying to understand what on earth Percy had been about. Kissing her in a carriage? All alone in a country lane? The man had his reputation to think of, irrespective of her own!

'But Gwen—'

'Hush! Here she is!'

The organ music had changed, the sound half lost in the rush of skirts as the congregation rose. Gwen quickly joined them, peering around to see a blushing bride in a delicate pink gown walk down the aisle.

A wallflower wedding…

Miss Pike was correct, in a way. It was a triumph. Gwen could hardly believe it had been achieved, but the proof was right before her.

As Lizzie reached her equally blushing husband-to-be, and the congregation took their seats, the voice of the vicar washed over her.

'We are gathered here today…'

A wedding. Gwen had never considered—or not with any seriousness—quite what that would mean. Standing there beside Percy, vowing to—

Beside Percy?

Now, where had that thought come from?

The vows were over far more swiftly than she had imagined, and Gwen rose hastily as the clearly ecstatic newlyweds swept down the aisle in a rush of lace. The church emptied slowly and the wallflowers were buffeted about. When Gwen finally made it outside, she stepped to one side of the porch and leaned against the wall.

There. She had managed to attend a wallflower wedding without drawing any attention to herself. She should be congratulated, really.

Someone nudged her shoulder.

'A duke!' Sylvia looked remarkably impressed. 'My word, Gwen, I must admit I did not think you had it in you when you first arrived at the Academy.'

'It is not like that,' Gwen attempted to say—but it was no use.

It was quite clear the wallflowers had had precious little opportunity to see one of their own attracting any attention—now they needed to revel in all the details.

'Well, whatever it is like,' said Rilla, leaning on Sylvia's arm with a mischievous grin, 'I recommend seducing him as soon as possible.'

Sylvia and Rilla collapsed into hysterics as astonished gasps came from those around them.

'You know,' said a different, deeper voice, 'that is a wonderful idea.'

Gwen froze. Her heart stopped, her fingers turning to ice, as she turned very slowly to look past the crowd who had gathered around the happy couple, to where the voice had emanated from.

Leaning against the church door with a wide grin on his face, cutting an impressively majestic figure in coat and breeches, was Percy.

Gwen's legs quivered, and her mind was unable to think about what she might possibly do next. Run? Flee the churchyard? Flee the Wallflower Academy and never return?

There could be no other option. How would she ever live with herself, knowing that Percy had overheard such nonsense? How could she possibly return to the Academy, knowing they all believed her to be courted by a duke when she knew full well he could not offer her anything?

Worse, how would she ever be able to look Percy in the eyes, knowing he had said such words?

Sylvia's laughter had faded swiftly. The other wallflowers had disappeared, which Gwen thought impressive, for she had not noticed them leave, and Rilla was looking in his direction, he head tilted to one side.

'Do my ears deceive me?' she asked in a low voice. 'Is that the Duke in question?'

'Yes…' breathed Gwen.

How long has he been standing there?

How much of the conversation had he heard?

Gwen tried desperately to run through all the wild and inappropriate words.

His hearing even one statement would be too much, but there was naught she could do now.

Besides, if she was not careful Sylvia would start pestering Percy with uncomfortable questions. Gwen might only have known her for a few weeks, but she knew there was nothing that woman would not ask.

'Excuse me,' Gwen said quietly, stepping away from the church wall towards where Percy still stood, a wide grin on his face.

Forcing herself to ignore the whispered conversation now occurring behind her, between Rilla and Sylvia, Gwen tried to step past Percy and go back into the church. Into sanctuary. Surely nothing untoward could occur there?

He did not budge.

'Why, hello, Gwen,' Percy said, his smile still broad. 'How pleasant to see you.'

'Let me pass, please,' said Gwen.

It was most irritating. He was doing it on purpose merely to annoy her, she knew, and the trouble was it was working.

Percy Devereux, Duke of Knaresby, had a particular skill in gaining a rise out of her, and the worst of it was the sensation was not pure irritation. That would be far too simple. Added in was a medley of desire, desperation, and…

Percy straightened up only slightly, leaving a gap just small enough for her to pass through if she brushed past him.

The sensation of her gown moving against his coat would be heavenly, but Gwen attempted to ignore the thought of it. What would Miss Pike say if she saw such shenanigans? Surely she would reprimand her, and there could even be a letter home to her mother.

A mother with far too much power over her.

'Your Grace…' Gwen said, as the murmurs behind her increased in volume.

'Percy,' he said, his smile faltering. 'I think…no, I am sure… I want you to call me Percy.'

Gwen's heart had only just started racing again, and now it skipped a painful beat.

Percy? How could he expect her to address a gentleman—a duke, no less—by his Christian name!

It was outrageous. It was intimate.

It was precisely what she wanted.

'I only call my friends by their Christian names,' said Gwen with a raised eyebrow as she remained by the church doorway. 'And a friend would move aside so I could step through.'

Was he surprised by her response? Gwen could hardly tell. Her mind was whirling, trying to understand what on earth he was doing here, hoping he would ignore—or forget—Rilla's comment.

Percy nodded. 'I suppose a friend would. But I, Gwen, am not your friend.'

Gwen's stomach twisted painfully.

And there it was.

The confirmation she should not have needed. The Duke

was merely playing with her. Teasing her. She was entertainment, that was all. Really, she should be grateful to receive any attention form him whatsoever. It was far more than she had expected, and drastically more than she had deserved.

'I see,' she said dully.

'No… "Friend" would not be the right word,' said Percy, dropping his voice under the medley of congratulations and conversations about the wedding.

At least they were not alone, Gwen tried to tell herself. That truly would be scandalous.

'What would be the right word?'

His face flickered. Gwen could see the war within him between what he wanted to say and what he knew he should not.

'Gwen, despite my better judgement, I want far more than friendship from you. And friendship would not be sufficient to describe what I feel about you.'

Gwen swallowed and looked into his face. A dark sort of seriousness had overcome Percy now, and she could see a flicker of uncertainty, of doubt, that she had never seen in that proud face before.

It stoked something in her…something new.

Hardly aware where this boldness was coming from, and certain she would regret this later, Gwen stepped forward. Her chest brushed up against his and for a wild moment she felt his breathing, felt it in tune with her own. She could feel his heartbeat—although perhaps that was her own pulse, racing frantically as she moved her face to within a single inch from his.

Then it was over.

Gwen stepped through into the church, where sunlight was streaming through the stained-glass windows, and although her breath was inexplicably ragged, she was still standing.

Two small pink dots had appeared in Percy's cheeks and his hands were clenched, as though he had forced himself not to reach out and touch her.

Mere fancy, Gwen reminded herself as she took in the several people still in the church, chattering away. She was seeing what she wished to see. Percy certainly would not have desired to do such a thing. He was merely teasing.

He stepped closer and whistled. 'Dear God, Gwen, what do you want to do to me? Drive me mad?'

Gwen flushed. There was no helping it. There had been desire in his words in the doorway—there was no possibility of mistaking it for anything else.

He desired her.

Matrimony was out of the question, and it would be far better for her if she could put it entirely out of her head. The spectre of his brother would loom over his choice.

A pair of ladies ceased their conversation and moved towards the door, glancing at the two of them curiously. Gwen stepped out of their path, carefully not looking at Percy, now standing on the other side of the aisle. If Miss Pike was to find her here, with the Duke, having a private conversation…

Well, there was no limit to what the owner of the Wallflower Academy might think.

Gwen half smiled at the memory of the almost-kiss she and Percy had shared in his barouche just four and twenty hours ago. Perhaps Miss Pike would not have a completely erroneous idea of what was happening, after all…

'I have no intention of driving you mad, Your—Percy,' Gwen said hesitantly, stepping towards him and keeping her voice low. His name sounded sweet on her lips. Sweet, and yet shockingly forbidden. 'You have said I do not meet your criteria, that your brother would not approve. You were the one eavesdropping on my conversation.'

My private conversation, Gwen thought as Percy stepped towards her, closing the careful gap she had left.

Not that she would have shared her true feelings with the other wallflowers. No, Gwen was still trying to ascertain precisely what they were, and she could not yet comprehend sharing them with anyone else.

She had feelings for him, undeniably. Feelings that swirled and mingled. Fear, desire, and a need to be felt and seen and heard as she never had been before.

And they were real feelings. These were not imagined emotions after reading a novel, or hearing from her mother about yet another lady of her acquaintance who had found a match.

No, these feelings stemmed from a gentleman whose voice made the hair on the back of her neck stand up and every part of her want to be closer to him. Closer than was appropriate.

Gwen swallowed. This was ridiculous. Percy was a duke. He needed to marry well—far better than her level. Had he not been open with her, and honest about the qualities his wife would need to have? And the truth of why she was at the Academy… Well, that scandal would be the last thing a gentleman like Percy needed.

'I rather enjoyed hearing you and your friends discuss me, I will admit,' said Percy cheerfully.

A knot tightened in Gwen's throat. 'I—I wasn't talking about you.'

Percy raised an eyebrow. 'Goodness, should I be worried?'

'You should not have been eavesdropping in the first place,' said Gwen, choosing to sidestep his question. ''Tis hardly a gentlemanly thing to do. And outside a church!'

He shrugged with all the lack of care of a titled nobleman. 'If the conversation is about me, does it truly count as eavesdropping? I do not believe so.'

It was a careless counter, but Gwen found it difficult to argue with. The conversation had, after all, been about Percy.

She supposed she should be grateful she had not been overheard saying anything personal. Why, if she had even attempted to explain to the wallflowers how she felt about him...the attraction in every word he spoke, the way he had almost kissed her...and his kindness. The way he looked at her not as a wallflower, but as a woman.

Gwen swallowed. 'I think, g-given the kind of woman you must marry, and the woman I am—'

'A wallflower, you mean?'

It would be too easy to merely agree with him. Gwen tried to formulate the word 'murderess' but decided against it.

Too much honesty would be the end of her.

'Yes, a wallflower,' she said quietly. 'I just think... Well... You and I, Percy—'

'I like that,' Percy interrupted, and Gwen realised with a start that he was now merely inches away. How had he moved without her notice? She needed to step back, but her feet weren't working. '"You and I".'

There was a sound—a movement out of the corner of her eye. Gwen took a hasty step back from the Duke as a gentleman stalked past them, glaring at Percy most irritably.

'What on earth...?' Gwen murmured as the gentleman stepped out of the church.

Percy chuckled. 'Oh, he's just sore because I won a bet against him just a few weeks ago. Now, will I be seeing you for dinner?'

Percy? At the Academy for dinner?

Panic flushed through Gwen's veins like boiling tar, searing her heart and her stomach alike with painful dread.

Another dinner? She was not aware of any formal dinner that evening—and if she was going to suffer through another official Wallflower Academy dinner she would have appreciated more time to prepare.

Prepare for what, she could not think.

'There's one tonight? A dinner, I mean?'

Percy frowned. 'I had thought you would eat dinner every night.'

There was nothing Gwen could do to prevent the flush searing her cheeks. 'So…there is no formal dinner? It will just be you?'

The words echoed around the church in a most disobliging way, but there was naught Gwen could do to stop them.

Percy hesitated for a moment before replying, 'As much as I would wish it…no. The wallflowers will be there, of course. And the Pike.'

That at least forced a smile to Gwen's face. 'I… I asked you once what—what your intentions were. You did not answer me then.'

That boldness she did not recognise within herself had risen once more to the fore, and this time she did not look away from Percy's face as she spoke the words—not really a question, but a statement of confusion. A need to know more.

But the bravado typically within Percy's face had disappeared, replaced by something akin to uncertainty. He shifted his feet, and when he finally replied it was in a soft whisper. 'I don't know.'

Gwen stared. It was not the answer she had expected at all—far from it.

'I should not be here, waiting after a wedding service to see you. I should not want to—My brother would never have encouraged—All I know is that I cannot stay away from you, Gwen,' said Percy urgently, reaching for her hand. 'That I will not.'

'I do not want you to. Stay away, I mean.'

Her heart was racing, but there was nothing she could do to stop it. Was his racing too? Were the same desperate confusions whirling around his mind? If only Gwen could read Percy's thoughts and know whether this was a trick, a jest, or something more. Something deeper.

'I do not know where this is going…' Gwen breathed weakly.

Percy smiled. 'You know, for the first time, I wholeheartedly agree with you.'

Chapter Eight

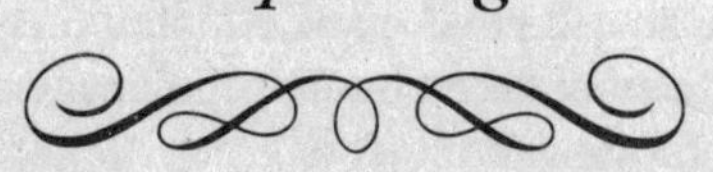

It was the ride, Percy told himself as he slowed his barouche along the drive towards the Wallflower Academy.

It was the ride. That must be it. There could be no other explanation for why his heart was pattering so painfully, why he could not concentrate on more than one thing for a matter of minutes before his mind meandered again.

Meandered to Gwen.

Percy clenched his jaw as the horses trotted along the gravel drive, but he could not help breaking out into a smile.

Gwen. Well, there was no point in trying to lie to himself, at least not in the privacy of his own mind.

He knew why his body was on fire, his mind unable to stop returning to the woman who had become the reason for his entire existence since he had first seen her.

Before he knew it, Percy had found himself visiting her almost every day. Playing cards, walking in the gardens, even putting up with those awful musical recitals from other wallflowers.

His stomach lurched. He was spending, in summary, far too much time here and not nearly enough time doing what he should be doing. Seeking a suitable wife.

Even now his desire had got the better of him. Approaching the Wallflower Academy with this wild idea? It was foolhardy.

Percy could not explain to himself why it was so important that he keep returning to the Wallflower Academy, but it was becoming increasingly painful for him to be away. The new idea, of course, had come to him only an hour ago, and it should have been immediately pushed aside. James would never have countenanced it. No, tonight's plan, concocted an hour ago, just as dusk had been falling, was far more audacious.

Which was why his presence here was just as much a surprise to himself as anyone else.

Percy pulled up his barouche outside the stables to the left of the main house. He was beginning to sound ridiculous even in his own head.

A stableboy scampered out of the stables as Percy's boots hit the gravel. 'Y'Grace!'

'Hello, Tom,' said Percy with a wry smile.

It was bad indeed that he was on first-name terms with some of the servants here at the Academy. But he was one step closer to Gwen. To seeing her, listening to her. Making her laugh, if he was fortunate. To making an even bigger fool of himself than he had already, if unfortunate.

'Back again, Y'Grace?' commented the stable lad with no shame. 'You're here an awful lot, aren't you?'

Percy glared. 'Not very often, I think.'

'At least three times a week at my count,' continued Tom with little fear. 'Don't you have other places to be, a great lord like you?'

Percy laughed weakly, but he could see the boy was not speaking to flatter. It was an honest question, one he would have to answer eventually—at the very least to his mother.

For he had not yet verbalised, even within himself, just why he could not stay away from Gwen. Why his chest tightened whenever he was away, as though his very lungs were unwilling to breathe air she did not breathe.

Why, his dreams were starting to become so scandalous it was surely not right for him to be coming to see Gwen at all. Not when the last time he had seen her in his mind she had been without clothes, without shame, and desperate…

Percy swallowed. The stable boy was still staring, wide-eyed, clearly intrigued by this strange duke who considered the Wallflower Academy the height of entertainment.

And the boy was right. He did have other places to be. Places his mother was expecting him to attend to meet the very best of eligible young ladies. He needed to find a wife—one who would confirm his place in Society now he'd inherited the title.

Well, he'd soon find himself in one of those places…

'I like it here,' he found himself saying to the boy. 'Tom, look after my horses, will you? I pushed them hard on the road.'

Because I was desperate to get here.

Percy made sure he did not say that.

Because every minute I am away from this place, I cannot help but wonder why. And being away from Gwen...

Percy clenched his jaw to ensure none of those words slipped out. The last thing he needed was the whole household thinking him a fool—not just the wallflowers. A grimace covered his face for a moment as he thought of the conversation he had overheard…

'I recommend seducing him as soon as possible.'

It was difficult to know who was more the fool: Gwen, for permitting his attentions when she knew there was nothing he could do about them, or himself for continuing to return, time and time again, to the woman he craved more than any other.

Craved, but must not have.

'I'll look after them,' said Tom placidly, clearly unaware of the turmoil within the Duke before him. 'Good day, Y'Grace.'

Percy blinked. He could not stay standing in the stable all day. He had to go and be a gentleman—and whisk Gwen away from the Wallflower Academy in a very non-gentlemanly manner.

How long he stood there before the redbrick manor house, his heart thumping painfully and his mind unable to decide whether to simply return home and avoid the shame inevitably coming his way, or enter and spend as many precious minutes with Gwen as he could…

Percy could not tell. He was sliding into trouble, he knew. No other lady of his acquaintance made him feel like this, made him question himself like this. Made him wonder whether it was worth it to throw it all away, leave the title and glory behind, and make Gwen his wife.

Gwen...his wife.

It was a heady thought. Percy found his fingers tingling and he clenched them, as though refusing to permit the sensation.

He was being ridiculous. Worst of all, he was playing not only with his heart but with Gwen's. What was he doing, if not hurting them both?

'Percy?'

He started. He had not noticed her step out, attired in an evening gown for dinner. *Excellent.*

'Marvellous, you're suitably dressed.'

Gwen frowned. 'Suitably dressed for—?'

'An academy dinner, I suppose?' Percy said, unable to help his interruption as excitement coursed through him. 'Tell Miss Pike you've received an invitation to Town for this evening,' he ordered.

She bristled. 'Who are you to be ordering me—?'

'I'm no one…no one to you,' he said, the words spilling from him. 'But I want to be.'

Gwen's eyes were wide, but she disappeared back into the Wallflower Academy without another word.

This was foolishness to the extreme! Percy knew he was running a risk with this plan, that it was one he should not even be contemplating, but there was too much reward to be gained. Besides, she had obeyed him. Not that he wished to make frequent demands of her…but surely if she had no wish for his company she would not have complied?

By the time Gwen stepped out again, a pelisse hugging her shoulders and a confused expression still in her eyes, Percy had made up his mind. Society be damned. He would take her.

'Where on earth are we—?'

'I'll explain when we get there,' said Percy, certain that Gwen would argue with him if he was so foolish as to reveal all now. 'Come on.'

The journey was swift, and for some unknown reason he found their silence more comforting than any conversation might have been. When was the last time he had truly enjoyed the company of a woman like this? In a delicate, unassuming way? It was most odd.

Only when his barouche rattled down King Street did Gwen turn to him with wide eyes. 'You have brought me to London!'

'I would have thought that was obvious,' said Percy with a snort.

Her cheeks darkened to crimson. 'I just—Well… Perhaps obvious to you. I have never been here before.'

Percy could not prevent his jaw from dropping. Never been to—? But London was the centre of the world—it was where everyone was! Anyone of importance, anyway.

'Never been to—?'

'It may have passed you by, Your Grace,' came the snapping retort, 'but the world does not revolve around London.'

Percy swallowed his indignation. The way she spoke to him sometimes—as though he was nothing! Well, this evening he would show her just how a woman should address a duke.

And then, whispered the irritating voice in the back of his mind, *you'll take her back to the Wallflower Academy and never see her again? Because this is a mistake. Your brother James would never have sanctioned this!*

'Well, here we are,' Percy said aloud, drawing the carriage to a halt. 'Almack's.'

It was Gwen's turn for her face to fall. 'No, you have not…? Almack's?'

'I have indeed,' said Percy with a grin. Dear God, it was pleasant to be rich. Rich, powerful, able to do whatever he wanted! 'I'm sneaking you in, so you had better be on your best—'

'But you can't—'

'There is nothing I cannot do,' said Percy easily, jumping down from the carriage. 'You'll soon see.'

He was rather pleased with himself. Almack's was, after all, one of the most delightful and exclusive assembly halls in London. Vouchers were issued by strict invitation by the most respected in Society. To be seen in Almack's was to be a part of the *ton*.

He offered his hand, but for some inexplicable reason Gwen did not take it. Stranger still, she was glaring.

'Don't you want to get out of that Academy?' he said.

She hesitated. 'Yes, but—'

'And haven't you always wanted to see how the better classes live?'

Percy had not meant his words to wound, but he saw a

spark of anger in Gwen's eyes, glittering with the reflection of candles.

'I've seen enough already,' she said darkly.

Percy blinked. Now, what on earth did she mean by—?

'Come on, then, let us get it over with,' said Gwen with a sigh, disembarking from the carriage while studiously ignoring Percy's proffered hand.

'Over with?'

Gwen marched up the steps, leaving Percy to suddenly realise he had been left behind.

How did this woman never cease to surprise him?

She was handing her pelisse to a footman with very bad grace by the time Percy reached her. He threw his great-coat to the same man.

'Gwen, I—'

'I think you'll find it's Miss Knox here,' Gwen said, arching an eyebrow. 'I suppose you have some sort of pretence for my being here?'

Percy hesitated. He supposed he should do, but—

'Devereux? I thought it was you. It was so kind of you to wait. Your mother has asked you to accompany me.'

His heart froze. He turned slowly on his heel towards the sound of the imperious voice, and his stomach lurched painfully when he saw it was indeed the woman he had feared.

The Dowager Countess of Staromchor. Finlay Jellicoe's mother. He was a friend from childhood—a rather elevated one at the time, considering Percy had had no title, but strangely lesser than him now when it came to rank.

Percy almost laughed. The vagaries of Society could alter so dramatically with just a few deaths.

But he had certainly not intended to meet the Dowager Countess here. What was she doing—and why was she so convinced his mother had asked him to go with her?

'Come now, sir, offer me your arm!'

He felt something strange and stiff brace within him. 'It's Your Grace, actually.'

'Oh…' The Dowager Countess raised an eyebrow, looking far too amused for Percy's liking. 'I suppose it is.'

Percy felt Gwen's eyes on him, but could say nothing.

The Dowager had done it on purpose, of course. All the old aristocratic families had been astonished when he had been elevated to their rank, and some were none too happy about it.

Not that they would say so outright, naturally.

'My darling boy is sadly occupied this evening, so it was not possible for him to accompany me,' said the Dowager Countess impressively as she dropped her pelisse onto the now almost buried footman. She leaned against the cane clasped in her left hand. 'You are here to make a match, I suppose? And quite right too. Almack's is the only place to find a woman of suitable breeding. And you are…?'

Percy opened his mouth but, traitorously, no sound came out.

'Miss Gwendoline Knox, my lady,' said Gwen, curtseying low.

It was painful to watch the Dowager Countess sneer so openly at a woman she evidently believed inferior to her—and not without cause.

Percy's stomach dropped. Had he made a grave error by bringing Gwen here? And the Dowager Countess was still holding out her hand to him, as though it was natural Percy that would abandon his companion and accompany her.

'My lady…' he said aloud.

Well, what choice did he have?

'I don't know what you are doing, loitering here in the hall, we will be much warmer inside,' said the Dowager

Countess, striding on impressively now she had her balance. 'You may have my arm.'

Percy put out his own automatically—well, he was not a complete cad—but he could not help but regret finding himself in this corner.

How was he supposed to speak with Gwen now?

Just out of the corner of his eye he could see her, watching him curiously. Oh, damn it all to—

'I must say, I have been reading such dreadful things about your family, Your Grace,' the Dowager Countess said happily. 'I can see why you need to wed—and swiftly. Your brother's death…what a scandal! Have they caught the culprit yet?'

Percy's jaw tightened. 'No, my lady. Investigations are ongoing.'

'Indeed? An inn, I heard? Though where such a place could be found I do not know.'

He said nothing—not even to correct her. His mother was right, though: he needed to marry. He should not be here, should not be dallying with wallflowers when he needed a bride, and a wedding to distract the gossips of London.

That certainty did not help now—particularly with Gwen following them so demurely. Knowing her place, Percy thought darkly.

When it became clear that he was not going to speak, the Dowager Countess said, 'I thought I might see you at the Wallflower Academy, for I hear gossip that you have made yourself rather popular there.'

Percy's jaw tightened. Dear God, the speed at which rumours could spread in this town! Now he would have to hope beyond hope that his reputation was not sullied by the connection, and that he would still manage to find a woman of whom James would have approved.

He was highly conscious of the heat on the back of his neck. Undoubtedly it was being warmed by the gaze of Gwen…

'Yes, I always knew being a patroness of the Wallflower Academy would provide me with sufficient entertainment,' the Dowager Countess continued as they walked towards double doors which opened to reveal spectacle and noise as they approached. 'But I had no comprehension it would be so thrilling. They are little darlings, aren't they?'

Percy smiled weakly, but held his tongue despite great provocation.

It was, after all, most infuriating. Not only was he being forced to remain by the Dowager Countess's side—unable to speak to Gwen at all, let alone privately—but he was also being forced to endure the banal conversation of a woman who clearly considered the wallflowers mere playthings.

Playthings! He would like her to spend more than five minutes in their company, Percy thought darkly. Sylvia had a tongue that could lash just as well as the Dowager Countess's, and Rilla was sharper than half the men in his acquaintance.

'They are most eloquent women,' Percy said as they stepped into the dance hall.

Much like White's, Almack's was unchanged. He couldn't imagine it being any different from the way it had been since the first time he had been given his vouchers: the elegant pillars, the tables covered in food and large punch bowls. A set of musicians were tuning their instruments at one end of the room, while Mamas cooed after their daughters, newly entering Society, at the other.

'Eloquent? I do not believe I have heard any of them string three words together,' said the Dowager Countess impressively, inclining her head at someone who had approached in a rush of fawning. 'Apparently there is a new one to view…most interesting. No real family, of course, and no connections. No real beauty either, I'm told.'

Percy's stomach twisted painfully and he could not help himself—he looked over his shoulder at Gwen.

She was furious. The same fury he had seen when he had accidentally knocked her down was visible in her eyes, and Percy could understand why.

Not that he could say anything. Oh, perhaps a man *born* the son of a duke…who'd had a duke's education, had been taught a duke's mannerisms, pride…perhaps he would be bold enough to directly challenge a woman like the Dowager Countess.

It was, after all, mostly true. Gwen had no family and no connections. She was a most unsuitable companion for a duke. She had beauty, yes, but Percy was not foolish enough to think that sufficient.

Perhaps, if James had not died…

Percy swallowed. Then he would not have been the Duke. Wouldn't have risen to the title under a cloud of scandal. Wouldn't need his advice at all.

But he was gone.

Percy's heart hardened. He was not about to disgrace his memory.

It was fortunate indeed that the Dowager Countess had released his arm to move away and chatter with the person who had approached. He was relieved not to have to disgrace both himself and Gwen by a half-hearted breathless defence.

No real beauty? Gwen? What idiot had shared *that* message? Percy could not conceive of anyone looking at Gwen, with her dark eyes, the cleverness within their pupils, the way her lips curled into a smile when she believed she was not being observed…

Percy's stomach lurched painfully.

Not beautiful?

'Well…' said Gwen quietly. 'That is breeding.'

A rush of exasperation roared through him. 'I cannot defend the indefensible, but you should think twice before speaking in such a way of your betters!'

Speaking to anyone in such a way a few months ago… it would not even have crossed his mind.

But he had changed, somehow, and it was only now that Percy realised it. Betters? Almost everyone had been his 'better' before the Duchy had fallen most unexpectedly into his lap.

Something curdled painfully in his chest.

Now they were words he might have spoken to anyone who had uttered such a disrespectful sentence. So why did Percy feel so traitorous saying them to Gwen?

They might have been such a perfect match. Before his title, before Society's expectations, before his mother had demanded the world…

Gwen would have been perfect. Bold, clever, elegant. Beautiful. Well-born enough for a man with no real fortune and no ambitions to nobility.

Indecision washed through him.

He should leave.

He should turn around, apologise to the Dowager Countess and her companion, if he could find the patience, and leave. Take Gwen back to the Academy. Forget about her.

Percy had come not to hear gossip but to be with Gwen—to get her on her own if he could. To make her laugh if he could. To dance with her scandalously before the *ton*, who would not know her humble origins. To lean close, breathe her in, finally kiss her, taste her lips…

'My betters? Right… So long as I know my place,' Gwen said with a glare. 'Well, we are here now—unless you wish to return me to the Academy at once. What does one do at Almack's?'

A pair of gentlemen overheard her question and shot her a puzzled, disapproving look.

Percy grimaced. He felt so foolish now. What had he been thinking, bringing her here?

'I'm sorry,' he said stiffly.

For a moment Gwen merely examined him, as though she could see within his mind, within his heart. Could she see the regret? Feel the anguish of the words which had slipped out?

'You don't even know the meaning—Forget it… You are forgiven,' she said quietly.

Percy frowned, examining her closely. 'Don't know the meaning of what?'

For some strange reason, Gwen would not meet his eye. 'It doesn't matter.'

'Anything you wish to say to me matters,' he said softly, his chest painful when she refused to look at him. 'Gwen!'

There was something intangible flickering under the surface. A passion, an intellect…something more. Something he had underestimated. There was far more to Gwen's thoughts than her mere words.

Gwen continued to talk, but he could not take in a word. He had acted rashly, yes, but they were here now, weren't they? Was it better to stay, attempt to make the best of the evening…? Or return her to the Academy? And what had she been about to say?

'Your Grace?'

Indecision paralysed him, preventing him from retreating, getting out of the place, or moving forward to dance with Gwen before the floor grew too crowded.

After all, there was always the danger that his mother might change her mind and attend tonight…

'Per—Your Grace?'

Percy blinked. Gwen was looking at him with a rather strange smile.

'I said, are you ready to accompany me in the next set?'

Percy swallowed. He should not even be countenancing such—

Fingers, warm and certain, slipped into his. He looked down. Gwen had taken his hand.

'I know I shall never come here again,' Gwen said in a low voice as the musicians played their opening notes. 'So I think it only right you dance once with me before we leave.'

His stomach relaxed and his heart sang as his eyes met hers.

Gwen.

It was criminal, the way he was being tempted. By God, Percy knew full well that he should leave. He certainly should not tempt Gwen's temper again. Once unleashed, it made her as fearsome and as eloquent as any man, let alone any lady of good Society.

Percy's feet took him closer, unconsciously. A flush crept across her cheeks.

'Well?'

'Oh, you must not mind His Grace,' said the Dowager Countess airily, waving a hand at Percy as she leaned away from her conversation partner. 'He is a duke, true, and far above your station, but you may speak to him if you wish.'

The colour in Gwen's cheeks was now a radiant crimson, and Percy would have done anything to help her escape. Every nerve in his body was on edge, but there was naught he could do. How could he disrupt Almack's? His reputation was only just being remade after his brother's outrageous death—he could not risk…

'I'll bear that in mind, thank you,' said Gwen sweetly,

before pulling Percy towards the set now being made in the centre of the room.

His heart was beating so rapidly he could barely hear the music—but that did not seem to matter. Gwen released his hand as she passed him, leaving him to stand in the line of gentlemen, and it was agony—agony to be without her.

This was too much…he was going too deep. He needed to step away and—

The dance began and the line of ladies moved forward. Percy's heart caught in his throat as Gwen smiled, her eyes flashing with mischief, and he knew then this was the most delightful mistake he had ever made.

He raised his hand and his stomach lurched as she met it with hers. It wasn't meant to feel like this, was it? He had danced before with countless ladies, all of them far superior in station to Gwen. At least, Percy supposed they had been. It was hard to concentrate on any other ladies now, with Gwen's hands in his as they promenaded down the set.

'You are so beautiful…' he breathed.

He could not keep the thought in; she had to know.

Gwen smiled ruefully. 'Is this the part of the dance where you compliment your partner?'

Percy swallowed. 'No, this is the part of the dance where I am supposed to find my senses.'

Because his hands burned as he touched her waist and ached as they left it. His heart was thumping so loudly he was certain she would hear it, and if he was not very much mistaken…

Oh, he would need an ice-cold bath after this.

Gwen glanced up through dark eyelashes as they stood at the end of the line, watching the other dancers promenade down the set. 'What did you expect, Your Grace, by bringing me here?'

Percy did not know. All he knew was that the mistake

was a glorious one. One never to be repeated, and so to be revelled in.

'Aren't you afraid?' she asked.

His stomach lurched as he lied, 'No.'

'Someone could recognise you…spread rumours…ruin your reputation,' Gwen said with a knowing smile as she stepped towards him.

Heat rushed through Percy as their bodies grew closer again. Recognise him? He had already crossed words with the Dowager Countess—it was too late for that. He would simply have to hope their conversation would not be mentioned to his mother.

Besides, he was not yet so famed in the *ton* to have his face noticed in a crowd.

'If they do, they will see naught but me dancing with a beautiful woman,' he said smoothly.

'A woman you cannot marry, though. Or even consider.'

'Of course not,' Percy said instinctively. 'You don't meet the—I mean…'

Damn. He had spoken without thought, giving the correct answer—the only response he could possibly give. And yet they tasted bitter in his mouth, those words which he would have said to any other woman who did not meet James's standards. And why did looking at Gwen make the words hollow?

And then the dance was over. The music stopped. Percy blinked, and heard gentle applause echoing around the room.

Gwen shook her head with a smile as she took Percy's unhesitating arm. 'I think we are agreed that I am not your future bride. So let us forget that. I had always worried I would never be able to dance in public.'

'In public?' repeated Percy, as though he had been hit over the head with a cricket bat. 'Yes…'

They were walking back to the side of the room—unfortunately, Percy saw too late, to where the Dowager Countess was now standing.

'I've never done such a thing at the Academy, anyway, and—'

'The Academy?'

Percy groaned inwardly as the Dowager Countess looked over at them.

'I know you cannot be talking about the Wallflower Academy. His Grace would never be so foolish as to risk his reputation by giving one of those girls any expectations,' the Dowager Countess said with a laugh that filled the whole room. 'Besides, they have little to recommend them, do they not?'

Bitter fire rose in Percy's throat. 'I believe the purpose of the Academy is to teach—'

'Oh, but you cannot teach the ability to talk to people, no matter what that woman says,' interrupted the Dowager Countess. 'What's her name? Miss Perch? Miss Pickle? And that must leave the wallflowers in a sorry position, must it not? Not that I am saying *you* are such a thing, Miss… I would never presume to insult you so. I mean to say, who would marry a wallflower?'

Percy could barely see, he was so furious, so desperate for this moment to be over. It was excruciating, standing before Gwen in such a conversation.

'I believe that with many wallflowers, as you call them, it is only confidence which is lacking,' he said quietly, trying not to catch Gwen's eye. 'With a little confidence—'

'Confidence comes from breeding, not lessons,' said the Dowager Countess curtly. 'Not that you'd know anything about that.'

Now it was Percy's turn to flush.

Of all the things she could have said—it was an outrage! Just because he had not been born to the Dukedom...

But he could say nothing. His mother's desire to remain in polite Society, let alone his own, required that he accepted the whispers and the murmurs about his sudden rise to the aristocracy. Why else was his mother so fixated on him making a 'proper' marriage?

'Have you nothing to say for yourself? Why are you so dull?' the Dowager Countess said lightly, flicking a finger at Gwen.

Percy's blood boiled—but he had no right to feel that way. He was not Gwen's relation, not father nor brother, to protect her reputation. He was not her betrothed and nor—Percy's stomach lurched—her husband to stand by her.

But by God he wished he was.

Mortified did not adequately explain the feeling in Percy's system, yet no words rose to Gwen's defence.

What could he say—what could he do?

Cause more rumours to flutter about London, to reach his mother's hearing, that he had fallen for a wallflower? Allow the whole of Society to believe he had been taken in by a woman who, in public, was unable to string more than two words together?

Worst of all, he might give Gwen hope that he would one day offer her something Percy knew he could never give her.

Gwen smiled coldly, no warmth reaching her eyes. 'My apologies, my lady, Your Grace, for being so devastatingly dull as to be considered a wallflower.'

'No, don't—don't say that,' said Percy wretchedly. 'Gwen—'

'You must understand, Your Grace, we are simply not prepared to speak to people of your elevated rank.'

Gwen's words were so icy she might have given his

mother lessons. Percy hated the way she spoke—without hope, without any belief that she was worth so much more than this rotten treatment.

'Do not say that,' said Percy again, stepping towards her. He wanted to be much closer, to bring Gwen into his arms, but he managed to restrain himself. Almack's was not the place for such expressions of passion. 'It is just that people of my rank, you know…we must speak the—'

'Truth?' interjected Gwen with a raised eyebrow. 'It is true. You and your kind, Percy—my apologies, *Your Grace*—look at us as like animals in a zoo. That's all we are to you—entertainment. Well, I have no desire to entertain you further today. I want to go home—I mean, to the Academy.'

Without another word, Gwen strode off towards the double doors, though she had the presence of mind not to slam them.

Percy stood there, hating himself and the situation he had allowed himself to be pulled into. Because Gwen was right. To others of his kind, the Wallflower Academy *was* merely entertainment—a way to be amused on a quiet day. His mother would certainly agree. He had been absolutely round the twist to bring her to Almack's. His father would never—

The thought halted in Percy's racing mind. Now he came to think about it, he wasn't sure what his father would have done. The man was a distant memory, faded, based primarily on the portrait of him in the hall. The man himself… It was James who had stepped into that role. James who had fleshed out the figure now living in Percy's mind, doling out judgement.

Percy swallowed. So what would James advise in this scenario?

And what was he to do with these growing affections?

Chapter Nine

'Have you nothing to say for yourself? Why are you so dull?'

Gwen swallowed and pushed away the painful memory from the day before and the fit of rage threatening to surface. She was not going to allow one conversation to overtake her mind, nor permit the words of one woman to colour her day.

But it isn't just one person's opinion, is it? a horrible, cruel voice in her mind reminded her, as each passing day brought more elevenses, luncheons, teas, dinners—though, thank goodness, no balls.

One after another they would continue, she knew, until she had managed to make a match her mother could be proud of.

Or, Gwen thought dully as she tried to focus on Miss Pike, *until her mother gave up hope of her marrying at all.*

How long? A Season? A year? Rilla had been here three years, she had revealed to Gwen, and her family had all but given up hope of a match.

'They have far more nefarious plans for me now,' Rilla had said darkly, only that morning, but though Gwen had questioned her politely she had been unwilling to say more.

'And the left foot forward!' Miss Pike said fiercely.

Gwen cleared her throat and moved her left foot, matching the other wallflowers in the line. That was the trouble with this particular class at the Academy. One could pretend to be attending when one was being lectured on etiquette. The ladies could have their own conversations when pretending to practise small talk. Even when learning the refinements expected at a dining table it was possible to ignore much of what Miss Pike said.

But not, evidently, in dancing lessons.

'Really, Miss Knox, I expected better of you,' said Miss Pike severely.

She was standing before the line of wallflowers in a room that anywhere else Gwen would have been described as a ballroom, though she had never seen it used in such a fashion. Still, the wooden floor was sprung, there were candelabras all along the walls and a magnificent chandelier above—at least, Gwen was sure it was magnificent. It was for the moment covered in a dustsheet.

'I do apologise, Miss Pike,' Gwen said quietly to the floor.

She tried not to notice the intrigued looks Sylvia was giving her, just to her right. As long as she prevented her mind from slipping back to the day before, when she had danced in a very different room and with a very different partner…

'Now—right hand up, palm straight, for you to meet the palm of your partner,' said Miss Pike, demonstrating.

Gwen started. She had become lost in her thoughts again—an inconvenient and all too repetitive problem of late.

That was the trouble with almost kissing dukes, she told herself sternly. And this particular duke had rather got into her head.

Still, it was not as though he had almost kissed her

yesterday—nor put up much of a defence at the Dowager Countess's words.

Gwen sighed and lifted her hand in the manner Miss Pike indicated. How they were supposed to learn to dance without partners, she had no idea. If only they could bring in a few gentlemen to dance with.

Any gentleman but Percy.

Even the thought felt like a betrayal. Though anger still roared in her veins, hot and sparking along her fingertips, she could not entirely quash the memory of his fingers on her skin, those tantalisingly unbidden desires—

She mustn't.

Yet the thoughts did not diminish.

Gwen's heart leapt at the prospect of dancing with the dashing Duke again. His hand pressed up against her, his steps following hers, that wonderful moment when he'd place his hand on her back, around her waist, and she'd look into his eyes and know…

Know.

Know what he wanted of her. What he felt.

It did not appear that Percy knew what he felt, but Gwen could not blame him. She hardly knew herself.

Besides, it was not likely she and Percy would ever dance together again. The Wallflower Academy never had balls—at least, Rilla had never known one in three years—and there was no possibility of returning to Almack's.

Gwen shivered. She needed to concentrate. Percy Devereux, Duke of Knaresby, was not her ticket out of the Wallflower Academy and she needed to remember that. If she wished to make a match—a respectable match, any match—she would need to leave Percy alone at the next afternoon tea or formal dinner and speak to other gentlemen.

Even if they did not raise her heartbeat like Percy did.

Even though they did not make her feel warm like Percy did. Did not make her long to be touched, to be held.

It made her realise he was one of the first people ever to have truly listened to her…

'One, two, three, four. One, two—Are you paying attention, Miss Knox?'

'Yes, are you paying attention?' whispered Sylvia with a wicked grin. 'Or are you thinking about that duke of yours?'

Gwen flushed. 'I am not—he is not my duke!'

'Enough talking there!' Miss Pike looked flushed herself. It appeared counting and moving was far more than her solid constitution could bear. 'Well, you know the steps now. Let me see what you can do. One, two, three, four…'

It was all rather dull, thought Gwen morosely as she stepped forward and back, lifting and dropping her hands on the correct beats. Pretend-dancing in preparation for gentlemen they'd never speak to and balls they would never be invited to.

It was all nonsense. All foolishness.

How did Miss Pike expect any of them to get married if they were never permitted to see any gentlemen truly as themselves? One could not simply transform a wallflower…

Perhaps it would be best if she did not see Percy again.

Gwen rebelled at the thought, but a part of her knew it was best. The best way to avoid pain and to reduce the agony of separation when Percy grew tired of coming here.

Because he would. He had almost said so himself. He could not marry her, could not court her—not properly. He had to make an impressive match. And she? She was a murderess. Hardly a suitable bride for a duke.

Gwen's heart contracted painfully, but she could not deny the truth of her thoughts. From today, she vowed, she would ensure she did naught to attract Percy's attention. If he even returned after that excruciating conversation between him and the Dowager Countess…

Trust her to make a fool of herself before a dowager countess!

No, from now on Percy could have nothing to do with—

'Good morning, Miss Pike…ladies,' said Percy brightly as he stepped into the ballroom. 'Practising a country dance, I see? My favourite.'

A slow smile crept over Rilla's face. 'My, my…' she said with clear satisfaction. 'Is that Gwen's duke I can hear?'

'He is not my duke,' Gwen hissed, hoping beyond hope that Percy had not heard those words—though it was too much to hope for if the grin on his face was anything to go by.

'I wouldn't be so sure, Gwen,' said Sylvia with a laugh.

'Ladies!' spluttered Miss Pike, astonished. 'Really!'

'Oh, I would not concern yourself, Miss Pike. They say far worse things about me when I am not around,' said Percy cheerfully. 'Well, we'll be off, then.'

Before Gwen could say anything, or even think about the confusion around her, Percy had leaned forward, taken her hand in his, and was pulling her towards the door.

'Off?' Miss Pike's stern voice echoed impressively around the room. '*Off,* Your Grace? Who do you think you are—stop manhandling my wallflower!'

Even with their difference in social station, it appeared the Duke could not resist a direct order spoken in Miss Pike's ringing tones.

Perhaps it was something to do with her being his governess, Gwen thought wryly as she stood, confused, by his side. All gentlemen of his class were raised by governesses, weren't they? Strong, determined, educated women, with stern voices carrying absolute command.

Perhaps Miss Pike had left her true calling.

'A problem, Miss Pike?' Percy asked mildly.

Gwen told herself she was not going to look at him—then immediately did so and regretted it. Why was the man so irritatingly handsome?

It wouldn't be difficult to resist his allure, his charming presence, if Percy was not so pleasant to look at—but as it was, she found herself utterly captivated.

He was everything she wanted.

Everything she knew she could not have.

'Y-You cannot simply abduct one of my wallflowers!' Miss Pike strode towards him, lowering her voice into a hiss, as though there were others within the room who might overhear and be shocked.

As it was, the other wallflowers looked remarkably entertained. Gwen tried not to look, but was then faced with two increasingly difficult options: gazing at Percy again, and allowing her heart to race most painfully in her chest, or looking at the ire of Miss Pike.

She compromised by staring at the floor between them.

'I cannot?' Percy raised an eyebrow. 'They are hardly prisoners. I promise to bring her back, Miss Pike, but beyond that I do not believe you can stop me.'

Once again, he took Gwen's hand in his own, and this time, with a thrill of excitement because she was both to leave the claustrophobic atmosphere of the Wallflower Academy for a time and spend time with Percy, she allowed herself to be pulled.

'Where are we going?' she asked breathlessly as Percy charged down the corridor and turned a corner.

He grinned as he glanced back. 'Anywhere but here.'

Gwen's heart soared, though there was a tinge of worry. What would her mother say if she was informed?

But there were moments—and this was one of them—

when she knew Percy understood her…really knew her. He understood her growing frustration at being cooped up like a child who had misbehaved. Why else had he taken her last night to Almack's?

Still, there was a prickle of discontent in Gwen's heart that she could not ignore as they reached the hallway and the protesting footman, who was roundly ignored by the Duke.

It had been not quite four and twenty hours since she had thrown angry words at him, and though she burned to think of them, Gwen did not regret their utterance.

She'd meant every last word.

There was too much to divide them, too much to keep them apart, even if Percy evidently did not wish it. Their stations in life and what was expected of them—and her dark past, which Percy simply could not guess—all should prevent any sort of attachment between them.

Gwen swallowed as she saw the Knaresby barouche once again stationed outside the Academy, horses snuffling in the cold air, their breath blossoming before them.

Only the smallest portion of her temper had been lost yesterday, and what had she done? Shouted at a duke, berated him for trying—and failing—to defend her from a dowager countess, then stormed out of Almack's, doubtless causing great upset and scandalous whispers.

It was a small mercy she had not raised her hand to him, Gwen thought wildly.

She was dangerous. She should not be spending any time with a gentleman like Percy, even if he was so arrogant. For his sake.

'Up you get,' said Percy briskly, lifting his hand and placing Gwen in the carriage before she could protest. 'There.' He strode around the barouche and within a moment was seated beside her. 'Off we go.'

Where they were to go, Gwen could not comprehend. Knowing not the lanes around the Wallflower Academy, it was impossible to guess. She could ask, to be sure, but after her outburst the previous day she found her words stuck in her throat.

How could she face him?

It did not appear, however, that Percy had much to say either. For a full twenty minutes, as London grew closer, they sat in silence as the hedgerows passed them at an ever-increasing pace, frost still picking at the corners of their golden leaves. They gave out as more streets emerged, and the clatter and noise of London roared about them.

Eventually, Gwen could stand it no longer. 'Where… where are we going?'

She shivered, though whether from cold or from uncertainty, she was not sure. If only she'd had time to collect her pelisse… If only she'd had time to ask more questions…

Yet time was not the problem here. Had she not, within this very hour, promised herself she would not spend any more time with the Duke who was fast securing her heart?

'I don't know,' said Percy shortly.

A thrill of horror rushed through Gwen's mind as the barouche turned a corner and rumbled down another street. She had believed Miss Pike to be far too agitated when she had accused Percy of abducting one of her wallflowers, but there was so much about Percy she did not know—huge swathes of his life she had never seen.

What was the Duke of Knaresby like when not at the Wallflower Academy? Was he taking her to his townhouse, where they would talk—where he would try to seduce her?

Gwen swallowed as her body warmed at the thought.

You are not supposed to desire such things, she told herself sternly.

Least of all with a duke who certainly could offer her nothing in the way of matrimony.

If only she had permitted him to kiss her when they had last been in his barouche…

It was a scandalous thought, but one Gwen could not help. The idea of being ravished by Percy, making love to him, his fingers on her skin… Though guilt clouded her mind, it did not diminish her desire.

A young lady should not want such things, she knew. A young lady should be chaste, and innocent, almost ignorant.

Gwen glanced at the gentleman beside her, highly conscious of his knee pressed up against hers. How would it feel if her skirts and his breeches were not in the way?

'You are cold,' said Percy regretfully, as she shivered again. 'I should have brought blankets. I did not… I just… I had to see you.'

That was perhaps the most endearing thing about Percy. When she had pictured a duke in her childhood days, even before she had arrived at the Wallflower Academy, she had envisaged an aloof, dry gentleman who never admitted fault and always blamed others.

But Percy was not like that. At least, he was sometimes. Arrogant and imperious and absolutely convinced he was in the right, no matter the subject of conversation. But at the same time he was…different. Warmer. Exactly what she wanted from a gentleman. From a husband. From a lover.

'We'll stop here.'

Gwen started as Percy nudged the horses to the side of the street and pulled them to a halt. Stop here? Where were they? And why had he brought her here?

Percy tossed a penny at a boy who was loitering on the pavement. 'See to my horses,' he said easily, 'and if they are well when I return I shall give you a crown.'

As she laughed at the boy's wide eyes, Gwen's cheeks were hot.

Here she was, in London, alone with a gentleman—with a duke, no less! What would her mother think?

'Rotten Row is just there—we'll go for a walk,' said Percy briskly. 'Come on.'

He seemed to be saying that a lot recently, Gwen thought sombrely, as she clambered down from the barouche, conscious of stares from those walking along the pavement. Well, he was a gentleman accustomed to barking orders. His rudeness was not rehearsed, but inbuilt.

'Here,' Percy said, moving his arm around her and pulling her close as he guided her forward towards what appeared to be the entrance to a great park.

Gwen's eyelashes fluttered as she was overwhelmed with the intensity of the intimacy. His warmth flooded her body as she was drawn to his chest. She could feel his heartbeat and it echoed hers—fast and frantic and untamed.

It was the most intimate she had ever been with a gentleman, and she wanted more. Unsatiated, Gwen knew that what she wanted was unthinkable. Yet it was certainly not unimaginable.

They passed through wrought-iron gates and she saw that there was, indeed, a park before them. A long path made predominantly of sand wended its way to the left, and it was there that Percy pulled her.

A number of other couples—all of excellent breeding, from what Gwen could tell from their outer garments—were walking in a similar manner.

Well, she thought wildly. *This is what it means to be a part of Society!*

How much time passed before either of them spoke again, Gwen was unsure. Her gaze drifted past the spires of churches and the roofs of tall buildings, looming against the autumnal sky. Other walkers looked at her curiously, their gazes flicking between her and Percy.

Her cheeks darkened. Of course they were wondering what she was doing with a gentleman like him!

'London,' said Percy with a sigh. 'I thought… Well, I thought it would be a chance to do something different.'

'I have never been to Town before. Except for last night, I mean.'

'Truly never been? I thought you were jesting.'

It appeared the idea was unthinkable to him, but Percy evidently had something else on his mind, for he asked no further questions.

Instead, after a minute of silence between them as they continued to walk, he said quietly, 'I must apologise for my behaviour yesterday. It was… There is no excuse. I can only ask for your forgiveness.'

There was clear tension in him as he spoke. Evidently the Duke had been punishing himself most severely for the way he had treated her and was unwilling to continue without an apology.

She swallowed. It all seemed like a dream now. The brilliance of the candles at Almack's, the silk gowns, the powdered hair, the sweeping movement of the dance…

Something of the way he had spoken echoed in her mind, and Gwen smiled. Her temper demanded that she rage, shout, even shove him to prove just how furious she was.

And she had been.

But no longer.

'You once said to me, at the first dinner we attended together, that when I had something to apologise for I would know it. You should recognise that in yourself, you know. And this…this isn't it. You have nothing to apologise for,

Percy. It was…regrettable. Regrettable, indeed. But not your fault.'

Percy sighed deeply and Gwen could almost sense the tension leaving his body. It was a surprise to see how greatly his apology had affected him, just as it had her. Why had he cared so much?

Why, if it came to that, were they in Town?

A terrifying thought struck Gwen.

He wasn't...he wasn't about to introduce her to his mother, was he?

Though the prospect frightened and intrigued her in equal measure, it soon became clear that Percy had no real idea of why he had brought her to Town at all. They meandered along Rotten Row and Gwen stared around her at London, loud and cacophonous, full of people and shouting and animals and noise.

'I thought of showing you the Queen's Palace,' said Percy with a dry laugh, 'but now I am wondering whether you would just like to stare at the people!'

Gwen's cheeks burned. 'I just—I had no idea London was so busy!'

'Far too busy, if you ask me,' Percy said with a shake of his head. 'Here, let us turn off here and I can take you through some of the busiest streets for your amusement.'

With the well-practised ease of a gentleman who had done it a thousand times, Percy guided her across the path of those well-dressed others walking along Rotten Row, out of the park, and onto the pavement of a bustling street.

Hawkers peddled their wares, someone was attempting to sell newspapers, a vicar stood on a box yelling at passers-by, and every minute another barouche or a chaise or a mail coach rushed past them.

Gwen could hardly take it all in, and fear curled at her heart. What if someone saw them? What rumours would flourish if the handsome, eligible new Duke of Knaresby was seen in public with a woman without a chaperon?

'Well, where shall we begin?' asked Percy, clapping his hands together.

Gwen laughed at her own ignorance. 'I just—Well, seeing anything, just the people in London, the noise, the excitement—'tis too much!'

Percy smiled as they started to meander. 'Truly, there is no particular spectacle you wish to see?'

'Sometimes you underestimate just how ordinary I am, Your Grace,' said Gwen with a teasing tone as they turned a corner onto a street that was, if possible, even busier. 'Most of us did not grow up as heirs to a dukedom.'

She had believed he would laugh, say something amusing about London and the people within it. What she did not expect was the dark expression that crossed Percy's face, as if a shadow had passed over the sun of his life.

'I… I thought that even if both my cousins had died without issue it would be James who…'

Gwen wished she could take back her words. Of course—how could she have forgotten? It was only by familial tragedy that his title had been inherited. How could she have been so thoughtless?

Percy laughed at the look on her face and shook his head. 'That is the trouble with you, Gwen,' he said quietly. 'Whenever I am with you I wish to remain in the present, not dwell on the past.'

'If it is too painful—'

'Oh, I can think on it quite well now,' Percy said easily, though Gwen was not entirely sure that was true. There was a catch in his voice suggesting otherwise. ''Tis only that… Well, I told you my uncle and cousins died most unexpectedly, and then my brother, and I inherited the title. But I did not mention in detail… I told you about him, my brother—my elder brother? He was a great deal older than me, so I saw little of him, and his death was quite sudden. Mysterious circumstances, to tell the truth. There were whispers of foul play, but obviously that was just talk. It was an accident. One of those accidents one can never predict.'

Gwen's heart seared with pain and she looked away. Was her life to be marked by such accidents? By these deaths of which at least one could be ascribed to her door?

She had not meant to—but then, had she? And he had died, that man. She was dangerous, that was what she was, and she should steer clear of any man she cared for.

If only she could stay away…

She had to get back. The Wallflower Academy might be dull, but it was safety. She must return.

'Gwen?'

Percy sounded astonished as Gwen removed her hand from his arm and turned around, pacing back the way they had come.

It was this way, wasn't it? Every street looked the same, and she had not been paying much attention to where they were going, most of her attention taken by the company she was keeping. She had to find her way back to the barouche…

'Gwen, what is wrong?' Percy caught up with her easily, a look of concern across his face.

'Nothing,' said Gwen, dropping her gaze so she did not have to look at him. She would not reveal the truth—not to him, not to anyone. Through a flustered breath, she said, 'The carriage—where is the barouche?'

'Gwen, come here.'

Gwen almost cried out as Percy pulled her suddenly to one side, into an alleyway she had not noticed. It was hardly wide enough for the two of them to stand in, and

Gwen leaned against the wall, ignoring its dirt, as her legs shook.

'You confuse me most heartily,' said Percy, his eyes searching her own.

Gwen could not look away. 'You confuse me every moment I am with you…'

Her breath was short in her lungs, and the world was spiralling, but for some reason concentrating on him, on Percy, kept Gwen grounded. His hands were cupping her face now, and she could not think how they had got there, only knew they felt as if they were home.

'Gwen…' breathed Percy, closing the gap between them and pressing against her, making it even more difficult for Gwen to draw breath. 'Gwen, I cannot stop—I cannot stop thinking about that kiss.'

Gwen swallowed, and Percy groaned as she whispered, 'Wh-What kiss?'

'The kiss that never was,' Percy said softly. 'The kiss we almost had in the carriage. The kiss I would take now, if you would let me. Oh, Gwen…'

It was hearing her name on his lips that did it. Overturning all her reason, Gwen gave herself up to the feelings she had so long suppressed and lifted her lips to be kissed. Percy moaned her name once more, and captured her lips with his own, gently at first.

The sudden shock of a gentleman's lips on hers was quickly overcome, and Gwen lifted her hands to clasp them around Percy's neck. And that was when the kiss deepened. He tilted her face, allowing his tongue to tease along her lips, one hand moving to her waist to pull her even closer, and Gwen's whole body tingled at the sudden pleasure rippling through her as she allowed him in.

'Gwen…' Percy moaned as he deepened the kiss, his tongue ravishing her even as his lips possessed hers.

And Gwen wanted more.

More of whatever he could give her, whatever they could share.

And even though she knew it was scandalous, kissing a duke in an alleyway as the rest of London passed them by, Gwen lost herself in the passionate embrace.

Eventually the kiss ended. Far too soon.

Percy looked into her gaze with a shaky smile. 'What have you done to me, you wallflower? You've made me want you all the more.'

Chapter Ten

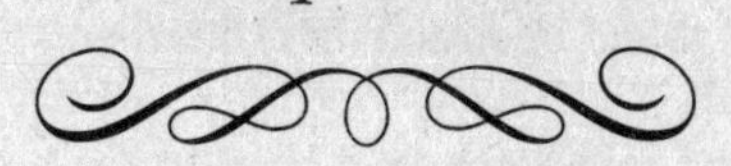

Gwen tried to concentrate. She really did. And it was not a lack of willingness to pay attention, but more an inability to—

'Miss Knox! Kindly refrain from permitting your horse to meander. We are keeping to the path!'

Gritting her teeth, and attempting not to tell the Pike precisely how difficult it was to direct a horse one had only met an hour ago, Gwen tried to smile sweetly. 'Yes, Miss Pike.'

The autumnal air made their breath blossom like steam, and perhaps in any other circumstances Gwen would have enjoyed the ride. After all, it was pleasant to leave the confines of the Wallflower Academy, even if she could still just about see the Tudor manor from where they were. Mostly it was hidden by the wide oaks, their leaves almost gone, and it was almost possible to believe she had escaped the place—though Miss Pike's continuous presence rather challenged that, unfortunately.

'Ladies!'

Her heart stopped. No, not stopped—but it skipped a beat most painfully. So painfully Gwen brought a hand to her chest.

It was as though she had dreamed Percy into existence as a perfect picture of genteel masculinity, with the breeze tugging at his riding coat and a haughty yet warm smile on his lips.

Percy Devereux, the Duke of Knaresby, rode towards the gaggle of wallflowers on a steed at least three hands larger than their own. Gwen heard a gasp. For a moment she thought it had been Sylvia's, but then she realised it was her own.

'Well met,' said Percy, still grinning as he brought his horse alongside Gwen's. 'What a fortuitous chance that we meet, Miss Pike.'

Miss Pike seemed utterly lost for words. Her gaze snapped to the Duke on his horse and the wallflower he was beside.

Gwen tried to hold the woman's gaze as boldly as possible, but she could no longer do so after a few moments. How could she when she was in the presence of both the woman who had been instructed by her mother to help her find a husband and the one man she…?

But she had to put those sorts of thoughts out of her mind. It would not do even to permit them, Gwen told herself firmly.

'Y-Your Grace,' stammered Miss Pike, evidently thrown by the sudden appearance of a man of such nobility. 'You honour us with your presence!'

'So I see,' said Percy, winking at Sylvia, who giggled. 'I wonder whether you will permit me to assist?'

'Assist?' repeated not only Miss Pike, but also Gwen.

She was staring at the man who, the last time she had seen him, had been kissing her senseless in an alley before they returned to the Wallflower Academy.

Just what did Percy think he was up to?

'Assist,' repeated Percy, his smile unwavering. 'It appears you are giving the ladies some practice at horseback riding, and I would imagine the addition of a gentleman for them to speak to would greatly enhance the challenge of the exercise. Why don't I take…oh, Miss Knox, say… on a route into the woodlands, and we can practise the art of conversation?'

Heat blossomed through Gwen's body and she hoped beyond hope that it would not be obvious to the eye.

Practise the art of conversation? She would have laughed aloud if she had not been so mortified. Did he really think the Pike so foolish as to—?

'What a wonderful idea, Your Grace,' simpered Miss Pike, inclining her head as though unable to withstand such cleverness. 'Miss Knox, I require you to attend on the Duke.'

'But—'

'*Now,* Miss Knox,' came the firm direction.

And what did it matter anyway? Gwen wondered, as she gently nudged her horse to follow Percy's down a path she had never explored before. What sort of argument could she possibly put up to prevent such an action?

If she even wished to…

The voice of Sylvia echoed behind them as Gwen followed Percy wordlessly into the woodland. The trees grew closer here, obscuring house, Sylvia and the Pike until they were alone.

Gwen shivered despite herself. Alone with Percy. Again. With a man who kissed like the devil yet made her feel like an angel.

Percy breathed a laugh as he slowed his horse to walk slowly beside hers. 'Goodness, what a stroke of luck.'

'You were too bold,' Gwen pointed out, her heart pattering painfully in her chest and a smile creasing her lips despite her surprise at seeing him. 'I never would have thought the Pike—Miss Pike, I mean—would agree to such a scheme.'

'What? Because your innocence might be in danger?'

The words were shot back so quickly Gwen hardly knew what to say in response. All she could do was look at Percy, see the desire and hunger in his eyes, and swallow.

Was it just as obvious in her own expression just how dearly she wished to be kissed again?

Which was a nonsense—because where could this go?

Oh, the woodland path would undoubtedly stretch for miles, disappearing off into the wilderness. Gwen was certain the two of them could endeavour to 'get lost' if they really put their minds to it, and Miss Pike would never think to question such an excuse if it gave one of her wallflowers additional time with a gentleman such as a duke.

But after that?

Gwen's mind whirled frantically as she attempted to understand.

One more kiss, yes—but what then? Percy could hardly make an offer to her. He had made that perfectly clear…

Until he had kissed her. Then he had been perfectly *un*clear.

'Did you hear that?'

'What?' Gwen said, turning.

There did not seem to be any movement in the trees, nor any sound to be heard. But Percy was looking around, his gaze narrowed, as though expecting to see someone's shadow flickering through the trees.

'Nothing, I just thought…' Percy swallowed. 'My mother says I'm getting paranoid. Expecting people to be talking about me.'

'And they're not?'

'Oh, they are,' he said with a wry smile. 'But my mother assures me it's only good things.'

Gwen tried to smile. Only good things… That was what she wanted from Percy, but even she could not explain what she meant. *Good things.* What would 'good' look like with Percy? What was possible? They were so different. So—

'Gwen?'

Gwen started. Percy had not only halted his own horse, but hers, too. His hand had reached out, unbeknownst to her, and caught the reins of her mare, drawing her to a stop. There was a look of deep concern on his face and, try as she might, it was difficult to ignore just how handsome he was.

She smiled weakly. 'Percy…'

'Walk with me,' he said quietly, dismounting.

'But I am supposed to be practising—'

'A pox on your practising,' Percy said, holding out a hand.

Gwen hesitated only for a moment. She liked riding, but the opportunity to walk with Percy, close to him, far closer than would be possible while they were mounted… it was too much to resist.

Gently sliding from her mare, Gwen found to her utter distraction that Percy had been standing so close she was now firmly wedged between the unmoving horse and his broad chest.

Her breath caught in her throat, her gaze was caught by his own, and there was a fiery look within his eyes she had never noticed before.

Or was it simply that it had not been there before?

'I have missed you, Gwen…' Percy breathed softly.

Gwen swallowed. She should not say anything, certainly not agree… 'I have missed you too.'

This kiss was different from those they had shared in the alley. Yesterday they had been unrestrained, hot, passionate, demanding of Gwen everything she was, and she had given herself willingly.

But this was different. Softer, gentler, no less passionate but with a different flavour of desire. More reverent.

Still, it fair took Gwen's breath away, and made it near impossible for her to stand. She would have fallen if she had not been so heavily pressed between man and mare.

'Come on,' said Percy quietly.

'You have a habit of saying that, you know?'

'I wouldn't need to if you would just follow me.'

Placing her arm in his, Percy gently tied the reins of both horses to a large oak tree and started to walk Gwen deeper into the woods.

'You have never kissed anyone before me, have you?' he asked.

Gwen's cheeks immediately flared with heat. 'What makes you say—?'

'Oh, I have no complaints,' said Percy quickly. His arm tightened around her own. 'Dear God, quite the opposite… No, it's just… I can tell. Something in the way you cling to me.'

This was going from bad to worse! How was Gwen supposed to keep a calm head on her shoulders with such—such a conversation between them?

'I was kissed once,' said Gwen, the words tripping off her tongue no matter how much she attempted to halt them. 'But I did not like it.'

What on earth had possessed her to say such a thing? They had vowed, she and her mother, that they would never speak of that night—not with anyone. Not even between themselves. Not ever again.

It had been painful enough to do so the first time.

Why would either of them wish to do such a thing a second time?

But something about Percy was drawing it out of her like…like poison from a wound.

Gwen had read once about drawing out the poison when one had been attacked by a snake in the wilds of India. And was this not the same? Had not poison settled in her heart, her treacherous heart, and would she not be whole again if it could be removed?

Percy was frowning. 'Dear me, was the gentleman unskilled?'

Gwen took a deep breath. 'The man—I will not call him a gentleman—was…was forceful.'

Forceful. That was all she could manage, all she was willing to say, but even uttering the word seemed to quieten a part of her soul she had not realised had been broken.

'Forceful?' repeated Percy, and then his eyes darkened. 'Gwen, you don't mean—?'

'I am still an innocent,' said Gwen hastily, her cheeks still pink. 'He did not—But he was forceful. I did not enjoy—I did not want—'

'The blackguard—I'll cut him through! I'll call him out! I'll face him across a field at dawn!' spat Percy, and she could feel the rage boiling within him. 'The brute! Who was it?'

Gwen swallowed, remembering the darkness of that night, the chaos, the desperate need to be free, to escape from the clutches of a man who smelt of drink and pain. How she had struggled, desperate, her temper rising, outraged at his treatment, overwhelmed until she'd pushed—

'I don't know,' she admitted.

It was the truth, even if Percy glowered. 'You do not have to protect him…'

'I know,' Gwen said softly.

She swallowed, tried not to think about the crack of the—

'I know,' she repeated. 'And I do not keep his name from you to protect him. I simply do not know it.'

'No gentleman would ever—The blackguard! Is he here? At the Wallflower Acad—?'

'No!' Gwen interrupted, her heart pattering painfully still. Oh, she should never have admitted such a thing. Her temper that flared and caused such terrible things to happen. 'No, it was b-before.'

After all, how had her mother put it?

'Where's the best place to hide a murderess, Gwen? In a garden of wallflowers...'

Percy's breath was still tight as leaves crunched under their feet. 'Well, I am glad you are well rid of him, Gwen.'

It was difficult not to exclaim at this, but Gwen managed it. 'Well rid of him, indeed. It is the way of the world; I am not unique.'

'And to think it happened to you! You, of all people!' Percy continued.

Gwen's stomach twisted as he spoke.

'I remember when my brother James first talked to me about women. Told me what to look for...what to admire. Why, he was such a gentleman. He knew the ladies far better than I ever could.'

A small smile crept across Gwen's face. Something had changed in Percy. She had felt it as well as seen it. It was as if a gentle relaxing, a warmth, was flooding through him. Comfort...a sense of peace.

'You truly admired him, did you not?' she asked.

'Oh, I don't think anyone who met James did not admire him, even if they didn't like him,' said Percy, chuckling under his breath. 'He was taller than me, yet one did not feel overawed by the man. He was generous with his time—arguably to a fault. There are times, you know... times when I think I shall never live up to him. To his charm, his cleverness. His memory. Why, I remember this one time...'

Gwen's stomach slowly began to unclench as Percy chattered happily about the brother he had so clearly adored. Well, she had managed it. It was as close a conversation as she'd had about the truth, and she had not revealed the shameful end.

Perhaps—just perhaps—she could go through the rest of her life without consequences. Without having to face the awful thing she had—

'Gwen?'

Gwen blinked. Percy had halted, and her own footsteps had halted too, but she had not noticed. His expression was strange, hard to read, though intensely focused on her in a way she found most disconcerting.

'Percy?' she said.

A smile spread across his lips. 'I like it when you say my name. You weren't listening, were you?'

Shame flashed through her heart. 'Yes, I—'

'So what did my brother purchase for my last birthday?'

Gwen opened her mouth, knew there was no hope of her guessing, and closed it again. 'You know I haven't the faintest idea.'

Percy snorted. 'Well, at least that's honest. What's distracted you, Gwen?'

She hesitated before answering. It would not be right, would it, to admit to the topic that had truly entangled her mind away from his company? And in truth there was more than one distraction in her heart, and one of them was standing right before her.

'You.'

It was a simple syllable, one hardly requiring any thought. It flowed from her, from the truth of her heart, and something changed in Percy's eyes.

'You know I would never do anything you did not wish me to do, don't you?' he said quietly, dropping her arm but only doing so, it seemed, to clasp her hand in his. 'You are…precious to me, Gwen.'

The moment between them was unlike anything Gwen had ever known. Safety and danger. The heat within her meeting the cold air in a rushing twist of desire she knew she should not give in to, but—

'Kiss me…' she breathed.

It appeared Percy needed no additional invitation. Pulling her into his arms, he kissed her exquisitely on the mouth, his ardour forcing Gwen to take a few steps backwards as she clung to him desperately, her body tingling as prickles of pleasure rushed through her.

And then she was pressed up against a tree, and she gasped as Percy's tongue met hers in a tantalising tangle of lust and something deeper, something far softer. She moaned…

'Gwen,' murmured Percy, his lips moving to her neck, trailing kisses to the collar of her pelisse as Gwen tilted her head back, unable to stop herself, eager for more. 'Oh, Gwen…'

'Percy!' she gasped, unable to say anything more, hardly able to think. 'Percy, I want—'

But any specific request—even if her brain had been able to think of one—was wrenched from her mind as Percy seemed to act on her very thoughts.

If she had been able to think such a scandalous thing, of course…

While his lips continued to worship her neck she melted into his arms. This was what it should be like, she could not help but think wildly, as memories of that less pleasant encounter were overwritten by his softness, his gentleness.

There was passion there, yes, but it was controlled. Determined, but not demanding. Eager, but not exacting.

Desire rose within her…a desire which had never been

sparked before. And she wanted to tell him, show him, just how greatly she desired him.

Without a word, he seemed to know.

Percy's fingers reached for her gown. Somehow—Gwen was not sure how, pleasure having removed all senses but touch—he had pulled up her skirts past her knee, and his hand now rested on her upper thigh—her actual thigh.

Gwen moaned. The sense of his fingers on her skin was overwhelming, intoxicating, and there was nothing she could do but cling to him and hope this moment would never end.

'Tell me if you want me to stop,' Percy managed on a jagged breath. 'You understand, don't you, Gwen?'

'Don't stop…' Gwen moaned.

All thought that they might be found, discovered perhaps even by Miss Pike herself, had been driven from her mind. All she wanted was to lose herself in this moment as Percy—

'Percy!'

She had not shouted—there was not enough air in her lungs—but Gwen had been unable to help herself exclaiming as he gently brushed her curls with his fingers.

Such a jolt of decadent pleasure, such an overwhelming sensation, Gwen had never known before. Head spinning, hardly aware how she was still standing, she whimpered with joy as Percy's fingers grazed her again.

'Gwen—'

'More…' That was all she could manage. 'More!'

He needed nothing else.

As Percy's lips returned to her own, capturing both them and her whimpers, his fingers grew bolder, one of them slipping into her secret place. Gwen could see stars, feel an aching heat building in her such as she had never known before, could never have imagined her body could contain, and then suddenly—

'Percy!'

That was what Gwen had tried to shout, but her mouth had been utterly captured by the man she now knew she loved, and as Percy's fingers stroked her into ecstasy there was nothing she could do but hold on…hold on to the man she had given everything to, would give anything to.

As the pleasure slowly receded like a tide, Gwen managed to open her eyes.

Percy was gazing adoringly straight into hers. 'Gwen—'

'Percy…' she breathed, hardly able to believe she had permitted him to do such a thing. 'I—'

'Hush…'

Gwen blinked up, unsure why, after such lofty heights, Percy had had to bring her back to earth. He was looking around as if he had seen something, heard something, though what she could not—

'Gwen? Gwen, the Pike says we must return to the Academy in time for dining practice. Where are you?'

Reality was a rather disappointing thing to discover after such sensual decadence. Gwen breathed out a laugh, dropping her head onto Percy's chest, and wished they'd had a little more time. More time to talk, to kiss, to—

'Damn,' said Percy dryly, neatly capturing her feelings in one word.

'Damn, indeed,' Gwen said, the bold word sharp on her tongue. 'I had hoped—'

'I should probably take you back,' he said, sighing, allowing her skirts to fall back to the ground. 'Although I would really—Gwen, I hope that was pleasurable for you?'

'Pleasurable?' she repeated.

How could the man be in any doubt?

A flicker of uncertainty tinged his face. 'I am sorry if—'

'Percy Devereux, I could happily have you do that to me every hour, on the hour, for the rest of my life,' said Gwen quietly, pushing aside the thought that her future could never contain that. She was dangerous; she would not hurt him. And his promise to his brother would divide them for ever. 'If I could—'

'Gwen? Gwen, can you hear me?' The indefatigable voice of Sylvia came through the trees.

Percy groaned. 'Gwen, I don't want you to go.'

Her heart was racing, and the temptation to tell him she had no wish to return either was teasing her heart. They could leave. They had two horses…they could make their own way in the world…

But they couldn't. She couldn't.

There was already one scandal in her past that she was attempting to escape from. It would not do to tempt fate and cause another.

'Your Grace,' she said primly, almost laughing at the groan Percy uttered as she released him. 'I believe it is time for you to return me to the Academy.'

'Blasted Academy.'

'Yes, that one,' said Gwen with a laugh.

Oh, it was glorious to see how disappointed he was, to see how very viscerally he wished to keep her… But it was no use.

'Oh. There you are.'

Gwen whirled around, stepping as far away from Percy as she could without it being too obvious—*was* it too obvious?

Perhaps. There was an uncomfortably knowing look on Sylvia's face as she beamed at the two of them.

'My apologies, Your Grace, for disturbing you, but I am afraid Miss Knox must return with me.'

'Of course,' said Percy smoothly, and Gwen both hated and loved it that he could so swiftly act as though nothing had happened between them when everything had—everything. 'Let me help you onto your horse, Miss Knox.'

Gwen tried not to notice how her fingers tingled as Percy helped her mount her mare.

'I shall see you soon, will I not, Your Grace?' she asked in a low voice as Sylvia turned her own steed around, heading back towards the Academy.

Percy's eyes twinkled. 'Soon? Oh, very soon. As soon as I can make it.'

Chapter Eleven

The first day, Gwen did not worry. Her mind was full of memories of tantalising touches, of kisses that lingered—and those that did not.

'Gwen!'

Gwen started. A piece of fried egg slipped from the fork she had been holding before her, evidently for some minutes, her mind entirely on other things.

Sylvia was staring, utterly bemused. 'What on earth has got into you?'

'Nothing,' Gwen said hastily.

The last thing she wished to do was reveal to the wallflowers precisely what had happened between her and Percy.

He had not needed to gain a promise from her of secrecy. The very idea of sharing the most intimate moment of her life with others…

'Is it just me, or is Gwen rather quiet this morning?' asked Rilla as another wallflower helped her with her breakfast.

'I am not—'

'Silence, ladies!' Miss Pike, at the head of the breakfast table, glared at them. 'I will not have bickering at breakfast. It is far too early for all that.'

And so Gwen moved through the day dreamily, even with Sylvia's uncertain looks upon her.

The second day, Gwen did not worry either. Well, it had only been a day, and Percy surely had commitments in Town that he was required to fulfil.

He is a duke after all, Gwen thought dreamily when she was supposed to be working on some embroidery.

'Ladies should always have a talent to discuss,' Miss Pike had said firmly, that very afternoon. 'And the only appropriate talents are music, embroidery, watercolour painting or remarking upon the weather.'

The embroidery of roses that Gwen was supposed to be completing had seen no change, however, in the hour during which she and the other ladies had been seated, ostensibly at their needlework, in the orangery as slow afternoon sunlight poured through the glass.

Her needle poked into the embroidery circle but then abandoned, Gwen smiled wistfully at the thought of the way Percy had kissed her.

He must care for her. She had not expected such affection from any gentleman, so to find it from him, a man so kind, so gentle… And yet on first meeting his haughtiness! His determination that his position required the perfect wife!

It was therefore on the third day that a prickle of concern started to creep around Gwen's heart. It was, after all, a long time to go without hearing a word from the man one had shared such a scandalous moment with. A very long time indeed after one had given him one's heart—and rather more.

No note.

Gwen had looked up eagerly when the post had been brought in that morning, but her shoulders had slumped as only one letter had been placed before her, her mother's handwriting adorning the front.

Gwen had given it little thought. She knew what it would contain. More crowing over her mother's neighbours, more exhortation for Gwen to marry well—but not too well—and more vague threats about revealing their secret.

It was still unopened upstairs in her bedchamber as she sat downstairs in the drawing room, listening to the dull monologue Miss Pike was now giving the wallflowers about the correct mode of address.

'Naturally, as wallflowers, you are nervous, and therefore more likely to make mistakes,' Miss Pike was saying so cheerfully. 'The best thing to do, if you are unsure, is wait until someone else has made reference to the person in question. Then you can see...'

On the fourth day, Gwen awoke with panic settled in her stomach. Why did Percy stay away? Worse, why did he send her no word?

She had been happy to acquiesce to silence, to secrecy, but not to solitude. The rambling Tudor manor felt acutely discomforting, both home and prison.

Perhaps she should have asked him more precise questions, Gwen could not help but wonder as she stood in a line in the ballroom that afternoon, trying to follow Miss Pike's erratic instructions for a new country dance.

Perhaps she should have clarified what they would do next.

Or perhaps there was no plan? Perhaps Percy had no intention of seeing her until he was bored with Town?

The very thought curdled in her stomach.

Gwen swallowed and turned left as the other wallflowers turned right.

'Really, Miss Knox, pay attention!'

'Apologies, Miss Pike,' said Gwen quietly, her gaze fixed on the floor.

'It's that duke of hers,' said Rilla. She had a ribbon in

her hand, her sightless eyes fixed towards the sound of the wallflowers attempting to learn new steps. 'He has been away a few days, now I come to think about it.'

Gwen's heart contracted painfully.

She would do anything not to hear her new friends discuss such things!

'He has probably gone to his estate for the shoot,' Miss Pike said soothingly, and Gwen looked up to see the owner of the Wallflower Academy doing a rare thing: smiling. 'I must say I did not think you had it in you, Miss Knox, but you certainly seem to have attracted his attention.'

Heat crept across Gwen's cheeks, but she said nothing.

Why, if Miss Pike could even guess what had truly occurred between herself and Percy!

It was on the fifth day that Gwen truly started to panic. Had she upset or offended him in some way? Worse, had he discovered the truth of her past?

When that thought occurred to her, as she was reading and Sylvia read aloud to Rilla, on the evening of the fifth day since she had seen him, Gwen was certain for an instant that she was going to be sick. The very idea that Percy might have discovered her terrible crime… She was dangerous and, worse, a danger to his reputation…

'You are very quiet.'

Gwen looked up. Not a single word on the page of her book had been taken in, and she was surprised to see not only the windows dark, but the lamps lit.

'What?' she said, distracted.

'I have noticed,' said Rilla. 'Something has changed in you, Gwen, and do not say it has not, for I am quite capable of knowing when I am being lied to.'

Gwen looked at her book rather than meet Sylvia's penetrating gaze. 'It's nothing.'

Sylvia snorted. 'Nonsense.'

Could...could they tell?

Gwen was not aware that feeling the heights of ecstasy thanks to a gentleman's fingers could change one's appearance, and she had attempted to participate in all the lessons at the Academy over the last few days. They should not be able to tell she was any different—at least, not by looking at her.

'You are upset,' said Rilla quietly, 'for you have not seen your duke in a while. Am I right?'

Thankful that Rilla was unable to see the flush that was surely on her cheeks, and hoping Sylvia would not remark upon it, Gwen said, 'He is not my duke.'

'Are you so sure?'

Gwen focused her gaze on the other wallflowers talking at the far end of the room—anything rather than give credence to Rilla's words.

But she could not help it. Rilla was right, even if she did not wish to say it. Percy was hers—her duke.

The idea of her having a duke was most ridiculous, and Gwen could not help but smile at the thought. But it was true. She owned him—or at least, she owned him as much as he owned her. He had possessed her now, body and soul, and she could as easily remove her own heart as untangle it from his.

'What I do not understand,' said Rilla, 'is what you are doing now.'

Gwen blinked. 'Now?'

Rilla nodded. 'He has not been here for several days. You are clearly eager to see him. Why are you waiting for him to come to you?'

It was only when her companion said the words that Gwen realised she had no idea. Why was she here, waiting for Percy to arrive at the Wallflower Academy, when she was no true wallflower?

Just because she had been sent to the Wallflower Academy it did not mean she had to wait for her life to start, unseeingly accepting whatever hand was dealt to her.

Her life—her real life... It could begin now. This moment.

Gwen smiled at the thought.

'I need to go,' she said, rising with a swish of her skirts.

Rilla smiled. 'I thought you might. Miss Pike mentioned she would be in her study upstairs, if you wish to speak to her.'

Gwen's shoulders tightened at the thought of the lie she would have to tell, but she jutted out her chin. 'Thank you, Rilla.'

'Anything to match a wallflower,' came the quiet reply. 'It is all I'm good for at my age.'

If Gwen had thought about it, she would have remained a moment, to ask Rilla precisely what she meant. But her heart had leapt at the thought of seeing Percy, so she did not pause when leaving the drawing room, and flew up the stairs towards Miss Pike's study.

Only when she reached her door did she hesitate. She knew the room's location, naturally—she had had it pointed out to her on her second day. But she had never received an invitation—or an order—to enter Miss Pike's study before. It was territory unlike the rest of the Academy: a place for Miss Pike and Miss Pike alone.

This was where the matches were agreed.

Swallowing hard, Gwen knocked on the door.

'Come!'

The door opened into a small but elegantly furnished room, rather like a small sitting room, but with an impressive desk in one corner. Upon the desk were piles of letters and paperwork—neat piles, but piles nonetheless.

Miss Pike was seated by a small fire, knitting needles

in her hands and a rather impressive shawl trailing to her feet. Her eyebrows rose.

'Goodness, Miss Knox,' she said languidly, not ceasing her knitting. 'What a surprise. How may I help you?'

Gwen swallowed, as though that might calm the frantic beating of her heart. It made no difference.

'I... I have received a letter. From my mother,' Gwen said hesitantly.

She did not like lying. It was something she did infrequently—especially since the night that had changed her life for ever and ended a man's life.

But still, it was hardly a lie. She had, after all, received a letter from her mother.

'I would like to borrow a carriage and go to Town,' Gwen said in a rush.

Miss Pike raised an eyebrow. 'Your mother would like to meet you in Town? She does not wish to visit you here?'

Gwen swallowed.

Everything she was saying was true.

'I would appreciate the loan of the carriage, Miss Pike, but I understand if it is not possible. I will merely write to my mother to inform her.'

It was delicately done, to be sure—but was it enough? Gwen could not tell. Miss Pike certainly would not wish any of her wallflowers to write home to their families to say they were not being given the opportunity to go to Town, especially when it was to visit a family member.

'When?' came the clipped question.

'Tomorrow,' Gwen said, with reluctance.

It was too late today, but the sooner she saw Percy, the better. Her heart needed to be soothed, and he was the only one who could achieve it.

Miss Pike examined her closely. 'The Duke of Knaresby

is in Town at the moment, perhaps? And your mother? Both of them?'

Gwen swallowed. So that was what the owner of the Wallflower Academy assumed. That she was orchestrating a meeting between her mother and the Duke who had marked her out as a favourite.

'I believe the Duke is in Town,' Gwen said, dropping her gaze to her clasped hands.

A moment of silence, then… 'I have no wish to speak out of turn, but from your mother's correspondence…' Miss Pike's voice trailed off. 'Well, I do not have the impression that she is an easy woman to please.'

Heat blossomed up Gwen's chest. It was an understatement. Her mother was demanding, cruel, argumentative… and the holder of her great secret. A secret she had held over her head more than once, with delicate threats as to what might happen to disobliging daughters.

'You have my permission to borrow the carriage,' said Miss Pike impressively, not waiting for her to reply. 'Well done, Miss Knox. Well done, indeed.'

Gwen left the study quickly and quashed all concerns about lying, deceit and being caught out.

As soon as breakfast was over the next morning, she was outside and the carriage was waiting.

'Thank you,' she said breathlessly as the driver helped her up into the chaise and four. 'The Duke of Knaresby's residence, please.'

It was all Gwen could do to calm herself as the carriage rumbled along the road, slowing as the noise of London rose around it. She was almost there. After almost a week—a terribly long week without the sight of Percy's face—she was surely only minutes from seeing him. The man she loved.

'Here y'go, miss.'

Gwen started.

They could not possibly have arrived already, could they?

The driver turned and poked his head through the small opening at the front of the carriage. 'Shall I wait here, then?'

'I—I… Yes, please. Thank you,' mumbled Gwen.

She had given no thought to the driver at all, in truth. All her thoughts had been focused on one man. But those thoughts were chased away now, as she stared up at the building.

The door was imposing. Tall, wide, painted a beautiful red and with a shining brass knocker, it sat at the centre of four large bay windows.

Gwen swallowed. This townhouse of Percy's—his second home, or perhaps even his third—why, it was larger than her own home…larger than the inn itself.

A prickle of hesitation caused her hand to stay before knocking. He lived such a different life from her. In a different world…in the spotlight. Was she truly ready to risk it all—scandal, perhaps imprisonment—by drawing attention to herself and stepping into his circle?

But impulse pushed her forward and she knocked. She had to see him. She could not bear to be without him any longer.

When the door opened, Gwen said impetuously, 'Percy!'

An elderly man in servant's livery blinked. 'I beg your pardon, young lady?'

Gwen flushed. 'I—I mean… I have come to see the Duke.'

The servant, probably a butler, stared. 'Indeed? And who shall I say is calling?'

If only she had considered this beforehand. There had been plenty of time in the carriage, if she had put her mind to it, and yet she could think of nothing to say beyond the obvious.

'Say…say it is a lady.'

The butler nodded—and closed the door in her face. Gwen blinked. Was that intended as a reproof, a rejection of her request? Or was it common practice for a butler to close the door before a guest entered?

Uncertainty stirred in her stomach.

Just another example of how very different they were, Gwen thought wretchedly. The more she tried to ignore their differences in station, the more obvious they appeared.

When the door was opened again it was by Percy, who looked confused—then horrified.

'Percy!' Gwen said with a wide smile. 'I thought I would surprise you!'

It was indeed a surprise. Gwen could see the astonishment on the Duke's face. But it was mired by rather different emotions: panic, confusion, and…

And something akin to embarrassment.

Her gaze dropped and the excitement that had filled her ebbed away.

'I… I did not know when I was going to see you again,' she said, filling the awkward silence that Percy did not appear to have any wish to end. 'So I… I thought you might like to go for a walk. See the Queen's Palace, as we did not see it last time. Or…or visit any alleys or trees which are close by.'

That had been rather daring of her, it was true, but Gwen's boldness rose whenever she was with Percy. He made her more herself, somehow.

Yet the Percy she knew did not appear to be present today.

Flushing darkly, he stepped out of the house and closed the door behind him.

Gwen stared. *Was she not going to be invited inside?*

'You have to go.'

Percy's voice was low, soft, as though he was terrified of someone overhearing him.

His words did not make sense to Gwen—so little that she repeated just one. 'Go?'

'Yes, go,' said Percy, just as quietly. 'Now.'

'I… I came all this way to see you,' said Gwen, confusion twisting her heart. 'Why would I go before I have properly seen you?'

'It is a shame, but unfortunately you have arrived at a most inopportune time,' said Percy quickly, his voice low. 'I am sorry to say I have another appointment.'

Another appointment. *Of course he does,* Gwen thought dully.

It would be far too much to assume that Percy would have nothing to do today, or any day. He was a duke. There would be many calls on his time, unlike on hers.

'Go, now,' said Percy, turning her around by the shoulders and pushing her forward, back on to the pavement. 'I… I will come to see you.'

'Soon?' asked Gwen, unable to understand quite what was happening. 'Percy?'

'As soon as I am able,' said Percy, glancing back at the house as though concerned they were being watched.

Gwen looked up at the large bay windows.

Were they?

'Go, Miss Knox,' said Percy in clipped tones. 'Good day.'

The door had opened and closed again, swallowing the Duke up with it, before Gwen could say another word, and she stood there in astonished silence.

Percy did not wish to see her.

More, he had made no definite appointment day or time to see her at the Academy. Worse, there had been no declaration of love, which Gwen had not only hoped for, but expected.

A flicker of doubt circled her heart, followed by that rise of that terrible temper of hers. Gwen tried to breathe, tried to ignore the rising passion tempting her to slam her fists on the door and demand to be let in.

It was all very strange. But then, he was a duke, and she a wallflower—at least in his eyes. Perhaps this was how a courtship of this kind was carried out…

Chapter Twelve

'You mustn't!'

'I have,' said Sylvia with apparent glee. 'And there is no point attempting to talk me out of it, so don't even bother. My half-brother says this was the best trick he ever played at his club!'

Gwen stifled a laugh as she sat by the fire in the drawing room, watching the imperious Sylvia raise a dark eyebrow at the other wallflowers.

'But you mustn't!' said Rilla with a snort. 'Sylvia, you'll be caught—and Miss Pike will be furious when she—'

'The Pike could do with loosening up a little. Not all of us are wallflowers, waiting around for our lives to begin,' said Sylvia smartly as she adjusted the door, left it slightly ajar, and beamed at her creation. 'No offence.'

'None taken,' said Rilla wryly. 'Describe it to me again.'

Gwen smiled, despite herself. 'Sylvia has got it into her head to play a childish practical joke upon our benefactress.'

'Benefactress?' Sylvia snorted as she stepped away from the door and dropped heavily into an armchair. 'Jailor, rather.'

'Either way…' said Gwen hastily. Anything to avoid an argument, with Sylvia clearly feeling particularly bold today. 'Sylvia has carefully balanced a bucket of water over the door—'

'Ice-cold water,' Sylvia interrupted with apparent relish.

Rilla laughed dryly. 'You are always one for the dramatic, Sylvia.'

'Well, if not now, when?' the prankster demanded. 'Here we are, stuck inside unless we are able to catch the eye of a duke—and Gwen still won't reveal how she managed that.'

'And when the door opens for Miss Pike as she joins us before dinner…' Gwen said hastily.

The less said about Percy, the better.

She still could not get that kiss from her mind, nor the way he had spoken to her…

'The door will open, the bucket will fall, and the poor thing will be absolutely drenched.'

'I am not sure I would characterise her as a "poor thing",' said Rilla with a mischievous smile. 'Not after her nonsense yesterday about me not being able to dance. Has she even seen me attempt it?'

'No, she has not,' Sylvia said emphatically as a smile crept over Rilla's face. 'This will serve her right, I say—and all of you must swear not to reveal that it was I, or it will be the same for you when you are least expecting it!'

'You really shouldn't!' said Gwen.

But she knew well enough not to attempt to change the young woman's mind. With a smile across her lips and a knowing glint in her dark, almost black eyes, Sylvia was not a woman to have her mind changed for her.

'I'm bored,' Sylvia said dramatically. 'Bored with waiting around for gentlemen to come and view us as though we are pastries in a shop, deciding to choose which one of us to be their boring wives. I'm just trying to bring a bit of merriment into our lives.'

'Even if we wished to stop you,' Rilla said softly, 'could we?'

Gwen glanced at Sylvia, who grinned. 'No. Miss Pike will get wet—and it's only water. She can go upstairs and change easily enough.'

'Then the real fun will begin,' said Rilla, a hint of trouble in her tones. 'A card party this evening, isn't it?'

Gwen sighed. 'A card party? I truly do not understand how I will bear it. Gentlemen playing at cards…trying to pretend we are in any way interesting to them…'

Her voice trailed away. She had not thought to ask if Percy was attending. Her thoughts had wended in quite a different direction. How had he dared speak to her like that? Why hadn't he invited her inside? Had his deathbed vow to his brother finally come between them?

Then at other times—when she permitted herself to forget that he was a duke, forget the promise he'd made to his brother, forget her past—she would wonder whether they could find again that little nook in the woodland near the Wallflower Academy, where they'd shared more passionate kisses… She would think of the way he'd touched her under that tree…ponder if those kisses would ever lead anywhere…

Despite the heat of the fire, a greater fire rushed through Gwen, turning her cheeks pink and making it impossible for her to contribute to the ongoing conversation.

Rilla was laughing. 'You're acting like a child, Sylvia!'

'Perhaps I am. But I'm tired of being stuck here, tired of never getting my own way, tired of being treated like a child by the Pike!' Sylvia retorted. 'We're adults! We're ladies, women of wit…'

Gwen only half listened. If the other wallflowers knew just what she and Percy had done… It had grown, hadn't it? Grown into something far more than a lady of good repute should even conceive of!

Young ladies did not kiss dukes in carriages—and certainly not in alleyways. Wallflowers did not get taken to ecstasy after a horseback ride, with a gentleman's body pressed up against her.

Gwen had been able to do nothing but cling on for her very life as Percy had taken her on an adventure to pleasure she had never known possible…

And, worse, Gwen was certain there was more. So much more. More that she and Percy would inevitably never share.

'Shush—shush! Here she comes!'

Gwen blinked. Sylvia was waving her hands around to get the others to stop talking, and now they could all hear footsteps approaching across the hall.

Her heart leaping into her mouth, Gwen could not help but glance between Sylvia and the ajar door as the footsteps grew closer. Any moment now the door would open, and Miss Pike would receive the shock of her life!

There was indeed a startled yelp as the door opened and the bucket of freezing water fell onto the unsuspecting entrant into the room—but it was no lady in skirts unexpectedly doused.

Percy blinked through his sodden hair as the bucket fell to the floor with a clatter. 'Wh-What…? Water…?'

Gwen gasped as Rilla fell into raucous giggles. The Duke was absolutely soaked: his jacket drenched, his cravat dripping, his breeches covered in water.

'My—Your Grace!' Sylvia rose, mortification across her features. 'I did not—I thought it was—You are so wet!'

'So very wet,' said Percy with a laugh, pulling at his cravat and twisting it before him so that water ran down onto the carpet. 'Oh, dear, Miss Pike won't like her carpet being so damp…'

Rilla snorted. 'Am I to suppose Sylvia's victim is not who we thought?'

'Sylvia's victim, you say?' Percy raised an eyebrow through his wet hair and turned a sardonic look at the woman now spluttering incomprehensively. 'Is it you, Miss Bryant, I have to thank for this sudden bath?'

Even Gwen had to laugh.

Really, it was most ridiculous!

How had they not considered it might be a gentleman arriving for the card party who might fall victim to Sylvia's trap?

Percy shook his head and flicked water across the wallpaper. 'I do not suppose there is somewhere I can change?'

Rilla was laughing too much to be of any help. Sylvia appeared unable to replicate human speech, and the other wallflowers had all looked away in astonished embarrassment. That left...*her.*

'Here,' Gwen said quietly, rising. 'I can show you somewhere you can remove those wet things.'

Why did her cheeks have to flush at such a statement? It was hardly as if she had offered her own bedchamber, which certainly would have been outrageous.

Yet even though she knew she was doing nothing wrong, Gwen could not help but feel disgraceful as she approached the dripping wet Duke.

'Thank you. That would be most welcome,' said Percy, brushing the water out of his eyes and grinning at Sylvia. 'And you and I, Miss Bryant, will talk about this another time. For now, I would suggest you remove the bucket. Anything to avoid awkward questions from the Pike, I am sure.'

He strode out of the room, squelching on the carpet, and Gwen followed him, trying not to laugh.

'You are laughing at me, Gwen,' Percy said ruefully as he walked soggily beside her up the stairs.

Gwen giggled. 'Serves you right after the way you sent me away.'

She had not intended to speak so directly, but her words did not appear to upset him. Quite to the contrary.

Percy smiled ruefully. 'I deserved that,' he said, shaking his hands. Water scattered about him. 'Well, not this, but your reprimand. My...my mother was visiting me, and she is quite...well.'

Gwen nodded. That was all that needed to be said. His mother would certainly have got the wrong impression if she had walked in—after all, there was no future between herself and Percy. Not unless his brother came back from the grave and changed his mind.

'I... I understand. You are here for the card party, I suppose? I shall enjoy watching you explain the damp patch on your seat to Miss Pike.'

'Perhaps you will,' he countered, although there was no anger in his voice. 'Dear me, what am I going to wear?'

'The only thing I can think of is something from the footmen's store,' said Gwen, thinking quickly.

It took her but a moment to retrieve a footman's outfit from the cupboard at the end of the corridor, though Percy frowned rather doubtfully at the breeches, shirt, waistcoat and jacket she handed him.

'So I can be footman and bar the door to all other gentlemen?'

Gwen grinned. 'Do you want to?'

She should not have spoken so boldly. Percy affixed her with such a serious look that Gwen was forced to look away and walk down the corridor.

How did he do that? Look at her with such intensity her whole body reacted?

'Here,' she said, hardly aware of what she was thinking, led by instinct. 'You can change in here.'

She had opened the door before she could stop herself and Percy had walked in.

The Duke looked around the small room, It was her bedchamber, with its large bed and bay window.

'A pleasant aspect in the daytime, I am sure,' Percy said quietly, placing the footman's clothes on a chair in the corner. 'Whose chamber is it?'

Gwen swallowed, her lungs tight in her chest. 'Mine.'

Silence fell between them. A silence Gwen desperately wanted to break, but could not think how. What had she done? She had invited a duke—Percy, the man she wished to be kissing right at this moment—into her bedchamber.

Percy smiled. 'Well, I thank you. And now, if you do not mind…?'

He glanced at the clothes and, cheeks flushed, Gwen nodded.

Leaving the room without saying another word, she reached out to close the door behind her—but something outrageous within her slowed her movements, until the door was only almost closed, leaving a small crack through which she could see.

It was a perfect view. Percy had already ripped off his jacket, waistcoat and shirt—all sodden, all dropped to the floor. Gwen tried not to gasp, but it was difficult. Even in this small sliver of a view, she could see that Percy was a handsome man down to his skin. Broad shoulders, a strength in his arms she had felt but never seen, a smattering of hair trailing down his chest towards his breeches…

Gwen swallowed. Something was stirring within her—something she did not quite understand. But she wanted more.

Oh, so much more.

There was a twist, a change, a gasp—and Percy looked up and caught her gaze.

Gwen gasped too. At the sudden shock of being caught out. Caught staring at a half-naked duke.

It was quite clear from the look on Gwen's face that she was horrified at being caught—but Percy could not think of anything better.

There it was. The desire he knew was inside her, just waiting to come out. He'd seen it once and was desperate to see it again. First the temper, then the tension, now the temptation.

Excitement rushed through Percy as he saw Gwen's wide eyes. So she had been watching him, had she? And had she liked what she had seen?

After weeks of restraint, after stolen kisses in alleyways and in carriages, after being desperate to know her—all of her—this was his chance.

His chance to…talk.

Striding over to the door and opening it fully, Percy leaned against the doorframe and gave the woman before him a lopsided grin. 'Was there more you wanted to say, Miss Knox?'

'I shouldn't have—I should go. I should return downstairs,' Gwen babbled.

Percy caught her hand in his as she turned and started to walk away. There was a tension in that hand…a fierce passion held back. He shivered. Dear Lord, if there was such desire in her now, just from looking at him, just from knowing what he could do when he kissed her…what more could she promise?

'Come on,' he muttered in a low voice.

Gwen did not need encouragement. She slipped into the room with soft footsteps, and when Percy closed the door and leaned against it he saw a woman who knew both what she wanted, and the fact that it was forbidden.

Percy swallowed. He would have to tread carefully here. Just because he knew Gwen Knox had been won over almost from the first moment he had met her, that did not mean Gwen knew herself what she was craving.

Or just how far she was willing to go to get it.

It was time to be a little more direct. A little more obvious about his own desires, Percy mused. And James be damned. Oh, his brother had meant well, certainly—but with Gwen constantly on his mind Percy had to admit that perhaps his brother, in a very small and insignificant way, had been wrong about women such as her. About ladies in general.

He did not have to seek someone who fitted the perfect list of criteria.

He had found Gwen.

'Does it give you pleasure?' he said quietly. 'To look at me?'

To his great surprise, he heard his own heart thumping wildly and loudly in his ears. Percy looked carefully at the woman before him, at the delicate elegance, the shyness that had swiftly returned to Gwen's features the moment she'd realised she had been caught.

Yes, she was a wallflower. But there was something far more here than just a wallflower. Gwen was more than a simple label that diminished her.

Gwen was a wallflower and a warrior. A scandalous woman in some ways, and a most proper one in others. Percy was not sure he would ever get tired of trying to understand the layers of this woman. But he certainly wished to become better acquainted with some of the layers she was wearing!

Though Gwen was clearly scandalised by his question, and Percy knew she had every right to be, he could not help himself. She was a woman so lovely, so interesting—far more interesting than any of the insipid chits his mother had attempted to introduce him to.

Gwen remained silent, though unusually she had not looked away. So Percy decided to attempt a different tack: honesty.

'It gives me pleasure to look at you,' he said quietly. 'Though I admit not as much pleasure as touching you would.'

Gwen's lips parted, almost unconsciously, but she said nothing. Yet still she did not look away, her gaze affixed on his.

Her desires had won, Percy realised, excitement growing in his stomach and descending to his manhood, which was even now trying to stand to attention. She wanted him to speak like this to her…to tease her, perhaps even to touch her. To caress her.

'What do you want, Gwen?' Percy asked as he took a few steps towards her. When she said nothing, he said softly, 'I can tell you what *I* want. I want to kiss you. Touch you. Hold your hands—hold you close to me. Closer than you could possibly imagine.'

'Why are you doing this?' Gwen's voice held no reproach, just confusion and desire.

Percy smiled as he took another step closer. 'Because I… I was wrong.'

She stared. 'Wrong?'

It was as unnatural for him to say it as it was for her to hear it, Percy realised with a twist in his chest. But then, gentlemen of his breeding were rarely ever told they were wrong, were they?

And since he had inherited the title… Well, since then he could not recall ever being told he was wrong!

'I… There isn't a perfect list for what a woman is, Gwen,' Percy found himself saying. 'My brother was wrong in this one regard, I think, and it is a most important thing for me to realise. Oh, Gwen, I cannot stay away from you! I think no one has ever told you how winning you are, Gwen. How desirable you are. I want more than I think you can give me—certainly more than you should…'

He watched her swallow, watched her pupils dilate as he came closer. By God, she wanted him.

'I knew it when I sent you away,' he said quietly. 'I knew it as I bitterly regretted watching you get back into that carriage—that I never wanted you to do that again. And James…'

Percy hesitated. It was difficult to articulate, even to himself, but he had to try. Gwen deserved that. *He* deserved that.

'James would not want me to be unhappy,' he said, his voice breaking. 'My brother…he created the criteria, made me promise because he thought it would make me happy. But you do, Gwen. It's you.'

He saw the flicker of astonishment in her eyes, the amazement at his revelation—and the excitement at what might come next.

'I would like to kiss you, taste you…know precisely how you moan when I give you pleasure,' said Percy softly. He was standing before her now, probably too close—or perhaps not close enough.

Gwen took a small step forward. They were mere inches away from each other now. 'And…and what then?' she asked.

It was all Percy could do not to crush her to him, desperate as he was to end this tension, this dance they had been doing around each other. But not yet. *Not yet.*

'Then…' he said, in half a voice, half a growl. 'Then I would like to take off your gown and kiss every inch of you.'

'I like the sound of that,' whispered Gwen, her mouth

curling into a smile. A tantalising smile which made Percy wish he had the restraint he should have—*any* restraint. For the words in his heart were threatening to spill out, to shock both of them, in a rush of certainty he had never known before.

Marry me, Gwen. Make me happy. Let me make you happy.

If he'd had restraint, he would not have said the words that would take them past a turning point: once they'd passed it, there would be no turning back.

What was it she had once said? *'Least likely to win a duke.'*

'Why don't I show you just how likely you are to win me?' he asked.

Chapter Thirteen

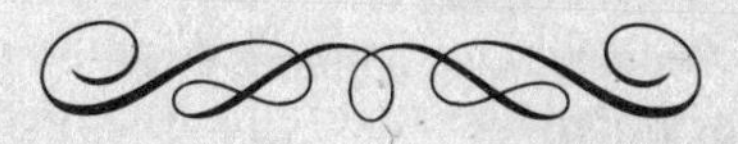

Gwen stared at the man who had asked her such a dangerous and delicious question.

She knew what it was now—this strange sensation in her chest, this anticipatory tingling across her body, the warmth between her legs.

Arousal.

She wanted Percy to make love to her, to kiss her and touch her and do all the delectable things he had said.

'I would like to kiss you, taste you...know precisely how you moan when I give you pleasure.'

But something held Gwen back, despite all the memories of tantalising pleasure, despite her imaginings of forbidden pleasure to come. Something that confused her.

It took a moment to understand what it was.

Fear.

As Gwen looked into Percy's eyes, his honest face, she knew it was not enough.

It was not sufficient to merely want another, to desire their touch. She cared for Percy deeply, and only now could she admit what those feelings amounted to.

Love.

She loved him.

It was a strange, new, imperfect love, to be sure—one that if she had been a titled lady might have grown into something precious and beautiful.

But she was not. She was a murderess—someone with no beauty nor wealth nor position in Society. And they were all precisely what Percy needed. She knew it; he knew it.

So when he offered her such things, such wonderful delights, it was as a mistress.

Gwen's stomach twisted painfully at the thought, but she could not ignore it.

While she might want to be his wife, marry him, spend the rest of her days falling more and more in love with the man before her… He did not want that. Percy needed to marry as a duke married, and those marital limitations pained her more than she could say.

It was too much. Too painful. Too excruciating.

Gwen knew she should step away…remove herself from such temptation.

But Percy's intoxicating presence was too much. His words were too much. His admission that his brother had been wrong, that he chose instead to be happy…

Although they were not even touching, Gwen was dazzled by the prospect of such intimacy. His naked chest was before her, crying out for her touch.

'Then I would like to take off your gown and kiss every inch of you.'

Something warm and aching slipped from her heart to between her legs. Gwen knew what she wanted: Percy. All of him. Not just his kisses, nor even his lovemaking, but his heart.

Something she knew he simply could not give her.

Besides, it would be scandalous to give in to such hedonistic desires! She was supposed to be a wallflower, not a wanton! No lady could permit herself to simply take the pleasures offered by dukes—even if they were as handsome and alluring as Percy.

'Gwen?' Percy said quietly. 'Are you quite well?'

Gwen opened her mouth, but nothing came out.

How could she speak? What could she say? It was impossible to conceive of any words that would make any sense to a man like him.

Surely he had experience in such matters?

At that very thought Gwen's gaze dropped, unbidden images of Percy with other women cutting through her thoughts.

The movement of her gaze did not help, however. Before it had been affixed to his eyes, something Gwen had thought far too intense, but now she was looking at the trail of hair disappearing into his breeches, under which there appeared to be a rather prominent bulge…

Ah.

Gwen's cheeks seared with heat as she realised what it was. Percy's manhood. He wanted her. His desire was obvious. This was no teasing trick.

But no duke should desire her in this way. Gwen was sure of that.

'I know why you are hesitating.'

Gwen could not help but laugh dryly at Percy's words. 'I do not think you do.'

How could he? Could a duke, or any gentleman, understand what it was to be so utterly overwhelmed? To be on the one hand overcome with desire for a gentleman—a desire Gwen knew she should not be feeling—and on the other hand believe that even if that gentleman made love to her it would not be meaningful unless it came with certain promises?

Promises Gwen knew Percy could not make.

She should never have shown him to any bedchamber,

let alone her own. She should not have watched while he removed his clothing.

She certainly should not have permitted such sensual conversation.

'I think I do,' said Percy. 'You want this to mean something. To be deeper than just physicality, I mean. A connection not just of bodies, but of hearts, minds, souls.'

Gwen looked up. Percy was not teasing her. 'You…you are right.'

How could she put it into words—or did she need to if he already understood?

Tempting as it was to reach out and touch that handsome chest, Gwen took a deep breath and tried to concentrate. It was important, explaining to him how she felt. He needed to know. There might never be anyone else she could explain this to.

'The…the act of lovemaking…' said Gwen. Her cheeks were flushing, but there was nothing she could do about it. 'Kissing, touching, c-caressing…any of that. All of it. I believe it should be…well, between two people who truly care for each other. Who are committed to each other.'

Had she said too much? Gwen's heart was pattering lightly but rapidly in her chest, making it difficult to think, to breathe, to know whether she had spoken too brashly.

There was a rather too knowing smile dancing across Percy's lips. 'You did not say that when you were kissing me in that alley, nor when I pushed you up against that tree.'

Gwen laughed weakly as he lifted a hand to push back one of the curls that had fallen over her forehead. Every inch of her skin came alive when he brushed it, as though for the first time. As though she would die if he did not touch her again.

'I did think it,' Gwen admitted in a breathless voice.

'It was just… I wanted you to keep kissing me so much I did not say anything.'

A flash of something she did not recognise seared across Percy's face. Was it desire? Desperation? Glory? A sense of achievement—or something else?

'I wish you had said,' Percy said. 'It… Gwen, it matters to me that you are comfortable with me kissing you. Touching you.'

Gwen's heart rose. He was a good man. She had known it before but had not been able to put it into words, nor had it demonstrated so clearly.

Gwen said quietly, 'I know. I… I truly care for you, Percy.'

Percy took a step backwards, widening the gap between them as he examined her. Gwen could almost feel the change in the air, the change in temperature as he retreated.

She should not have spoken so openly. Nothing good came of her voicing her opinions or letting loose her temper—Gwen knew that. And just at the moment when it was most important for her to be near him, to feel the reassuring presence of him being close, he had stepped away.

Of course he had, Gwen thought dully.

Dukes did not want wallflowers admitting they had feelings for them. They looked for quick and meaningless relief—pleasure, not partnership.

'Forget my words,' Gwen said hastily, turning away. 'I should not have said—'

'I will never forget them.'

Gwen's heart stopped, skipping a beat almost painfully. She turned back to look at Percy.

'I am relieved to hear you say those words,' he said softly, 'because…because I have known for too long that I care too much for you. Too long and too much.'

It took a moment for Gwen to take in what he had said.

It could not be.

Did the handsome man before her really care for her? It must be a trick of her hearing, even with those words about ignoring his promise to his brother ringing in her ears. Yet Gwen could not imagine what words she must have mistaken for such a declaration of affection.

'Could…could you say that again?'

Percy chuckled softly as he stepped forward. 'You wish me to make another declaration of my fondness for you?'

'Are…are you in love with me?' Gwen asked shyly, stepping into his arms and almost crying out as Percy's arms curled around her and pulled her close.

This was where she was supposed to be. After all this time, wondering why her mother had seen fit to send her to such a joyless place, now Gwen knew why she had been sent to the Wallflower Academy.

To meet him. Percy. To know him. To stand here, in his arms, as his smile became bashful upon hearing her words.

'Oh, I don't think I said that aloud,' Percy said, his gaze slipping from hers.

Gwen smiled, joy flooding her heart. Everything she might attempt to say now could be communicated in a much more delicious way.

This time when Gwen lifted up her lips to be kissed Percy did not start gently. No, he possessed her mouth as a thirsty man reached for water…as though without it he would surely die.

Gwen gasped into his mouth, heady sensations overwhelming her rapidly as Percy's naked chest pressed against her clothed one.

Just a few layers of silk, she could not help thinking, as her hands returned to the nape of his neck, as they had done when they had kissed in that alleyway. Just one gown, easily moved aside as it had been when he'd touched her by that tree. Just a few inches of silk and their skin would touch, would meet with the same passion and reverence they had enjoyed then.

The kiss ended, and still Percy looked bashful.

'You did not say it aloud,' said Gwen hesitantly, certain she should not speak these words, but knowing she would never forgive herself if she did not. 'But do…do you feel it? In your heart?'

At first it appeared as though Percy would avoid the question. But he certainly did not avoid another chance to kiss her lips, and Gwen shivered as his tongue teased greater pleasure from her than ever before.

But when he pulled away, eyes blazing and mouth clearly hungry for more, he murmured, 'Yes. Oh, yes, Gwen—I love you. I did not know it until it was too late to do anything about it, and even then…even then I did not want to. I love you, Gwen.'

It was everything Gwen had ever hoped the moment would be and more. Nestled in Percy's arms, with his strong hands on her waist, slipping towards her buttocks, her hands around his neck, keeping his mouth close, was precisely where she wanted to be, his words ringing in her ears…

He loved her.

Happiness was searing her heart, branding it and branding this moment in her mind as one she would never forget.

He loved her.

'I love you, Percy,' Gwen said shyly, growing in confidence with every syllable. 'I love you even if you are a duke.'

Percy laughed. 'Is that a problem?'

'No! No, I just meant…' Gwen tried to explain, then laughed when she saw his teasing smile. 'You are a most irritating man, Percy Devereux.'

'And you are a most tantalising woman, Gwen Knox,'

said Percy with a groan, his fingers finally reaching her buttocks, cupping them and pulling her towards him. 'I don't know how you've done it, but you've won me over.'

Gwen smiled, delight almost overwhelming her. She loved him. She loved Percy, and he loved her.

'Does this mean,' asked Percy, 'that you will permit me to do what I want?'

Her smile quickly disappearing, Gwen swallowed and tried to think calmly—something that would be far easier if she was not in the warm embrace of a half-naked duke.

What he wanted?

What he wanted was everything, as far as Gwen could tell. She was hardly well versed in the art of making love, but touching, caressing, touching every part of her skin…?

It would be a line crossed that she could never uncross. A departure from her life of good manners and well-behaved solitude. It would mean giving up any chance of keeping that part of herself for her wedding night.

The thought scorched her mind, but Gwen pushed it aside. She loved Percy and he loved her. To all intents and purposes this *was* her wedding night. Their wedding night.

'They'll come looking for us…' she breathed. 'The Pike. The card party—'

'I did not return my invitation, and I'm sure she'll be far too distracted by Sylvia to think of anything else,' Percy said, his gaze hungry.

Gwen nodded, easily convinced by his words. Yes, they were alone, and they would be left alone. And if she could not give herself to the man she loved, what was the point of all this growing love and affection within her?

'I want you,' said Gwen softly, 'to kiss me…everywhere.'

Percy's eyes widened.

She laughed. 'Ladies have desires too, you know.'

'Yes, well, that's all very well… But…everywhere?' Percy said in a half-whisper.

It was as though he could not quite believe his ears.

Gwen could hardly believe she had spoken the words herself, except she knew they had sprung from her own heart, her own desires.

If she could not be open and honest now, with the man she loved, when could she?

'I love you,' said Gwen quietly. 'And I want you.'

Percy did not need greater encouragement. Returning his lips to hers in an ardent yet reverential kiss, he moved his fingers from her buttocks—to Gwen's regret—and started to untie the delicate ribbons along the side of her gown.

Lost in the heady sensations of nibbling lips and searing hot tongues, Gwen was so lost in the pleasure of the moment she barely noticed when Percy had finished his work. It was only when her gown slipped to the floor, leaving her in naught but her stays and under-shift, that Gwen gasped.

'There,' Percy said, kissing just below Gwen's ear, making her shiver. 'And now…'

It was all Gwen could do not to moan as Percy's lips moved across her bare shoulder. Every inch of contact branded her as his and Percy claimed her…all the parts of her no one else had touched.

Now, no one else ever would.

'Percy!' Gwen gasped as his swift and knowledgeable fingers removed her stays and under-shift in but a moment, leaving her utterly naked.

It was a strange sensation. Gwen had never been so vulnerable before another person—had never had a gentleman see any part of her, let alone all of her.

Moving her hands to hide herself, she glanced nervously at Percy. There was such potent desire in his gaze that

Gwen found all her nerves melting away. It was not a disapproving look…

'I never imagined… You are so beautiful, Gwen. I can't stop myself—tell me if you want me to stop.'

There was no sense of demand in his voice, and Gwen could not think what he meant—until he stepped forward and gently pulled her across the room and against the door.

'Percy…?' Gwen whispered, conscious of only this narrow block of wood keeping them from the corridor.

But he did not reply—at least, not in words. Kissing her lips with a passionate moan, Percy left her mouth and kissed down her neck towards her breasts.

Barely able to stand, Gwen grasped the door handle and quickly turned the key in the lock. Her entire body quivered as pleasure soared between each kiss, peaking to an unimaginable height as Percy captured one of her nipples in his mouth, arching his tongue slowly around it.

'Oh, Percy!'

Gwen tried to stay quiet, she really did, but it was impossible once Percy descended to his knees, his kisses moving down her stomach and suddenly to her secret place. Through her curls, his tongue entered her, and Gwen arched her back against the door at the sudden rush of ecstasy consuming her body.

'Percy!' she gasped, hardly aware of what she was saying.

This was too much. When he had said he wanted to kiss her everywhere…

Percy seemed to take her quivering, twisting pleasure as encouragement to continue, and Gwen moaned and sobbed, clutching desperately at the door handle as his tongue twisted within her, sucked and then built a rhythm, bringing her closer and closer to a peak she remembered and ached for, until eventually Gwen cried out his name, with no thought to who might hear her, as her climax shook her entire body.

'Percy!'

His hands reached her hips, holding her there, preventing her from collapsing. Stars appeared in her eyes, and for a moment she was not entirely sure where she was.

After blinking several times, Gwen looked down to see Percy looking up, a desperate hunger on his face.

'I wanted to hear you come,' he whispered, 'and now I need to feel it. Get on the bed.'

Gwen obeyed—not because there was any threat in his request, but because she wished to please him. Oh, she wanted to please the man who could make her feel like that…

Percy had stripped off his boots and breeches by the time he joined her on the bed, and Gwen tried not to stare at that part of him she had never expected to see.

His manhood. Large, hard, stiff as Percy settled himself between her legs and into her welcoming embrace.

'I will go slowly,' Percy promised, kissing her lightly on the corner of her mouth.

Slowly? Gwen did not want to go slowly. She wanted the fast, desperate, hungry pace Percy had given her with his tongue, deep inside her. She was wet with desire as he slipped into her and started to build a rhythm she now recognised—the same rhythm which had taken her body to such heights only moments before—and Gwen's heart quickly rose in excitement at the thought of feeling that again.

At feeling everything again.

Everything he could give her.

'Damn, Gwen, you feel so good,' moaned Percy as he plunged himself into her once more, causing twinges of pleasure to ripple through Gwen's body.

She clung to his shoulders, unsure whether she should say something but actually unable to speak a word. Not when she was experiencing such pleasure—a pleasure that was building and building, as it had done before, and she wanted it, craved it, craved him, Percy, the man she loved—

'Percy…oh, yes!'

Gwen could not help it. She cried out for a second time as ecstasy overwhelmed her, and it appeared Percy had reached the same peak, for he thrust into her rapidly and then collapsed.

Clutching him, pulling him into her arms, Gwen tried to think, tried to concentrate on the breathing that felt difficult in this moment.

To think such things were possible…such sensation was just at arm's reach. How did anyone, once knowing the pleasure such desire could bring, manage to stay away from it?

'I could never have imagined it…' Gwen breathed, unable to help herself. 'Losing my innocence in such a way. In such a…a heated, delicious encounter that fulfilled all my wildest dreams.'

And more, she wanted to say, for she could never have dreamt of such sensuality.

Percy chuckled as he moved onto the bed beside her, pulling her into his arms. 'Good,' he said sleepily, his eyelashes fluttering shut. 'And now I have you right where I want you…'

Gwen snuggled into him, placing her face on his chest. His heartbeat was just as frantic as her own.

'Oh? And where is that?'

'Right in my arms,' said Percy quietly. 'And in my heart.'

Chapter Fourteen

It was cruel that he had to depart.

Percy told himself another few minutes would not matter. Why not stay here, in the comforting warmth of Gwen's bed, with her naked form beside him, lost in slumber?

He had awoken early—so early the sun was still not up. Birdsong drifted through the bay window, its curtains open. They had been so lost in their lovemaking, then fallen asleep swiftly.

Gwen's gentle breathing moved the blanket Percy had drawn over her and he watched, marvelling at her beauty. To think that he had seen, touched, those delicate fingers, those sensual breasts...had taken and given pleasure of all kinds with such a woman.

It was more than he had ever expected. Perhaps more than he deserved. Certainly more than he should have done. He had thrown out all decorum, Society's expectations, his brother's precepts, and his own knowledge of what he needed to do to cement his title's reputation.

But Percy knew there was little he could keep from Gwen now, even if he wanted to, now he had given her his heart.

His heart contracted, then relaxed, expanding with his devotion. She was a wallflower, yes, but a passionate one.

A woman who understood him, who cared for him—who loved him.

Joy blossomed through him. Love—something he had not expected and yet had found with this precious, beautiful woman. If only he could stay. If only this moment, these early hours, with the Wallflower Academy silent and their secret still their own, could continue for ever.

Percy sighed, his breath ruffling Gwen's long dark hair, draped over her shoulders and the pillow.

But it could not be. He had to leave—and quickly, if he was not to be spotted. And that meant leaving Gwen. His stomach rebelled, aching both from hunger and agitation at the thought of leaving her.

There was no other choice.

Percy reached out a hand and softly brushed away the hair from Gwen's shoulder. She stirred, her head twisting, and murmured gently, though her eyes stayed closed.

He smiled.

So, Gwen was not a morning person.

There was still so much to learn about her…so much to discover. He would never grow bored with this tempestuous wallflower.

'Gwen…' Percy whispered.

That seemed to be enough to draw the drowsy woman from sleep. Gently, Gwen's eyelashes fluttered, and she looked up. For a moment there was stillness, and then a broad smile crept across her face.

'Percy…' she breathed.

'Hello, my love,' said Percy.

It was instinct leading him to speak in such a way. Why not speak words of love to the woman to whom he had given his heart? And he had been offered hers so openly in return.

Difficult though it was to accept that they must now be apart, Percy clenched his jaw and forced himself to say the words he knew must be said—even if they pained him. 'I must go.'

Gwen blinked, and then a sharpness appeared in her pupils and a line appeared between her eyes. 'Go? Now? Why?'

Percy jerked his head towards the window. 'Day breaks, and if I am to leave the Academy without anyone seeing it must be now.'

For a moment it appeared Gwen would disagree, debate the fact, but then a look of sorrowful resignation covered her face.

'I suppose so,' she said, but then a mischievous smile crept across her lips. 'Although if you stayed here I could always make it worth your while.'

Her fingers crept towards him, pulling him closer, and Percy groaned.

What had he unleashed within this woman?

Heavens, if he was not careful, he would make love to her again, and doubtless wake the whole household with her cries of pleasure.

His manhood jerked. It was not the worst idea he'd ever had…

'No—no, Gwen,' Percy said regretfully as he captured her fingers in his and held them tight. 'I really must go.'

Gwen's mischievous smile softened. 'I will miss you.'

'I know,' said Percy heavily, wishing he could remain here for ever, in the safety and sanctuary of her affections. 'I will miss you too.'

He allowed himself one kiss, one dipped moment of connection, and his whole body quivered as his lips touched hers. This was more than love, more than affection. It was an intimacy he could never have conceived of…beautiful, perfect.

It was with great regret that Percy broke the kiss. Gwen

appeared to feel the same, leaning up in an attempt to prolong the connection for as long as possible.

'Gwen…' said Percy quietly.

'Percy…' said Gwen, leaning up for another kiss.

He leaned back. This was important, and it could not be said in the middle of sleep, nor while affectionate kisses were addling their minds. He had to make sure she understood—or there would be consequences, and not ones he could control.

Percy took a deep breath. 'Gwen, we will need to keep this…what's between us…between us. Do you understand?'

Perhaps he should explain more clearly, he thought wryly. It was, after all, very early in the morning, and Gwen had given him no sign of being particularly awake yet.

She frowned. 'Keep what's between us, between us?'

Percy swallowed. 'I mean…our lovemaking…the fact we love each other—'

'I do love you,' said Gwen with a sleepy smile.

Percy's stomach twisted. James's list of conditions for a wife—to be elegant, refined, distant, wealthy—had always seemed right, naturally. It was James's list. Only now could Percy see just how cold and isolating a woman like that would have been.

A woman James would have approved of…

He could not imagine her now. Not with Gwen before him.

She was everything he wanted: gentle and loving, passionate and wild. So ready to accept his touch, All the things he had never expected to find in one woman—let alone one so beautiful.

'Gwen,' Percy said firmly, half to get her attention, half to focus his own. 'No one can know—do you understand? It's not the right time. Not yet. This must stay between us.

Our lovemaking, our declarations of love…they must stay a secret. For the moment.'

Because, Percy thought darkly as he watched the words sink into Gwen's sleepy mind, *he had no idea as yet just how to broach this with his mother.*

The idea of telling her that her son, her only remaining son, had given himself away to a chit of a wallflower with no connections nor refinements…

He would find a way, Percy told himself, and then he would declare his passion and affections for Gwen and they would be married. It would all come right, eventually. They just needed to be patient.

'I suppose that makes sense,' said Gwen quietly, yawning. 'We will need to think about how to tell my mother, and Miss Pike—goodness, and *your* mother, I suppose.'

The knot of tension which had been building in Percy's stomach had not consciously been noticed by him before—not until Gwen spoke those words and the knot started to fade away. She understood.

'Precisely,' he said with a sigh of relief. 'Thank you, Gwen.'

Percy kissed her again, unable to resist the allure of those soft, inviting lips, and groaned as Gwen placed her hands around his neck to pull him closer.

'No—no, Gwen. I must away,' Percy said regretfully.

Gwen sighed as she nestled herself into the pillows. 'I suppose you are right.'

'I am not so sure,' Percy said ruefully as he entwined his fingers with hers. 'The very last thing I wish is to leave you here, but I… I have no choice.'

And that was the truth, Percy thought as he looked at the most beautiful woman he had ever seen. *No choice.* No choice but to love her…no choice but to be devoted.

Even if his mother would never have made this choice.

Even if it was going to be one of the most difficult conversations he had ever had, trying to convince his mother to accept Gwen as her daughter-in-law.

And if she did not? If she refused to give her permission? Refused to accept that Percy was going to invest his marital prospects—the prospects of a duke, no less!—in a woman with no dowry, family or prestige?

What if—heaven forbid—he received the Cut from Society? And his mother, in similar fashion, was cut from her friends, her connections, her very reason for living?

The knot of tension had returned, but Percy could do naught about it. He had no idea how he would solve that problem, and a problem it was.

He swallowed, then kissed Gwen lightly on the nose. 'We'll see each other again soon. Last night…you won my devotion, Gwen.'

'I already had it,' Gwen said sleepily, her eyes closing as she drifted back to sleep.

Percy's heart fluttered painfully before continuing in a regular beat.

He might not have started this with…well, with the best of intentions. When everything within him had told him being near Gwen was both terribly wrong and painfully right. But there was nothing he could do now to prevent the loss of his heart.

He would have her. No matter what happened.

Gwen had almost fallen asleep by the time Percy slipped out of the bed into the cold morning air. It took him but a few moments to put on the footman's outfit, finding the breeches a little short but otherwise sufficient. It was a pain, truly, that his clothes were still damp.

But then, Percy thought, *I did not exactly spend much time last night worrying about drying them.*

He had been far too interested in removing Gwen's clothes than looking to his own.

Percy almost made it to the stall where his mare had been lodged overnight without discovery, but as he opened the door to the stables a young voice shouted after him.

'Hi, there!'

Percy sighed. It had been too much, it appeared, to expect to be able to leave without detection.

Turning on his heel, he saw Tom, the stable boy, approaching him with a frown.

'You're not a footman here,' the boy said in an accusatory tone. 'Who are you? A thief come to steal from the house using your trickery?'

Percy stared. It was incomprehensible that the boy should not recognise him—but then he was dressed very differently from the way he had been in their previous encounters.

Oh, the shame...to be taken not even for a footman but for a thief!

''Tis I, Tom,' Percy said in a low voice.

The stable boy frowned, evidently recognising the voice but unable to place it. 'You? Who *are* you?'

Swallowing heavily, Percy saw there was nothing for it. He would have to reveal himself and hope for Tom's natural deference.

'The Duke of Knaresby,' Percy said softly, as though a lower volume would make it less scandalous. 'I had to— My clothes were ruined. I needed to borrow… Just let me get to my horse!'

Striding past the astonished stable boy, Percy reached for the tack and quickly saddled his horse. Tom appeared to be so utterly astonished he was unable to speak. Only when Percy had mounted the mare, wincing slightly as the footman's breeches stretched painfully, did Tom finally say something.

'But…but why are you dressed like a footman?'

Percy sighed. How on earth was he to explain the series of events which had led him to be dressed like this?

Well, he should probably start at the beginning.

'Sylvia—'

'Say no more, Your Grace,' said Tom hastily, cheeks flushing. 'I quite understand.'

That was remarkably simple, Percy thought as he nudged his horse forward.

'Marvellous,' he said in a low voice. 'And no word to Miss Pike, if you please.'

Tom nodded, and was rewarded with a smile—Percy, of course had no coin to give him. Everything was still in his waistcoat, tucked under his arm. He would have to remember on his next visit.

The ride back to London was unpleasant, to say the least. Percy made a variety of discoveries while on his horse in the freezing cold morning air. Firstly, he knew that he would never criticise his tailor again, for he now knew the value of well-fitting clothes. Secondly, footmen had rather a difficult lot, being forced to wear these ridiculous clothes. And thirdly, he could manage to trot down the streets of London to his home and pass the reins to his astonished stable master so early almost no one would be up.

His good fortune, however, did not last. Percy ought to have expected something to go wrong, but his confidence peaked as he slipped into his London townhouse by the back door, closed it as quietly as he could manage, and leaned, exhausted, against the wall.

Well, he was home.

In less than half an hour he could be in a hot bath, left to think only of his delightfully disreputable encounter with Gwen Knox. And he had managed it all without his mother—

'Percival William Devereux—what are you wearing?'

Percy straightened hastily, pulling the ill-fitting jacket down, and smiled weakly at his mother, who was striding down the corridor towards him.

Ah. Now there was a morning person—more was the pity. It would be difficult to explain this away to her as easily as to Tom, the stable boy.

'Good morning, Mother,' Percy said brightly, as though cheerfulness might prevent his mother from seeing the state he was in. 'It is very early, is it not?'

'You are wearing the clothes of a servant, Percy—and not a servant of this house,' said Lady Devereux severely, stopping before him and frowning. 'Dear me, this is a livery I admit I do not recognise. What interesting piping on the sleeves.'

Percy's smile froze on his face. 'Ah. Yes, well, the thing is—'

'Dear Lord, is that the livery of the Wallflower Academy?' The frown on his mother's face deepened as Percy's stomach twisted. 'Percival William Devereux—what on earth were you doing there? I thought you were attending the Kenceysham ball last night?'

'Well…' said Percy awkwardly. 'The thing is—'

'And returning in a servant's outfit!' Lady Devereux shook her head. 'Percy, what am I to do with you? You spend far too much time at that place. If I have said it before, I have said it a thousand times!'

'You have indeed,' said Percy heavily.

'And with all this threat of scandal in the newspapers, your brother's death still unexplained, I would have thought you would take your responsibilities as the new Duke of Knaresby more seriously!'

'I am,' said Percy urgently. Did she think he did not care? 'Which reminds me… I thought I would go to the inn where James was killed—the Golden Hind, I think it was called—and ask—'

'No,' said his mother firmly. 'No. I forbid it.'

Frustration stirred in his chest. Did she not wish to know more? Questions about his brother's last moments had always whirled through his mind. 'I have never understood why you have no wish to know—'

'Is this what you call taking your requirement to marry well *seriously*? Wearing the clothes of a servant? Percy, really!'

Blast. It was too much to hope that his mother would understand the hilarious circumstances in which the wearing of the outfit had occurred.

Explaining about Gwen, he thought darkly, *was not a good idea—not now.*

He would shelve that for another time.

'You see, the thing was,' he said, with what he hoped was a light-hearted smile, 'one of the wallflowers—a Miss Sylvia Bryant—played a trick involving—'

'I do not want to hear it,' his mother said sharply. 'I hardly need further proof that you should not be visiting the Academy—if one could even call it that. You are better than that, Percy. Always were. And especially now. You have your title to think of!'

Percy swallowed, but said nothing. He well knew his mother's opinion, and could only guess the response he would receive if he revealed that he had fallen for one of the Academy's occupants.

Fallen and fallen hard.

Love is a powerful force, Percy thought. *Oh, yes, Gwen—I love you. I did not know it until it was too late to do any-*

thing about it, and even then...even then I would not have wanted to. I love you, Gwen.

Something stirred within his heart—something bold, brash—and he determined to make a clean breast of it to his mother. He loved Gwen. That was not going to change. And the sooner his mother could start reconciling herself to that truth, the better.

'Mother,' Percy said firmly. 'I must tell you. I have decided I will marry—'

'Yes, yes, I know. And all we have to do is find the right lady,' said Lady Devereux, waving a hand. 'That is precisely why you need to hurry.'

Percy smiled. 'Well, actually, there is no need to hurry. I have already found—'

'When I say you need to hurry, I say it advisedly,' said his mother sharply. 'Go now, upstairs, and get changed. They'll be here in less than an hour, and I cannot have you wandering around looking like a servant.'

Percy blinked. 'Who will be here in an hour?'

'*Now,* Percy!'

Kissing his mother on the cheek, he nodded. Well, what else was there to do? Arguing with his mother was rather like shouting at a mountain: one might feel better afterwards, but the mountain would be unchanged.

A bath, however, would be welcome.

Sinking into its almost scalding embrace, Percy sighed heavily and leaned back. It was strange to think how far he had come in only the last few hours. This time yesterday he'd had no thought of revealing his feelings to Gwen.

In truth, he'd had no idea how deeply they went until he had seen her watching him undress.

There is such an attraction, he mused, *in seeing attraction in another.*

Now he had shared his affections, and Gwen hers, and

they had shared in delightful lovemaking, all he had to do was find the right time to speak to his mother.

With guests arriving in less than an hour, now was certainly not the right time…

After a quick shave from his valet, and the relief of getting dressed in his own clothes, Percy felt a little more human again. He descended the stairs hastily as he looked at his pocket watch. Almost eleven o'clock—an early visit, indeed. But then his mother had never seen the point in wasting the day away.

'Well, Mother,' Percy said as he entered the morning room. 'I hope you will find this outfit more accept…'

Eyes wide, he stared at the scene before him and wondered whether he had entered the wrong room—the wrong house. This appeared to be far more like a scene from the Wallflower Academy than his own home.

His mother was seated in an armchair by a small table, where a tea tray had been laid, and was smiling broadly. Opposite her, standing in a line, were three young ladies, all dressed in their finest gowns. One had even put a flower in her hair. They were staring as though they had been waiting for hours. One was flushed. Another fluttered her eyelashes coquettishly.

'Ah, there you are, Knaresby,' said Lady Devereux smartly, using his title name as they were in company. 'See—I have three very eligible young ladies for your viewing.'

Percy opened his mouth, but no words came out. How could he speak? What could he say to such nonsense? To such a way of shoving him towards an appropriate marriage?

What on earth was his mother doing, speaking about these ladies as though they were not here?

'Now, the Honourable Miss Maynard—that's the one on

the left—she comes from a very good family, with sufficient dowry but nothing too impressive,' began his mother, pointing at the first young lady.

Percy saw Miss Maynard's cheeks flush as his mother spoke of her so callously.

'Whereas Lady Rose has a very impressive dowry, but rather unimpressive brothers,' continued Lady Devereux, with a knowing look at her son. 'If you chose her, you would have to do something about their behaviour, I declare. For one of them would soon bring us down in Society if left unchecked. And Miss Middlesborough—'

'Mother!' Percy said, mortified, as he shut the door behind him and strode towards the seated women. 'Really!'

This was awful—worse than the way the Wallflower Academy treated its inhabitants. Why, what was she thinking, having them standing there, listening to her nonsense, lining them up as though at a cattle market!

'Oh, you care too much,' said his mother, tapping him lightly on the shoulder. 'These young ladies knew what to expect when they received my invitation—did you not, ladies?'

'Yes, m'lady,' came the murmured replies.

Percy's stomach clenched. 'Nonetheless—'

'Nonetheless, nothing,' said his mother sharply, her eyes affixed on her son. 'Mark my words, Percy—Knaresby. When a duke marries, he must consider all these things. He marries not for himself but for the betterment of the family and the title. There is a great weight of responsibility upon him. 'Tis not as though you will have a love match. We seek a marriage to benefit both parties.'

Percy opened his mouth, but his typically eloquent tongue failed him. How could he speak when his mind was clouded not with reasonable arguments against the nonsense before him, but instead on how each of these ladies was nothing compared to Gwen?

He found them wanting, despite their superior breeding and their dowries. He felt nothing for them. There was no comparison to Gwen.

'And besides,' his mother said, her gaze still fierce, 'it is what your father would have wanted. Would have *expected*.'

Percy closed his mouth as his heart sank. He would?

In his vague recollections of his father he had never spoken to him of such things. Why would he? Percy had been nothing but a child when his father had died.

'What would James have wanted?' he blurted out.

His mother's eyebrows rose. 'James? What on earth does your brother have to do with this?'

Percy hesitated. He knew he could never express to her the tumultuous emotions turbulent in his heart. How was he ever to explain them to his mother, who surely would never accept a mere wallflower?

Chapter Fifteen

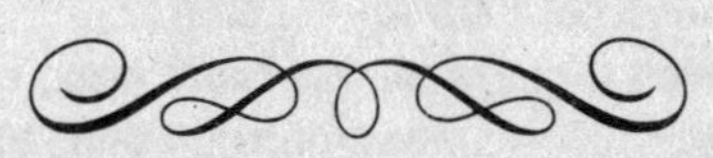

'We are going out for afternoon tea,' Miss Pike announced grandly, as though she had just given the wallflowers a precious gift as they sat around the luncheon table. 'With members of the aristocracy.'

Sylvia's eyes widened.

Miss Pike nodded approvingly. 'Indeed, you may look impressed, Miss Bryant,' she said grandly. 'I have worked especially hard for this afternoon tea to be a perfect opportunity for you ladies to make an impression on a gentleman with a title—take a leaf, perhaps, out of Miss Knox's book.'

Gwen flushed as the owner of the Wallflower Academy nodded impressively in her direction. Her hands twisted in her lap, her plate of cured ham and potatoes abandoned.

How could she eat? How could she act as though everything was normal, as though her life was perfectly ordinary, when she knew it was not?

Worse, the one thing Miss Pike was apt to praise her for—attracting the attentions of a duke—made her heart so unsure of the future?

The remembrance of Percy's heated touches, his clever fingers, crowded Gwen's mind and made it impossible for her to follow the conversation now circling around the table.

'Gentlemen of note do not all need to have titles, surely?' Sylvia was saying.

Rilla laughed. 'Are you honestly telling me you would decline the advances of a gentleman merely because he had a title?'

'That is not what I am saying at all…'

Titles, Gwen thought wryly. True, when she had been a little younger, a little more foolish, she had daydreamed about being taken away by a gentleman with more riches and titles than he knew what to do with.

Until that fateful night.

Until the whole of her world had fallen around her because of what she had done.

Until her mother had discovered her.

Since then, it had been easiest to keep her head down and be silent. A wallflower, indeed, even if it was merely because she was afraid of being found out.

But Percy was that imagined perfect gentleman, was he not? Wealthy, with a title, but kind, too. With something deeper in him she had never discovered in any other man.

Of course they would not wish to announce their engagement before he had spoken with his mother—so did his absence mean Percy's mother had taken against her? It had, after all, been almost a week.

Seven days without him. Without a word. After giving herself to him so willingly…

Perhaps she had been foolish to consider herself worthy of him, to think their union would not be endangered by the truth of the past. But she loved him. Oh, how she loved him. And a very real pain twisted in her stomach at the idea of never seeing him again.

From the moment Gwen had seen Percy—admittedly

she had been on the gravel of the drive—she had been unable to resist him. Resist his presence. Resist the growing attraction budding inside her…

Even when he had acted so haughtily against any union between them at the start.

And after giving herself to Percy it was a cruel separation.

'Many members of the aristocracy—at least ten—have confirmed their attendance at tea, and there are more I hope will attend,' Miss Pike was saying. 'We will enter the carriages half an hour after luncheon.'

Something stirred in Gwen's memory.

'We'll see each other again soon.'

Was this what he had meant? Gwen's heart fluttered at the hopeful thought which now invaded her mind. Had he been thinking of this afternoon tea?

A smile graced Gwen's lips, if only for a moment.

Oh, if only he would be in attendance today.

She had not paid attention to the place where they were going, only taking in the fact that it was a lady's home in London. A chance, Miss Pike had said, to practise their manners.

And if Percy was there…

They would have the opportunity to talk, to laugh. Perhaps he would move his fingers across hers. A sense of anticipation rushed through her. Perhaps, if they were very careful, they would be able to slip away together.

Gwen swallowed the scandalous thought, but now it had occurred there was no way to ignore it.

Picking up her knife and fork in the hope that the other wallflowers and Miss Pike would not notice anything amiss, Gwen lost herself for a few minutes in delightful imaginings of Percy pulling her aside while no one was looking, the two of them running up the stairs hand in hand, slipping into a bedchamber and making love, hastily and passionately, trying desperately to muffle their moans of joy…

And then, Gwen thought wistfully, *they would talk—properly talk.*

Talk of when their wedding would be, and where they would live, and how happy they would be. For they would be happy, wouldn't they? It would be glorious to be together for the rest of their lives.

A prickle of guilt interrupted these pleasant thoughts.

As long as the truth of her past could remain hidden.

That was vital, of course—but what was the point in waiting? They had given themselves to each other, Gwen thought with a smile. What was left but their marriage?

'Gwendoline Knox!'

Gwen started. 'What?'

Miss Pike was shaking her head. 'You really are lost in the clouds at the moment, aren't you? I asked how was your visit with your mother and your…gentleman friend? You never did tell me, but I have not forgotten.'

Gwen swallowed. So far she had been able to relate the details of her excursion without lying. Only Rilla knew the truth of her intentions, and even she did not know the awkward reality of her journey.

'It was without incident,' Gwen said quietly, looking to the expectant face of Miss Pike, who now nodded approvingly.

'That is what I like to hear. Take notice, ladies! "Without incident" is a great accomplishment for any wallflower. Next, I would appreciate a little announcement, Miss Knox…you know the sort I mean. After all, you know whose home we are visiting today…'

Cringing inwardly at this pointed reference to a wallflower's inability to navigate social situations without embarrassing herself, and still utterly at a loss as to where they were going, Gwen held her tongue rather than add to the Pike's irritation.

Thirty minutes did not feel adequate to prepare herself for returning once more to London—to the place where she had danced with Percy, had been kissed by him for the first time.

But this would be different, wouldn't it?

Gwen tried to convince herself of that as she and the other wallflowers gathered outside the Academy, taking turns to step into the carriages waiting to take them to Town.

As it happened, the first carriage was full, so she stepped towards the second, where Rilla stood waiting.

'There you are, Gwen,' she said.

'How did you know?'

Rilla snorted. 'You think I cannot hear someone coming? I often don't know who they are until they speak, but Miss Pike said you'd be in my carriage. Here, help me up.'

It was a relief to be settled in the carriage with Rilla and no questioning Miss Pike or Sylvia, Gwen thought ruefully.

With a sudden jerk, the carriage moved forward.

'Well, then—are you ready to talk?' asked Rilla.

Gwen swallowed. 'I don't know what you mean...'

Rilla snorted. 'Wallflowers usually hide in their bedchambers before this sort of thing, but I think you need someone to talk to. Something's changed, hasn't it?'

Gwen flushed at the very idea of someone as innocent as Rilla knowing that she had lost her own innocence. Why, it was wild indeed just to have done it—but for it to be *known*!

'Look,' said Rilla quietly as the carriage rattled on, 'I am blind. And that does not mean I become a savant in the other senses—that is just a story told to children. But

I do have other senses, and, Gwen, I smelt the Duke's cigars on you the day after he was soaked by Sylvia's jest. I am not mistaken, am I?'

It had been delicately done, but that did not mean Gwen was not mortified. Rilla had smelt Percy's cigars on her... Well, of course she had—he had been pressed up against her! Even now she could remember his heady scent.

'And you did not come downstairs to the card party after you showed the Duke upstairs,' Rilla continued in a low voice—so low that Gwen could only just hear her. 'The following morning you said you'd had a headache, and no one questioned you, but...'

Her voice trailed away delicately, and Gwen's heart thumped so painfully it echoed in her ears.

'You...you won't tell anyone?' she managed. 'Please, Rilla—'

'I will not betray you, I promise—'tis not my secret to tell,' said the blind woman with a smile. 'And I do not believe anyone else has noticed. At least, they have said nothing to me, and I am sure if Sylvia even suspected it would be all she could speak of.'

Gwen laughed weakly. Yes, that was a fair comment. If Sylvia had any inkling that the newest arrival at the Wallflower Academy was now no longer an innocent it would be her primary—perhaps only—topic of conversation.

Streets were starting to appear through the carriage windows, and the clouds of the wintry day were heavy in the sky.

'The question is, what are you going to do about it?'

'Do about it?' repeated Gwen. The idea of *her* doing anything, when Percy was a duke... 'I... I don't know.'

What was a wallflower—a murderess wallflower, no less—supposed to do after such an encounter? When they had shared their mutual love not only in words but in ecstasy?

The carriage was drawing to a stop. They were here, and that meant she might only be a few minutes away from seeing—

'Wallflowers!'

Gwen winced as Miss Pike's cry echoed up the street. Surely it was bad enough that they had been brought here under the inauspicious description of a wallflower. Did Miss Pike really have to shout out such a moniker right in front of the row of impressive townhouses they had halted by?

'Well, I suppose it's time…' murmured Rilla.

The carriage door was opened by the driver, and Gwen helped Rilla out. The other wallflowers had collected by the front door, nervously standing close to each other. She could see the fear on their faces.

Another day…another set of forced encounters with eligible gentlemen.

Another expectation of gaining a proposal.

Gwen's heart pounded painfully in her chest.

Another hope of seeing Percy.

'Here we go again,' said Sylvia with a dry laugh, stepping over to them. 'Will we be seeing your duke, Gwen?'

'He is not my duke,' Gwen said, with the strange sensation that she had said that phrase too many times.

It was not as though she did not want him to be her duke.

She did. Desperately.

But it was all so complicated, and she'd had no word from Percy as to what they would do next.

Gwen squared her shoulders. 'Let us see what type of gentlemen Miss Pike has managed to accumulate for us.'

Sylvia laughed as Miss Pike led the wallflowers towards the door and rang the bell. 'If there *are* any gentlemen.'

Rilla frowned. 'What do you mean?'

'Well, did you notice Miss Pike used her words very carefully?' Sylvia said as they walked forward, entering an impressive hall. A chandelier tinkled above them as the door was shut. '"Aristocracy", not gentlemen. We could be about to attend a gathering of ladies, not men.'

It appeared Sylvia's suspicions were well founded.

When they were ushered into a drawing room there were elegant piles of cakes and sweets on platters around the room, along with steaming teapots and many cups.

There was also a plethora of ladies.

'Hmm…' said Sylvia knowingly, glancing at Rilla and Gwen.

Gwen's shoulders slumped. From what she could see there were a number of older women seated around the room, their conversation halting, clearly talking about the wallflowers as they entered.

But no gentlemen.

More importantly, no Percy.

He was nowhere to be seen and Gwen's heart sank.

Well, she would merely have to enjoy this opportunity to escape the Academy—and the room where they stood was certainly elegant and refined. The latest in printed paper adorned the walls—a delicate blue with a flower motif. A console table made of marble hosted several teapots, cups and saucers, and the rug by the fire looked to be antique, from what Gwen could make out.

Yes, here were all the trappings of respectability and wealth.

So, whose home were they in?

'There's our hostess,' Miss Pike hissed, her cheeks slightly flushed and her hands waving in the general direction of at least four finely dressed ladies. 'Gwen will introduce you, I am sure. Won't you, Gwen? Go and thank her, ladies, for she is doing you an eminent service by—No, Sylvia, absolutely not!'

Miss Pike strode off to pull Sylvia away from the window, where she was waving at the passers-by, before clarifying who precisely it was who had invited them. Gwen was mystified. Why on earth would *she* be able to introduce their hostess to the wallflowers? She knew no one in London.

Besides, every moment was pointless if Percy was not in it with her.

Would this feeling ever pass? she wondered as she took up a position by another of the large windows overlooking the bustling street. Or would it fade over time as they became more accustomed to each other?

As we live happily together, Gwen thought with a brief smile, *how will that happiness change?*

The door opened and she turned eagerly towards it—but a gentleman she did not recognise, with large teeth and a haughty laugh, entered. After two successive entrances by gentlemen, she was still disappointed.

It appeared the Duke of Knaresby would not be attending this particular gathering.

It was only when she had reconciled herself to the fact that he would not be attending, and she would simply have to learn to be patient, that Gwen was finally rewarded.

'Ah, Knaresby!' The large-toothed gentleman strode forward to clap Percy's shoulder as he came in and Gwen's heart leapt. 'Never expected to receive an invitation from your mother. What an honour!'

Curiosity overcome her shyness, and Gwen peered across the room at the woman who would soon be her mother-in-law.

Impressive. That was the only word Gwen could think of when looking at the woman who stood beside Percy wearing a conceited expression. She was dressed in the most fabulous gown, with more ruffles and delicate embroidery than Gwen had ever seen on a single skirt. There was a string of pearls around her neck, and she looked around the room as if she was rather displeased.

'Yes, I should think it *is* an honour,' said Lady Devereux imperiously. 'But then I am always doing what I can for the unfortunate. Inviting these poor wallflowers to Mayfair House is nothing at all. Percy, bring me some tea.'

No one appeared astonished at the lady of the house ordering her son about, rather than calling a footman. Perhaps that was just how it was with nobility.

Delight tempered with astonishment curled at the edges of Gwen's heart as she watched the man she loved step across the room to pour his mother some tea.

Mayfair House…this was Lady Devereux's home? Oh, now there could be no mistaking it. This tea party was a kindness for her, surely! Percy must have told her, quietly, and the two of them had cooked up this excuse to meet her.

Gwen's stomach lurched at the very idea.

He was here.

With his mother, admittedly, which Gwen had not foreseen.

Miss Pike had surely not mentioned it was Lady Devereux who had invited them for afternoon tea—but that was no matter…not now.

It would certainly be a discomforting sort of encounter, this first time—and in public too. And she had not prepared herself emotionally for meeting the mother of the man she loved—but still… It was a start.

After all, Percy had had ample time to acquaint his mother with the truth of their affection.

Although, Gwen thought hastily, *not perhaps the whole truth.*

Just enough for Lady Devereux to know she would soon be acquiring a daughter-in-law.

And that meant eventually Percy would have to meet her own mother.

The thought caused a shudder to rush through Gwen, which she forced aside. She would not enjoy that.

Perhaps Percy was uncomfortable—perhaps that explained why he had not looked over at her, or taken the chance to introduce them immediately.

Gwen took a deep breath, smoothed her skirts, and tried to ready herself for what was to come.

Her first meeting with Lady Devereux.

All she could hope was that it would go well.

It was about as bad as Percy could imagine—and he had imagined some rather awful scenarios. But this was the worst, and it was all his doing. His dishonesty. His idiocy.

He had not even mentioned Gwen by name to his mother, nor referred to her in any way.

This whole afternoon was a mistake—and he had been unable to convince his mother to call it off when she had first revealed what she had done not an hour ago.

'But you cannot! Mother, you must send a messenger to the Wallflower Academy immediately and rescind the invitation,' Percy had argued vehemently.

His mother had only raised an eyebrow. 'What a thing to say, my boy. Rescind my invitation? I have never done such a thing in my life and see no reason to start now.'

Now Percy swallowed, his heart thumping, as he saw the wallflowers in his mother's drawing room. This was a mistake—and now there was no opportunity to stop Gwen as she meandered her way towards them.

If Gwen was about to do what he thought she was—introduce herself to his mother, on the assumption that the introduction would be welcome—everything would fall apart.

Tension crept across his neck, and Percy's heart pounded painfully in his chest, but nothing could stir him to move. His mother sat on the sofa beside Lady Windsor, and just as Gwen reached them Percy spoke, words he could not hold back spilling out of his mouth.

'Are you quite comfortable, Mother?'

Lady Devereux looked up. 'Comfortable? Well, as comfortable as I could hope to be, I suppose, surrounded by such people.'

The tension around his neck increased. Percy could almost feel the indignation rising in Gwen, but could neither acknowledge her nor comfort her.

This had to go well—but how could it be anything but a disaster?

'Indeed, I reconsidered whether this was something I wished to do. After all, the parks in London are teeming with the very best of people,' Lady Devereux continued, even as Percy winced at her disdain for those around her. 'But then, you are a duke now, and must do your best for the unfortunate.'

Out of the corner of his eye Percy saw Sylvia bristle at those words. He stepped to the right, to prevent his mother from seeing the ire she was creating in the wallflowers of the Academy, but unfortunately that took him further away from Gwen. From the one person in the room who could give him any sense of peace. If only they could be alone…

'All these unwanted daughters,' his mother said loudly, taking a sip of tea.

'Mother,' said Percy hastily, trying not to look at Gwen. 'Really!'

'Do not attempt to say they are otherwise, Knaresby. It does you no benefit to pretend they are other than what they are,' said his mother impressively. She nudged her companion on the sofa. 'Some poor gentlemen will eventually be trapped by them, I suppose…'

If only the ground would swallow him up here and now, thought Percy desperately, preferably taking Gwen with him—or, better, if only it would swallow up his mother!

The room was starting to quieten as people listened to the harsh words his mother was saying, and Percy tried to laugh loudly as a way to distract them. That was the trouble with hosting an afternoon tea; people were wont to actually pay heed to your words.

If she could just stop there, he thought frantically, glancing at Gwen and seeing the rising anger he knew dwelled within her. *If his mother could just hold her impertinent opinions—*

'What did you say, Your Ladyship ?' asked Miss Sylvia Bryant sweetly, stepping around Percy despite his best efforts to get in her way. 'I am sorry, Your Ladyship, did you say we are here to entrap gentlemen? We came on *your* invitation.'

Now everyone in the room was listening. Percy felt the pressure of their gazes, and the discomfort of his stomach stirred as he tried not to notice the whispers of the gentlemen.

This was precisely what he had not wished for.

'I am sure that is not what you meant, Mother, is it?' Percy said pointedly, conscious that his mother had not replied. 'There are many ladies of quality here, and—'

Percy was not sure how, but his mother managed to cut him off with a sniff.

'Well,' she said coldly. 'I am not so sure, my dear. This is an occasion for charity, not matchmaking. I doubt very much that a wallflower could entrap a duke, even if she wished to. A wallflower is not an appropriate wife for a duke, and I should not have to be the one to tell you that.'

A movement just out of the corner of his eye made Percy turn and he saw that Gwen had taken a step back, as though retreat was the only option when facing such an onslaught.

Perhaps she's right, Percy thought wildly. Perhaps he and Gwen should just leave, abandon his mother to her terrible opinions and—and run away together!

But he did not move. Despite knowing what his mother had said was rude, arrogant and hurtful, he said nothing. James would have agreed with his mother, likely as not, and the idea of forming a contrary opinion to his brother was painful in a way Percy had not expected.

Lips clamped shut, mouth dry, heart pounding, he found he could not contradict his mother in public. Not in her own home. Could not bring shame upon her when all she had done ever since he had ascended to his title was attempt to calm the rumours about his brother.

'Wallflowers,' Lady Devereux said then, 'can be very pretty things—and a few are, I see. But they are decoration, Knaresby. One plants wallflowers for a season, and then one grows tired of them and they are replaced. They are not what one has a garden *for*. They are not roses.'

Percy's pulse was ringing in his ears, and his gaze was pulled inexorably to the one person he did not wish to hear such things: Gwen.

She was pale—far paler than he had ever seen her. Her eyes were wide, flickering between him and his mother as though she was expecting him to do something.

Yes, do something, Percy's mind craved, and yet he stood motionless.

Perhaps this was his punishment. If he had just been brave enough to speak to his mother before the wallflowers had arrived, at any point in the last few days, he would not be suffering the agony of bringing Gwen this hurt.

But he had not spoken to her. Years of obedience… years of following James and never having to make a stand against his mother… Only now did he realise what that had bred into him.

Inaction.

Well, no longer.

Percy swallowed. No. He would not allow it. 'Mother, I must say—'

'Lady Devereux, these cakes are delicious,' Miss Pike said hastily, rushing over to their hostess, cheeks crimson. 'Your cook must tell mine precisely how the delicate sponge is able to—'

Percy could wait no longer. His mother's attention was diverted, if only for a moment, and this was his best and perhaps only chance to speak to Gwen. He took her hand, pulled her away. Ignoring Sylvia's gasp and questioning look, he opened the nearest door, stepped through it, and took Gwen with him.

It was the dining room.

Percy shut the door heavily and did what he had wanted to do the moment he had seen Gwen by the window. Cupping her face with his hands, he kissed her desperately, as though everything could be wiped away as long as they were together. As long as their love was at the centre.

But the kiss did not last long.

Gwen pushed him away violently, cheeks now scarlet. 'How can you kiss me?' Gwen hissed, even as murmurs of the conversation in the next room flowed under the door. 'How can you kiss me after permitting your mother to… to speak about me like that?'

Percy shrugged helplessly, his hand rubbing absentmindedly at where she had shoved him. Quite forcefully, as it happened.

Respect, honour, love, affection… They were at war within him. He could not respect and honour his mother while also loving Gwen.

She waited for him to say something, a quizzical eyebrow raised, and then her expression changed. Her fury hardened into something more akin to coldness.

'I am wanted back in the drawing room, I am sure,' she said icily as she strode past.

'You are wanted here!' Percy said desperately.

How could he make her see how impossible this was? Make her understand that it was difficult, and would take time. Time he knew he didn't deserve, but so very desperately hoped she would give him.

Gwen examined his face for a moment, then shook her head. 'I am not so sure. After all the things you said…after what we shared… I am wanted, you say? I am accustomed to being the least likely to win your true affections, Percy. Be sure, next time I see you. Be sure of what you want. I would hate for that meeting to be our last.'

The door snapped shut.

Percy leaned against the wall, his chest tight, as uninvited emotions swirled within him. This didn't feel like winning the heart of his future wife…

Chapter Sixteen

'*Wallflowers can be very pretty things, and a few are, I see. But they are decoration, Knaresby. One plants wallflowers for a season, and then one grows tired of them and they are replaced. They are not what one has a garden* for. *They are not roses.*'

No matter what she did, Gwen could not prevent Lady Devereux's cruel words ringing in her ears.

Over and over again, even as the days slipped by, the words would not leave her alone. They were relentless, appearing in her dreams, preventing her from rest and paining her heart as she saw the completely insurmountable pressure that was on their love.

She cleared her throat, as though that would clear the painful remembrances from her mind, but it was no use. They plagued her.

It was as if the library echoed with the sound, then the book-lined walls absorbed the noise and left Gwen once again in silence.

Silence and solitude. That was what she craved.

Ever since the afternoon tea party Gwen had attracted the great ire of Miss Pike—for her impertinence and her stubbornness.

'You have refused to attend even one of my evening parties for five days now!' Miss Pike had snapped at dinner the evening before. 'Really! It is most unbecoming of you to be so rebellious, Miss Knox. I never would have expected this from a wallflower! I should write to your mother!'

Gwen had clenched her jaw, tightened her grip on her fork, but said nothing.

What could she say?

That she had never been a wallflower to begin with, but had been sent here because her mother knew her to be a murderess?

That she had no intention of ever attending another of the Pike's foolish events, for if there was even one single chance she could see Percy again…

Gwen snapped shut the book in her hands. She was barely taking in a word anyway—and besides, the library had been stocked with severely dull books that Miss Pike evidently thought wallflowers should be interested in.

There was nothing more Gwen needed to learn about how lace was made in the French style, or the way roses needed to be arranged, and everything else was dull, dull, dull.

Standing and meandering down the shelves, Gwen gently brushed the spines of the books with her fingertips. There must be *something* interesting in this library that would capture her attention for at least half an hour. Distract her from the thoughts that were swiftly overpowering her.

Gwen swallowed. It was not enough, it appeared, that Percy's mother had spoken so harshly—words that could have come from her own mother's mouth…a feat remarkable in itself. No. The encounter had also reinforced all her fears about Percy and their love for each other—a love fragmented as soon as it had formed. He wanted her, yes. But not for marriage. For a tup.

She would not see him again.

Gwen knew that deep within herself, and although it pained her to be away from him it was surely a lesser agony than what she would suffer if she was in his presence again.

Whatever they had, it could not be love. Lust, perhaps. Desire, certainly. But nothing that could last, or surmount the growing pressures of parents and prestige. Her past would not permit it.

Gwen sat heavily in an armchair by the bay window and looked listlessly at the gardens. Winter had arrived with a vengeance, and the trees were now almost bare. The wind rattled them, shaking the last few leaves which had managed to cling on.

Her parents had never been particularly demonstrative in their affection for each other. She had hoped, foolishly, for a match of happiness. That would bring her something…*more.*

'This is the library, isn't it?'

Rilla was standing in the doorway, the cane she used to feel her way around the corridors when alone in her right hand.

'It is,' said Gwen with a wry smile.

Even when she wanted to be alone it was impossible. Discovered by a blind woman—who would have thought it?

'Ah, there you are, Gwen,' said Rilla with a laugh as she stepped into the library. 'Any possibility of helping me to the sofa?'

Gwen rose. 'Of course.'

When Rilla was seated, she patted the space beside her. 'Come, join me.'

Gwen hesitated, not immediately accepting the invitation. It was solitude she sought, not company—rather ironic, now she came to think about it, as she would likely be spending the rest of her life alone.

Still, it would be rude not to join Rilla.

Gwen sat slowly on the sofa and folded her hands in her lap. She knew sometimes Rilla merely wished to have the sense of someone's presence around her. It did not necessarily mean she wished to talk about anything, let alone—

'Your duke is by the front door, you know,' Rilla said conversationally.

Gwen sighed heavily, her shoulders slumping as she fell back into the sofa. 'He is not my duke.'

'So you keep saying,' said Rilla. 'I am astonished that you keep protesting, you know. No one believes you.'

Gwen took advantage of the woman's blindness to glare at her.

'Don't give me that look.'

It was impossible not to splutter at Rilla's retort. 'How did you—?'

'You think I need to see to know precisely how you will react?' Rilla laughed. 'I'm blind, not mute. You are, if you will forgive me for saying so, Gwen, a rather predictable character. Now you're going to tell me that you do not want to see him.'

'But I don't want to—'

'Protesting again?' cut in Rilla with a smile.

Gwen frowned, a growing knot of irritation twisting her stomach. 'So if I say I do not want to see him, and that he is not my duke, that merely means I do want to see him because he is?'

Her companion smiled. 'I know… It is rather a contradiction in terms.'

Gwen had never considered the matter much but, if asked, she would have said it would be easier to lie to a blind person than someone with sight. So many clues in one's body language, one's face, would be missed. It did not appear that mattered to Rilla.

'I truly have no wish to see the Duke of Knaresby,' she said finally, as aloofly as she could.

'I do not need to see to know you are lying.'

'You heard what his mother said!' Gwen could not help her outburst, and they were alone in the library. 'You heard her! All that talk about wallflowers trapping men, and being useless, a-and—'

'And a lot of other things we wallflowers have heard our entire lives,' Rilla completed.

'You heard what Lady Devereux said,' Gwen repeated, her heart contracting painfully at the memory.

Rilla was quiet for a moment. 'Yes. But I did not hear her son say it.'

Gwen stared. Although Percy had never said anything of the kind, his silence had cut deeper than any blade.

'He has almost knocked down the front door, you know,' Rilla said quietly. 'The footman says he demands to speak to you. The Pike is furious that you won't see him.'

Gwen almost smiled. Oh, if only that passion, that desire, could have come from *Mister* Percy Devereux—the same man, but without all the challenges that came with a title, without a reputation to maintain, a dead brother to honour, a mother to please. Just a man who could love her. A man without the need to protect his nobility.

'He has brought you a letter. I have it here.'

Startled, Gwen looked around. 'What does it say? I mean—' She had to laugh. 'I do apologise, Rilla.'

But her friend merely smiled. 'Oh, it does not matter—but I too am intrigued by the contents. Will you do me the honour of reading it?'

Gwen tried not to think about what the letter might contain as she took the small envelope from Rilla. It was sealed with a wax dollop formed into the shape of a very elegant K intertwined with a D.

Knaresby. Devereux.

Gwen swallowed. It was disgraceful, receiving a letter from a gentleman to whom one was not formally engaged—but then, their…entanglement, for want of a better word, was far more intimate than many engagements.

It could not be wrong, could it, to receive and read such a letter?

'I don't hear any opening of a letter.'

Gwen sighed and shook her head. 'You are a menace, you know.'

'I know,' said Rilla cheerfully. 'Perennially underestimated—that's me.'

When Gwen had pulled apart the seal and removed the letter from the envelope her first emotion was disappointment. The letter was short—a scrawl, really—clearly written in haste and with terrible penmanship.

Gwen—

You must let me explain.

Let me apologise.

I know not how to convince you that nothing my mother said was...

I am still navigating my responsibilities as a duke, and the expectations placed upon me, but one thing I do know, and that is I have always been forbidden from contradicting either of my parents in public. It is a hard habit to break.

But I am not a child now, I am a man, and I should have defended you. If I could take back her words—

Perhaps that would not be enough.

Meet with me, and I will show you just how devoted I am,

Your humble servant,

Percy

Gwen's throat constricted.

How could she believe a single thing he had written? How could she countenance the idea of meeting with a gentleman who gave her so little respect?

No, Percy had been pained by her parting words when he had written this, but that did not mean he could make any change within his circumstances to make this…this love…this marriage…a possibility.

Pain seared Gwen's heart, but she knew she could do nothing about it. She had given her heart, entirely, to a gentleman who could not keep it.

Percy was a duke.

She was a false wallflower with a secret in her past that would risk not only her reputation in Society but his own. The wife he needed was one with wealth and connections, and she had none.

Worse, her secret…what she had done that fateful night…it was too much. She would ruin not only Percy, but the Knaresby name. There were too many obstacles. Too many walls to breach if they even attempted to seriously consider a future together.

Something strange tugged at her memory and Gwen glanced at the letter again. Although Percy had only written a short amount, almost all of it was taken up with his mother. There was no declaration of love, no formal offer of marriage, no commitment of any kind.

Worse, his request to see her was surely only an attempt to seduce her once again!

Matrimony was a topic never mentioned by either of them, Gwen thought, and wondered, her heart pattering painfully, that she had never noticed before.

How had she permitted herself to be so undone, so vulnerable—giving away her innocence, the most precious thing she could bring into a marriage—without any sort of promise?

Yes, he had spoken of love, Gwen thought wildly, and of wanting, of desire…but not anything more tangible.

She was a fool. A fool easily taken in by a handsome face and a dream of marriage to a man so delicious as the Duke.

'Miss Gwendoline Knox!'

Gwen rose hurriedly from the sofa, heart racing, to see an irate Miss Pike glaring from the doorway.

'Miss Pike…?' she ventured.

What could she have possibly done this time?

'There is a duke at my front door,' said Miss Pike, her eyebrows raised.

Gwen fought the desire to snap that it was not her fault. 'I am aware, Miss Pike.'

'What I am aware of is the fact that you have not seen him!'

Of course, Gwen thought darkly. No one would understand why she was not falling over herself to secure a duke.

'He is damaging my front door!' Miss Pike glared at Gwen. 'I command you to speak to him. He is a *duke*, for goodness' sake!'

'That is no reason why I should speak to him,' Gwen said, as calmly as she could.

Rilla moved her head from side to side, following the sound of the conversation.

But Miss Pike was not finished. Affixing Gwen with a glare, she hissed, 'This is the entire reason you, Miss Knox, were sent to the Wallflower Academy in the first place! To find a husband! Do you not think a duke might be a suitable option?'

Gwen opened her mouth, hesitated, and closed it again.

What could she say? It was true—any lady would consider herself lucky to receive the attentions of a duke—any duke—and Percy was a very likeable gentleman.

If only it was not so complicated.

Gwen was not sure she could even explain it fully to herself.

Still, that left her with but one option.

'Fine,' she said testily, returning Miss Pike's glare with her own. 'I will see him.'

Miss Pike breathed out slowly, as though she had been fighting a great beast, and placed a hand on Rilla's shoulder. 'Come away, Miss Newell.'

Rilla said nothing, but rose and followed Miss Pike's guidance out of the library. Gwen beseeched her with her expression to stay, but there was nothing she could say in Miss Pike's presence and the door was shut behind them.

It did not remain shut for long. Given hardly a minute to compose herself, Gwen gasped as the door slammed open and Percy appeared.

'Gwen,' he said, shutting the door behind him and stepping forward.

Gwen curtsied low. 'Your Grace.'

'Don't give me that. We have never treated each other—'

'Perhaps that was our first mistake,' interrupted Gwen, hating herself for doing so, but knowing it was the only way. She had to show him how impossible this was. 'Perhaps if I had treated you as a duke and you had treated me as a wallflower—'

'I no more think all men should be treated one way than that all wallflowers should either,' Percy said, with a grin that unfortunately made him incredibly handsome. 'Come on, Gwen, you know I am not like that.'

Gwen glared, but said nothing for a moment. This conversation had to be brief, to the point, and above all without tears. If that was possible.

'Your Grace,' she began stiffly, 'when your mother—'

'Forget my mother.'

'You think I can so easily do such a thing?' Gwen snapped, her temper rising. 'You think it is easy for me to brush aside the indignities spoken to me? To all of us?'

It was clear Percy regretted his words. Biting the corner of his lip, he said, 'I have already apologised for her. I regret to tell you I think it unlikely she will offer an apology herself.'

'It is not your mother I am…upset with,' said Gwen, heat whirling in her throat, making it difficult for her to speak. 'It is you.' Gwen's temper flared. 'You should have defended me, Percy—Your Grace—and I don't buy your story of always obeying your mother as a child, because you are not a child, you are a grown man, and your mother was rude!'

'I should have said something…'

Gwen waited for more, her heart desperate, willing him to share something that would convince her, that would put the entire situation in a different light.

But nothing came.

'You are the sort of gentleman who always gets what he wants,' Gwen said with a dry laugh, her bitter temper finally unleashed. 'But in this situation you should have known better. Another duke would have known better—hell, any gentleman would have known better.'

It was as though she had physically slapped him.

Percy's mouth fell open, his eyes went wide with pain, and he took a staggering step back.

'I had not known your temper was so violent,' Percy said quietly.

Gwen blanched. That he would say such a thing—and to her! But then he did not know, did he? No one did. She had been sure, when she came to the Wallflower Academy, that no one knew of her terrible past.

'Dear God,' said Percy, a puzzled expression on his face. 'Why do you react so?'

'Because…' Gwen knew she should not answer, knew she should keep her counsel, but it was too much. Her heart was breaking, and her head hurt, and the tirade she knew she should not let loose came pouring from her lips. 'Because earlier this year I killed a man!'

She clasped her hands over her mouth in horror, but it was too late. The words were said.

Percy stared at her as though unseeing for several seconds in silence, then said, 'Killed a man?'

'I did not mean to, but he…he had stolen from us… my family…'

Gwen knew not from where these words came—knew she should laugh, pretend it was all a jest, make Percy love her again. But he could not love her. He could not love a murderess.

'My family's inn…the Golden Hind. My mother said she saw the body…she knows I did it! He stole from us and then he tried to kiss me, to force me to—I told you before. I fought him off.'

'The Golden Hind?'

Gwen stared. Of all the things she had said, the admissions she had made, the confession that she was a murderess… And Percy was more interested in the location of where her crime had taken place?

She nodded. 'My parents' inn—my mother's now, I suppose—'

'The Golden Hind in Sussex?' Percy said urgently, stepping away.

Gwen nodded again. What did it matter? The deed was done, the man was dead—not because she'd wished to do it, but to protect herself.

'You killed my brother.'

Gwen blinked. She could not have heard those words. She had imagined them.

'You killed James,' said Percy dully. 'Oh, God… To think for all these months we have wondered… He was found outside the Golden Hind inn…dead from a blow to the head. Murdered by a common harlot.'

'It was not like that,' whispered Gwen, feeling stinging tears enter her eyes. 'The man would not pay…and he grabbed me…he tried to kiss me. His hands were all over me—I told you before—and I pushed him. And when he fell—'

'I have heard enough.'

Percy's gaze had slipped away, was now focused on a point just above her shoulder. He straightened his jacket.

'Dear God, I never would have expected… Thank you for this information, Miss Knox, it will finally put my mother's heart at rest. We will not meet again. Good day.'

Chapter Seventeen

Well, he should have guessed he would end up here, Percy thought hazily as he hiccupped for a second time in a row.

Did not all dukes end up this way eventually?

Was it not the one direction every duke took: towards drink?

The glass in his hand was resting upon his stomach as Percy sat lazily in his armchair by the fire. It was seemingly empty. That could not be. He had filled it with brandy but five minutes ago… Was it five minutes ago?

Percy glanced at the grandfather clock in the corner and was astonished to find the clock was moving.

No—no, wait. That was him. He was moving.

After reaching to clutch at the arm of the chair, Percy was struck by the unfortunate realisation that neither himself nor the clock were moving. But his room was.

How many brandies had he had?

Percy reached to the floor, where he had left the brandy bottle, and was surprised at the ease with which he could lift it up to his eyeline.

That was because it was empty.

'Dear God…' Percy groaned into the silence of his study,

and wondered whether his hangover would be as bad as he was already imagining.

Probably. Perhaps worse.

Perhaps then his body would feel as awful as his heart, with that twisting pain, the agony and the heaviness he could not shift from his soul. Perhaps then it would all align and he would feel as appalling as he knew he should.

Rising in a swift movement, then staggering forward, Percy sighed and sat down again. Maybe retrieving another bottle of brandy was not a good idea. Perhaps it was safer to merely sit here, alone, watching the dying embers of the fire disappear, taking the warmth with them.

When so much was wrong with the world, why not sit and experience the simple things?

'Because earlier this year I killed a man!'

Percy's jaw tightened. He should have known. He should have known the minute he had walked into Gwen and received her tirade for knocking her down.

It was all too good to be true.

A wallflower with that sort of temper…the way Gwen's eyes brightened when she became passionate…the way she became more beautiful when aroused…

All too good to be true.

And just when he'd thought he was close to happiness—finding that Gwen desired him just as much as he desired her, and that their mutual attraction sparked into a pleasure that was riveting—his inability to stop his mother talking had led to a revelation he could hardly ignore.

Percy dropped his head into his hands. He had thought the most difficult challenge to surmount would be his mother and Gwen never seeing eye to eye—but to find himself face to face with the woman he loved, who was also his brother's murderess!

It was too much. No one would blame him for finding a little liquid solace.

Not when the woman he wanted to hold on to for dear life...the woman he knew, loved, had bedded...was not just a wallflower with a temper...

No. Gwen was so much more.

Percy would never have been lumbered with this title and all the rules and restrictions that came with it if it had not been for Gwen.

It couldn't be.

There had been times, in the five days since Gwen had made her startling revelation, when Percy had believed himself confused. He must have misheard her, he had tried to convince himself in the dead of night, with sleep eluding him.

What word sounded like murderess?

Countess?

Actress?

No. No, it was no good. Percy knew himself to be a fool, certainly, but not that kind of fool. He had not misheard. He just did not wish to believe, as well he might not, that the woman who was still overtaking his thoughts at every moment was the woman who had taken the life of his brother.

That temper of hers.

That fiery blaze, always just underneath the surface.

Percy laughed bitterly as he sat up and shook his head, looking into the fire. He had seen it—it had been there the whole time. Not always visible, but when one knew where to look—there it was.

He had known she was no wallflower from the very beginning. He should have trusted his instincts. But instead of doing so he had fallen in love. There was this pain in his heart, this twisted devotion, this desire to see her even now...even after knowing she had murdered James...

What else could it be, if not love?

Percy sighed and wondered what the time was. Glancing at the grandfather clock, he saw to his relief that it had stopped its merry dance and was now showing near eleven o'clock.

He had given his heart to a woman who could hate as strongly as she could love, whom he certainly should not love, and he was late.

Percy chuckled in the darkness, the only light the amber flickering of the fire.

Late? He was far more than late. Terminally late.

Lady Rose would surely have put the card tables away by now…disappointed, he was sure, at missing her chance of hooking the Duke of Knaresby.

Well, he was in no mood to be accepting pretty compliments or agreeable charms. Not when he wanted to see the delicately frustrated expression of Gwen, when debating with him about the right way to drive a horse, or laughing at the way Miss Pike attempted to orchestrate impossible matches.

His stomach twisted and he placed a hand upon it. He would never recover. Gwen had a piece of his heart now, even if he did wish to have it back.

'More brandy, I think,' Percy muttered.

The door to his study opened behind him.

'Do not disturb me,' he snapped at whatever servant had entered the room.

'There is no need to speak to me like that,' said Lady Devereux curtly as she stepped around him to glare into the eyes of her son.

Percy swallowed. There was an unwritten rule in the townhouse that he would not enter the parlour without his mother's permission and she would not enter the study without his. Having Mayfair House made that easier. Most of the time his mother stayed there.

It was entirely different at the estate in the country, of course. Percy was still learning his way around the place, more in need of a map than mere directions, and his mother had an entire wing to herself. Apparently the Dower House was insufficient.

But here, in Town, it was important to have different spaces.

It avoided awkward scenarios like this, for example, he thought darkly as he placed his empty glass hastily down beside the empty brandy bottle and hoped his mother would not notice.

'Ah,' he said aloud, as though that would clarify things.

Lady Devereux raised an eyebrow. 'Ah, indeed.'

Well, it was his own fault for being the worse for wear, Percy thought awkwardly as his mother settled herself in a chair opposite him.

'Well, you were greatly missed at Lady Alice's, of course—but then you know that,' said his mother impressively, her gaze still affixed to his own.

Percy swallowed. 'I do.'

'You do,' said Lady Devereux pointedly, 'because you were not there.'

Blast and damn it. He should have known better than to think his absence would go unnoticed. He should have attended for half an hour or so and then slipped away, convincing his mother later that he had merely been in a different room.

As it was…

'What is wrong, then?' asked his mother curtly. 'Come on—out with it.'

Percy knew what the correct answer was, of course. 'Nothing is wrong. I merely felt tired and wished to—'

'Poppycock.'

Percy's eyes widened but his mother said nothing, waiting for him to continue.

As though he could continue.

What was Percy supposed to do? Admit to his own mother that he had fallen in love not merely with a wallflower—a type of person she clearly disliked—and not only with a woman with no title, no connections, nor anything to offer the Knaresby title, but with the murderess of her eldest son?

No. Percy was not a cruel man, and he saw no reason to inflict this pain upon her. Lady Devereux had buried her brother-in-law and her son in the last year. He would not force her to bury all her hopes for his marriage.

''Tis as I say,' Percy said stiffly. 'Nothing.'

Lady Devereux examined him for a moment, and when she spoke again it was in a far softer voice than he had expected. 'I am your mother, you know.'

It was such a different line of attack—one Percy had not been expecting—that he found he had once again dropped his head into his hands.

'Nothing is wrong,' he said, his voice muffled, knowing how ridiculous it was. His mother was no fool.

She snorted. 'I raised you, Percy Devereux, long before you were ever destined to become a duke. I know when you are lying. Now, I demand to know what the problem is. It surely cannot be any worse than my imaginings.'

Percy lifted his face and looked straight into the eyes of his mother. Could she understand? Would he ever be able to make her see just how awful the whole thing was?

Lady Devereux blanched. 'Perhaps it *is* worse than my imaginings.'

'I…' Percy hesitated, but he knew the truth had to come out eventually.

She would need to know why he wanted to shut up the London townhouses and disappear to their country estate. There would be questions. Society would talk…wonder why. At least this way his mother would have answers.

Unless she decided to stay, of course, and face them.

Percy took a deep breath. 'I… I have broken things off with a woman I… I truly cared about. There. Now you know.'

Lady Devereux gasped, a hand moving to her chest. 'A woman you—? Percy Devereux, had you offered marriage to this woman?'

'Yes—No,' corrected Percy quickly, his mind whirling.

How had that never occurred to him before? He had never noticed till now, but in truth he had never mentioned matrimony to Gwen. It had seemed so obvious, so clear that he wished for it. Had she expected him to offer directly? Had she been pained, perhaps, that he had not spoken the words?

He pushed aside his concerns. What did it matter? She'd killed his brother. Gwen did not deserve such loyalty, such consideration.

'But I did not know you were even courting anyone!' Lady Devereux looked most put out. 'There I was, parading ladies before you for your choice, when you had already made it!'

'Well, I have unmade it,' said Percy hastily, and felt a wrench pulling through his heart. 'Which should make you happy.'

His mother was silent for a moment. 'And the young lady in question was…?'

Percy did not know what made him do it. He only knew he must keep the truth of Gwen's identity to himself. What good would it do now, to name her to his mother, when she was not only no longer to be her daughter-in-law, but was confirmed as her son's killer?

Still, it was impossible to withstand the glare his mother was subjecting him to for long, and Percy found himself saying, in some sort of defence, 'One of Miss Pike's ladies.'

Percy waited for the onslaught of criticism. He should never have gone in the first place...should never have talked to those ladies...should never have compromised his affections...

He could well imagine the criticism his mother was about to level at him.

As he'd expected, Lady Devereux groaned. What was unexpected, however, was her words.

'Oh, Percy, I wish you had said something at the time! I must have offended her so deeply—I do hope the breach between you is not on my account!'

Percy blinked. He waited for the words to realign themselves and mean something different, with more clarity, more like what he'd been expecting.

But they did not. And now he came to look more closely Percy realised there was a flush of something that might be shame upon his mother's cheeks.

What on earth was going on?

'Oh, I have deeply regretted my words since that afternoon tea ended,' said his mother, shifting uncomfortably in her seat. 'I wish I had spoken differently, to be sure, and that was even before I knew I could be doing you such harm.'

'What—? Harm?' Percy could not help himself; he was bewildered. 'What do you...? Mother, I have never known you to regret speaking in your life!'

'When you have lived as long as I have, my boy,' said his mother sharply, 'you will find there are more than sufficient ways to embarrass yourself. But I had hoped I was past the worst.'

Percy could not understand it. Perhaps it was the brandy, but he was certain that in living memory his mother had never apologised for anything she had said or done.

And this was to be the first time?

'The truth is, I always feel a little awkward around wallflowers,' his mother said with a heavy sigh. 'They never do or say anything, do they?'

Memories of Gwen flashed before Percy's eyes: Gwen laughing, Gwen challenging him to a game of cards, Gwen teasing him at the dinner table or in the carriage, telling him how much she cared for him…

'Well,' he said dully, 'you do not have to worry on that score any longer. As I said, I have broken things off with her.'

'And why, precisely, is that?'

Percy tried not to laugh, but it was difficult not to. It was not a laugh of joy, but one of desperation. How could his life have descended into this…this pit of despair?

'Because she has no dowry, no title of any kind, no family, no connections and no prestige in Society. She does not fit any of the criteria James would have wanted, and she also,' Percy said quietly, unsure if he was brave enough to speak these words, 'has guilt on her hands.'

Lady Devereux frowned. 'Guilt on her hands?'

Percy nodded.

His dear Gwen...the woman he had given his heart to...

'She is a murderess.'

His mother's mouth fell open. She sat for almost a full minute, then managed, 'I—I beg your pardon?'

Nodding again, Percy found he could say nothing else. There was nothing more to be said. The woman he loved—a woman he could never have imagined doing such a terrible thing—had committed one of the most heinous acts a person could.

She had taken a life—and not just any life. The life of his brother.

'And who, precisely,' asked Lady Devereux icily, 'was the woman in question?'

Percy swallowed. 'Miss Gwendoline Knox.'

He had no real expectation of what his mother would do with this information—which was why it was most alarming when his mother's cheeks turned pale and she rose so hastily that her gloves fell to the floor.

She strode across the room, opened the drinks cabinet, and pulled out a bottle of whisky and a glass.

'Hang on, there,' protested Percy, 'that is my whisky you are—'

'It is for both of us,' interrupted Lady Devereux calmly, returning to her seat and opening the bottle. 'Pass me your glass.'

Percy obeyed wordlessly. His mother drank alcohol, of course, just like any lady with taste. But it was usually a delicate sweet wine in a small glass, on a Sunday evening after supper.

He watched in silence as his mother poured a generous helping of the amber liquid into each of their glasses, drank hers in one, then replenished it.

'Steady on, Mother,' Percy said quietly. 'I do not think there is any need for—'

'You have just told me you've fallen in love with a woman you believe has killed,' said Lady Devereux succinctly. 'Killed, as I suspect you know, your brother. I believe there is every need.'

Percy blinked. He was dreaming. That was it. He had fallen asleep on the sofa after his brandy. Though even he would never have expected his mind to concoct such nonsense.

How on earth did his mother know?

'Oh, Percy, you were always such an innocent,' said his mother heavily.

Percy straightened up on the sofa. 'I would not say I was—'

'I am your mother. I shall decide,' Lady Devereux said smartly. 'And you always did idolise your brother, no matter the… Well, the rather unsavoury habits he developed as he grew up. He was so much older than you, wasn't he? Eleven years… What a difference that can make.'

Percy swallowed. James had been quite a bit older than him, it was true. It had felt like an insurmountable distance when they were boys, but as they had both grown Percy had hoped to spend more time with him.

Then it had been too late.

'James was away so often—at Cambridge, then the Inns of Court as a lawyer,' Percy said hoarsely. 'There was never much time to—'

'He was not at Cambridge,' interrupted Lady Devereux, a painful note in her voice. 'Not for long, anyway. Nor at the Inns of Court, I am afraid. All lies. All untrue.'

Percy stared. It was not possible. 'But James said—'

'He was not a good man, Percy. It pains me to say it, but there it is,' said his mother. 'Sometimes one has to accept that the boy one has borne and raised is not the man one would have hoped he'd be. He got himself into… difficulties.'

Percy leaned forward. He had believed Gwen's revelation to be the greatest shock of his life, but clearly he had been wrong. 'Difficulties?'

A nerve twitched in Lady Devereux's jaw. 'With money. With ladies. He was…disrespectful. He attempted to… Well, the less said about that the better. But I was forced to give quite large sums of money to ladies who had suffered his attentions being pressed just a little too hard.'

Nausea rose in Percy's stomach and mixed with the brandy, making his head spin. No. No, it was not possible, James would never—

'He was not a good man, Percy,' Lady Devereux said again. 'Lord knows, I should have spoken to you about this earlier. His behaviour… I would not call it merely bad. Criminal, perhaps.'

Percy could not speak—he could barely breathe. James had never thought much of obeying the rules, to be sure. And there had been that streak in him… Not cruelty. Not exactly…

'When his body was discovered outside an inn, a gash across his head and a rock—an immovable rock, mark you—stained with his blood,' said Lady Devereux calmly, 'with the daughter of the house hysterical and shouting about how she would not permit him to touch her… Well. That was an end to it.'

Silence fell in the study, although Percy was sure he could hear the pumping of his heart, the twisting of his lungs as they worked hard to keep him alive.

Gwen.

Gwen and James.

He had tried to…

'It was her,' Percy mumbled. 'Gwen. He tried—'

'The important thing is that he did not,' said his mother curtly. 'I looked into the matter, of course. The Knox family—mother and daughter. The daughter was well spoken of, well liked, though very shy and quiet, and withdrawn after the…the incident. I had thought her kept quietly at home…'

'But she was sent to the Wallflower Academy,' said Percy, his eyes wide. 'And that is where she met—'

'You.' Lady Devereux sighed. 'Oh, Percy, I hope I did not

offend her. I wish you had told me of her before you went bumbling in and got the wrong end of the stick.'

Percy stared at his mother.

She could not be serious.

How was this his fault? All he had done was fall in love. Was that his doing? How could he have prevented such a thing from occurring?

'You are a fool,' said his mother.

'Me a fool?' Percy spluttered. 'Why on earth do you say—?'

'I have heard about your Miss Knox, and from a very reputable source,' said his mother with a dry laugh. 'Yes, Miss Pike cannot stop singing her praises. Rather unusual for that woman. I now see why. She obviously believed I knew of your feelings. You would be lucky to have her, Percy.'

He was definitely dreaming. Percy could well remember all the lectures he had endured from his mother about how to find a wife who would further the Knaresby name, a woman who had the elegant breeding of the very best of Society, with money to boot.

'But all the gossip…the newspaper reports and the questions about whether I am a suitable heir to the line,' Percy continued wildly. 'Do you think marrying a woman with nothing to recommend her will help?'

'No, but—'

'You were the one who said I needed to marry for the Knaresby line,' Percy reminded his mother. 'For money and prestige all the things Gwen does not have!'

Lady Devereux fixed him with a beady eye. 'Yes, I did, didn't I? But I married for love…and it brought me nothing but happiness with your father.'

Percy smiled ruefully. His father. Gone these seven and ten years now. His memories of his parents together had faded, yes, but the colour had not gone from them. Neither had the sense of happiness.

'That was different,' he said weakly.

His mother raised an eyebrow. 'You are right. You are a duke now. You have responsibilities and you currently have no heir. I have seen arranged marriages blossom into love, and I have seen arranged marriages wither with no children, for they could barely stand the sight of each other. Answer me this, Percy. How will the Knaresby line continue if you do not marry someone you truly love?'

Chapter Eighteen

Gwen had never looked at the ceiling of the orangery before. It was not the sort of thing one paid a huge amount of attention to, not really, but as she lay there on the cold, calming floor, she was remarkably impressed by the intricacy of the lattice work.

'You are overreacting.'

'I am not overreacting,' said Gwen firmly from the comfort of the floor. If anything, she was underreacting. She had just admitted to murder, to a duke—the duke she had fallen in love with, no less—only to discover that the killed man in question had been his own brother.

What a disaster.

She could not have imagined a more devastating blow to the growing love they had been desperately trying to keep alive—and it was too late now. It was over.

Movement.

Her gaze flickered away from the orangery ceiling to see the face of Sylvia.

'You don't have to lie there, you know,' she pointed out as she looked down.

Gwen shrugged from her prone position on the floor. 'I

don't have to lie anywhere. I don't have to do anything. Nothing changes anything. Nothing matters.'

The dull ache in her heart had settled there the moment Percy had turned his back on her, refusing to hear her explanation—as though it would have made any difference—and disappearing from her life.

After holding him at arm's length for days, for fear of him not being able to love her, and fear of his mother's disapproval, Gwen thought it was poetic justice that it was her own actions which had finally torn them apart.

And she hadn't cried. No matter how much she had attempted it, alone in bed at night, upstairs in her lonely bedchamber, Gwen had not been able to force a single tear to fall.

Perhaps that was why she felt so adrift in the sea of life. What did it matter whether gentlemen came to the Wallflower Academy to view them, take tea with them, dine with them?

None was Percy.

None would ever accept a murderess for a wife.

She was going to be here, at the Wallflower Academy, for the rest of her life.

A foot nudged her—not painfully, but enough for Gwen to wince. 'Ouch!'

'Didn't see you there,' said Rilla placidly, from her seat beside Gwen on the floor. 'And I don't know what you're so upset about.'

Gwen glared, though she knew it had little effect. 'You don't?'

'It is not as though you would ever have been able to convince Lady Devereux of your suitability for her son,' Rilla said plainly, her face expressionless. 'Even if you hadn't revealed whatever it was that made the Duke leave so suddenly.'

A heavy weight settled in Gwen's stomach. 'You are not very comforting, you know.'

'I am doing my best,' countered Rilla. 'You've not given me much to go on.'

Gwen sighed and turned back to look at the ceiling of the orangery. That was certainly true, but nothing any of the wallflowers said would convince her to reveal precisely why Percy, after banging on the front door for nearly an hour and demanding to see her, had spent less than ten minutes with her before storming out.

He had not returned to the Wallflower Academy.

He never would, Gwen was sure.

'Perhaps it was best to break things off,' said Rilla, her voice softer now. 'I mean…before things became too serious.'

A tear welled up in Gwen's eye and slowly trickled into her hair.

Too serious.

Rilla had only guessed at what she and Percy had shared in her bedchamber—and she had clearly underestimated just how intimate they had been.

Too serious.

Gwen could not imagine anything more serious than her feelings for Percy, complicated as they were, tinged with sadness and confusion after his mother's words, affection and desire after their conversations and kisses, pain at his brother's death, frustration and hurt…

'I am doing all I can,' muttered Rilla above her. She was speaking to Sylvia, who was whispering rapidly into her ear. 'No, I will not tell her to buck up!'

Gwen sighed. No matter how hard the other wallflowers tried, she knew it was not possible to restore her spirits.

'Well, does she *look* comforted?' Rilla's voice was irritable. Evidently she was exasperated by the harassment Sylvia was subjecting her to.

'You should have a good cry,' said Sylvia, matter-of-factly, as though she had survived several heartbreaks and lived to tell the tale. 'A good cry will do you the world of good. Then eat cake. All the cake we can find.'

Gwen blinked. It was not the worst idea she had ever heard. Truth be told, of all the wallflowers at the Academy at the moment, Sylvia was the last one she had expected to be so…so understanding.

She looked up at the concerned face of the woman.

Sylvia smiled wryly, her black eyes glittering with what might have been tears. 'You are not the only one of us to have had her heart broken. It happens to all of us eventually.'

Gwen opened her mouth to ask the question. Had she had her own heart broken?

But approaching footsteps, smart and purposeful, halted her tongue. There was only one person who walked like that at the Wallflower Academy.

'Miss Gwendoline Knox,' said Miss Pike sternly, leaning over her wallflower. 'What are you doing?'

Gwen's heart sank. It was not enough that she was to be heartbroken, left here to fester as a wallflower until the end of her days. No, she had to be criticised for it into the bargain.

'When can we expect the pleasure of His Grace's company again?'

Gwen swallowed, tasting bitterness on her tongue. It was all over. It was too cruel, too harsh to make her say it again, but she would. She would say it until the rest of them believed her. Percy was never coming back, and in a way she could not blame him.

She had no siblings, no one to protect or feel protective of. But Percy had adored his brother.

There was no possibility that Percy would find it in his heart to forgive her—none at all. The more she hoped for it, the less likely it would be.

She needed to come to peace with it, Gwen thought as she drew in a deep breath, *and that meant being frank.*

Until she could speak openly about it without tears, without fear of overwhelming emotion, she would be a captive to this pain.

'I am sorry to inform you, Miss Pike,' said Gwen quietly, still lying on the floor—well, she had not been instructed to rise, had she?—'that I have broken things off with the Duke of Knaresby. I do not believe he will be visiting the Academy again. He will wed another.'

The thought cracked her heart in two.

She had not considered it until the words had tripped out of her mouth, but that was likely, wasn't it? Whether he found her here at the Wallflower Academy, or at Almack's, or in someone's dining room, or at a card party, Percy would meet someone else. Another lady he would learn to love, who would not have the ignominious past of having murdered someone he loved.

'B-But…if an invitation was sent to him—'

Gwen sighed. 'Miss Pike, I regret it, but there it is. I do not believe an invitation even from your own hand would be sufficient to entice the Duke of Knaresby back to the Wallflower Academy. That is my opinion, of course, but I share it advisedly.'

Not after revealing my terrible secret, she thought wretchedly, tears threatening and prickling at the corners of her eyes again. Not after she had finally answered the question which had clearly plagued Percy for many a month: who, precisely, had murdered his brother?

If only it had never happened. But Gwen had known, deep down, that the moment would one day come back to haunt her. She could not be let off with merely the fear of being discovered; she would be punished, somehow, and now she knew how.

In a strange way, it was a relief. Now at least she would not have to concern herself with the fear of being found out. The worst had already happened. Percy would be protected from her and her terrible temper. She would never have to fear that one day she would lash out and hurt him, too.

Who knew what scandal might have occurred if she had married him? The Duchess of Knaresby…murdering the heir to the Knaresby line. It would have been terrible.

'Miss Knox, I am ashamed of you!'

Gwen's gaze focused on Miss Pike as her words echoed around the orangery like a death knell. 'A-Ashamed?'

Miss Pike rose to her full height, which from the floor of the orangery was a great deal, and affixed a most malignant stare to the unfortunate wallflower. 'Miss Knox, I cannot prevent myself from berating you, you shameless woman! Losing the affections of a duke…perhaps the best marriage offer you could ever have had!'

Out of the corner of her eye, Gwen noticed that Sylvia had taken Rilla's hand and quietly begun leading her out of the orangery.

Evidently they had no wish to be witnesses to another scene of Gwen's shame. She could not blame them. She did not particularly wish to witness it herself.

'And to think the only reason you are here is because your mother wishes you to find a husband!' continued Miss Pike, eyes blazing. 'What ingratitude to show her…when you were on the brink of securing for yourself the finest husband any wallflower here has ever attained!'

Gwen bristled and sat up to glare directly at Miss Pike. *Well, really!*

Her mother had only wished to be rid of her, and if Miss Pike had ever taken the time to get to know her she would have known that her mother would be mortified if her daughter had married someone as impressive as a duke! Her daughter? Outrank her? It was not to be borne!

Besides, it was scandalous, the way Miss Pike was talking. She spoke of husbands like—like fish! Specimens to be caught—to be mesmerised into falling onto hooks, scooped up out of the water and displayed like prizes!

Percy—if she had been fortunate enough to become his wife—would have been far more! Far more than just a trophy…a prize to crow over with other women!

'You may have lost,' said Miss Pike, lowering her voice but losing none of her intensity, 'the one and only chance you will ever have at happiness.'

And that was it.

Gwen could take no more.

Her heart had been bruised, battered, squeezed beyond belief, then broken. She had tried desperately to cry tears of agony, had railed against the darkness of her life, had wished she had never even been there that night at the Golden Hind.

But this was too far. How dared Miss Pike criticise her for her own heartbreak?

Though her heart had been ripped from her chest, while it was still beating, Gwen was still certain she had done the right thing.

Her confession had spared Percy from a lifetime of misery as her husband—and through it all she loved him. She loved him too much to condemn him to a lifetime of defending himself against a scandal he had never been informed of.

Percy deserved better. That was her gift to him.

'I am very disappointed in you,' said Miss Pike, with feeling.

Gwen rose to her feet. Every inch of her body was humming with rage, a rage she could barely keep inside, but she would do her utmost to make sure she was calm and collected.

She had a certain few things to say to Miss Pike, and as they were alone this was the perfect opportunity.

A small smile crept across Gwen's face. She was going to enjoy this. Her temper rarely had an opportunity to be released, particularly since the incident at the inn, and it had been fizzing inside her for far too long.

She would relish the chance to tell Miss Pike a few home truths.

'The trouble with you, Miss Pike,' Gwen said quietly, 'is that you think there is nothing more important in the world than mere marriage.'

Miss Pike blinked, startled. She had evidently never heard such a measured, yet forceful statement. 'I—I… I beg your pardon?'

'The Wallflower Academy is not the be-all and end-all of the world, Miss Pike,' said Gwen triumphantly, warming to her theme.

Oh, it felt wonderful to finally stand up for herself. She could not recall doing so since first arriving at the Academy, when...when Percy had knocked her down.

Speaking her mind, her true opinions, with no malice but merely honesty, was a balm for her broken heart.

'Yes, I have lost the affection of the Duke of Knaresby, and arguably for good reason,' Gwen said calmly, hoping beyond hope that Miss Pike would not enquire just what that reason was. 'And, yes, I loved him—still love him, in fact, far too much to tie him to me when he is unwilling. But he is not my last chance of happiness!'

Miss Pike's mouth was opening and shutting in the same fashion as her namesake, but no words came out.

Gwen took a step forward. Power crackled in her bones, as though she had been given the gift of speech after being forced to be mute for decades.

It was wonderful to say these things—but it was even more wonderful to mean them.

'One's happiness is not merely tied to a husband. One should not be defined by one's connection to a man! They do not own us—we are not possessions! I admit I would have loved to be Percy's wife,' said Gwen, a little emotion tremoring in her voice. Miss Pike's eyes had widened at her use of the Duke's first name, but Gwen continued onward before the owner of the Wallflower Academy could interrupt her. 'Perhaps I may not marry, and I will find a different kind of happiness then, but there is every chance someone else will want me. They will. Because I am a fine match for—for anyone. Duke or not! I may be the least likely to win a duke, but perhaps a duke is least likely to win me!'

Her last words echoed around the orangery, and Gwen could not help but feel victorious as she spoke them. Because she was only now starting to believe it. Someone, one day, would recognise her worth, her value. See that she was a good person, and could be an excellent wife. For someone.

'I am worth winning,' Gwen said, smiling at Miss Pike. 'And I would never wish you to forget that, Miss Pike.'

'I could not agree more,' came Percy's voice. 'Well said, Gwen.'

Chapter Nineteen

The shock and surprise on Gwen's face was palpable, and Percy regretted for a moment that he had allowed his tongue to be so unguarded.

If only he had thought—had stopped himself from speaking so quickly. If only he had pulled Gwen aside after her conversation—or rather, altercation—with Miss Pike. He could have taken her into a quiet corner, gained a moment to remember his words, and had the pleasure of her presence alone.

But it was too late. The astonishment on both ladies' faces was a picture of surprise that anyone had overheard their rather stern words, and Percy's stomach twisted.

He had not expected Miss Pike to be a potential audience to his declarations...had intended to make them private, not public.

But as his pulse sounded a hasty drum beat in his ears, Percy found he was starting to care less and less about the way people looked at him. As long as Gwen looked at him. Her startled eyes were wide, her pupils fixed on his, and Percy's heart soared to see the connection there. However faint. However much it had almost been destroyed.

A glimmer of hope fractured his heart.

Yes, Gwen was a fine match. Far more than she could possibly understand, and far more than he had understood until yesterday.

Percy was not going to make the same mistake again. He had lost her twice. He was never going to lose her again. Not if he had anything to do with it.

'Gwen…' he said, rather weakly.

It was not what he had intended to say. During the unendingly long ride Percy had prepared a speech so impressive, so wonderful, Gwen would have no choice but to accept him. To believe him. To love him. To understand that his heart had been bruised, but so had hers. And, while he had been dishonest, foolish, idiotic to the extreme, she had done nothing but defend herself against a man who, Percy had to accept, was not what he had thought.

It had not consisted of the single word 'Gwen'.

Miss Pike's eyes were flickering between them. 'I—I… I don't… Y-Your Grace!'

Percy smiled awkwardly. How long would it take him to truly become accustomed to hearing 'Your Grace' instead of Devereux? A lifetime, perhaps.

If he was fortunate, a lifetime with Gwen.

The orangery was starting to chill as he stood there in the doorway to the garden, so Percy stepped inside and closed the door behind him.

There was another doorway, open into the main house, and just beyond it appeared the faces of Miss Sylvia Bryant and Miss Marilla Newell, not to mention every other wallflower in the place. They were all listening carefully.

'My word…' said Sylvia, not attempting to keep her voice down.

Gwen whirled around and coloured. 'Sylvia!'

'Sorry, Gwen,' said Sylvia, with absolutely no hint of

actual remorse on her face. 'We wanted to hear what the Pike—what Miss Pike had to say.'

'Sylvia!'

'Sorry, Miss Pike,' came the uncontrite words.

'Gwen,' said Percy again, wishing beyond anything to be alone with her. This was not exactly the reunion he had expected.

'Ah,' said Rilla with a knowing smile. 'Your duke's back.'

Gwen coloured, her cheeks flushed pink, but she said nothing.

Percy grinned.

So he was her duke, was he?

Well, if fortune was with him, by the time he finished this conversation with Gwen he would be.

Though it could all go so wrong, even now.

Percy clenched his jaw. He must make it work. He was not sure how he would be able to go through life without her.

'Good,' said Rilla with apparent relish. 'Is he here to make an honest woman of you?'

'Rilla!'

Percy took a hesitant half-step back, almost against his will.

Now, that was unexpected.

Gwen had told the wallflowers, then, precisely what they had shared together—*well, hopefully not precisely.*

It was a disconcerting thought.

Making sure not to catch anyone's eye at all, Percy swallowed, and discovered to his surprise that he did not care.

Let them know.

Let the world know.

He had nothing to hide except the fact that he had been such a fool. Before knowing that Gwen had been in any way mixed up with James's death, Percy had been foolish enough to permit his mother to sow seeds of doubt in

Gwen's heart—seeds which should never been permitted to take root.

But he was here to change that. He needed her. More than Society and reason should dictate.

And, seeing her here, Percy knew just how deeply he cared.

Gwen did not belong in the Wallflower Academy, being berated by Miss Pike for being true to her own heart. She was no wallflower—not really. She had been forced to be here…forced into silence for an accident that had not been her fault…

Percy's stomach clenched. A dark deed had been committed that night, but it had not been by Gwen's hand.

'Gwen…' he said softly.

As though she had been waiting for his very breath, Gwen turned to him, eyes wide and brimming with tears, though he could not tell whether it was because he was here or because he had stayed away.

Oh, to think he had risked not having Gwen in his life. It was intolerable. He would regret these few days he had been without her for the rest of his life.

'Percy…' Gwen whispered, a single tear trickling down her cheek.

Without a word, without invitation, Percy stepped forward and brushed away that tear, cupping her cheek and lifting her chin.

Oh, when she looked at him… He could have melted right there and then.

There was something about the woman he loved… something more important than he was, than the promise he had made.

His life was only complete with her. His body craved hers, yes, but it was his heart, his very soul, that demanded she be his. He could not be without her—would not permit anyone to separate them.

There was only one person who could make him miserable now, and that was Gwen herself.

If she was still resolutely against him...

Gwen was stammering. 'B-But you cannot be here—Wh-What are you doing here?'

He glanced around them. Miss Pike looked triumphant, as though she had somehow managed to orchestrate the entire thing, Sylvia was gawping, mouth open, and Rilla had inched closer, in the clear hope of hearing more.

They could not stay here.

There were things he had to say to Gwen Knox, Percy thought darkly. *Things not for the hearing of the general public.*

'Come on,' he said, offering his hand with a twist of a smile.

Without hesitation Gwen took it, and Percy's heart soared.

She would not be so trusting, would she, he thought wildly as he pulled her out of the orangery and into the garden, *if she had entirely decided against him?*

After several minutes of striding through the freezing garden, with Percy feeling Gwen's hand in his but refusing the instinct to look at her, knowing he would do nothing but kiss her if he succumbed to that temptation, he finally found somewhere he was certain they could speak without being overheard.

Though he would not put it past Sylvia or a few of the other wallflowers to creep out into the garden and attempt to overhear them, Percy thought with a wry smile.

He could hardly blame them.

'Gwen,' he said quietly.

Gwen pulled her hand away as they stopped in the rose garden. Most of the roses were over now; only the rose

Gwen had admired so much the last time they'd been there still had a flower remaining.

'Percy,' she said, just as quietly. 'I mean, Your Grace.'

Percy waved it aside. 'Oh, Gwen, do you not think we are far beyond that?'

A rueful smile crept across Gwen's face as she stared at the lawn. 'I… I thought we were. But then we went further still, and seemed to circle back to civility. And now…'

'Now?' Percy had tried not to speak too eagerly, but he had not succeeded.

Gwen swallowed. 'Now…'

After waiting for a moment Percy became certain she was unable to speak, so took matters into his own hands. It had been by his brother that Gwen had been so injured in the first place, forced to bear the burden of a murderous misunderstanding, and he and his mother had merely compounded the injury.

It was time for him to make amends.

'I am sorry.'

Gwen looked up, her sparkling eyes meeting his. 'Why on earth would you say that? After what I have done—'

'You have done nothing,' interrupted Percy, taking a step towards her, but halting as Gwen took a step back.

She was not ready—not yet.

'Gwen, I assumed the worst in you when you told me of your…your difficulty with my brother. I was wrong. I knew you. I should have known better.'

Gwen appeared overpowered by emotion. A mere nod of her head seemed all she could manage, and Percy knew why. She still believed herself a murderess…someone who had taken a life. And that could no longer continue.

No matter how complicated his emotions towards James were—and he would undoubtedly spend the rest of his life unpicking them—Gwen should not have to live with unnecessary guilt.

Not if he could do anything about it.

Percy swallowed hard before he tried to speak. It was still painful. One did not lose a brother in mysterious circumstances, and then discover one's beloved was mixed up in the sordid detail, without taking time to heal.

'Your mother would not wish you to be here.'

Percy almost laughed at Gwen's words, and saw surprise in her eyes as he said, 'It was actually my mother's idea for me to ride out here at once. But do not mistake me. I would have been here by luncheon regardless of her advice.'

Because he couldn't hide from the truth for ever. No matter his rose-tinted memories, Percy knew Gwen's words had rung true. It had not been easy to accept his brother had not been as he believed. But now, although it had taken time, the path that lay ahead of him was clear.

It went to Gwen.

'But—but I do not understand,' said Gwen, a crease across her forehead. 'Percy, you should not be here!'

'I could not stay away!'

The words echoed around the garden. Percy had not intended to speak so loudly, so vigorously, but it was too late. He simply had to speak. Had to show her what he felt.

'Gwen, do you think I could live life without you?'

Percy stepped forward and this time Gwen did not step away.

'Life without you…painful and lonely…with the greatest absence of my heart dragging me down to misery? You think I could live like that?'

'But I am no good for you!' Gwen's voice was taut with emotion, pain etched across her face. 'No good for you at all! Do you not think marrying your brother's murderess would be a mistake? My mother has made it perfectly plain—'

Percy took a shuddering breath and tried to collect his wits. She was in pain, and so was he, but together could they be healed. He was sure of it.

The question was, how could he convince her?

Percy turned away, desperately trying to think, and then turned back to the woman he loved. 'I assumed the worst of you, and that was wrong.'

'I am rather good at assuming the worst of myself,' admitted Gwen with a dry laugh. 'But…oh, Percy…do you think I would permit you to bind yourself to me? In every possible way, I am the very last person you should be considering as a wife!'

'No!' said Percy, stepping towards her, panic filling his heart. He would not let her escape him again—he had to be with her. 'No, Gwen, you don't understand—'

'I think you are the one who does not understand!' Gwen said, her voice sharp. 'You say you wish to spend your life with me, but I would bring shame upon you, upon your family, even if we…even if you offered me…'

Percy saw her hesitancy, knew it would be painful for her to speak the word which had rested on his heart for so long. 'Marriage?'

A flush darkened her cheeks as a cool wind rushed by. 'You said it—not me.'

'I know I said it,' said Percy with a smile. 'Do you think the word has not been nestled in my heart since the first moment I kissed you?'

Gwen's flush deepened, and it was enough to give Percy hope.

She has not walked away.

She had not cut him off, told him icily that it was impossible and left. She was still here. Gwen was still here, wanting him, wanting this to work.

He would make it work.

Percy stepped forward, only about a foot from her, and Gwen did not retreat. 'You…you apologised to me once, and I told you that if I ever gave you a reason to apologise, you would need to mean it.'

Gwen laughed—a coarse laugh with as much joy within it as pain. 'At the Wallflower Academy dinner. I remember.'

'Since that moment you have never given me cause to hear an apology from your lips,' said Percy seriously, his gaze affixed to hers. 'Even…even for my brother.'

A look of agonising pain flashed across Gwen's face and she made to move, but Percy was too quick this time. He grabbed her hands, keeping her close, desperate to make her see.

'Let me go!'

'You were not the cause of James's death,' Percy said quietly.

Gwen ceased her struggling, though tears had once again pierced her eyes. 'You don't know that. You did not even know I was there. It was my family's inn—'

'It appears there are quite a few things about my brother I did not know,' Percy said bitterly.

To think he had revered the man...a blackguard who had attempted to force himself upon unsuspecting young ladies.

If James had been any other man Percy would have wanted him shot. Perhaps it was a good thing he had never known.

'My mother told me… Well, she told me quite a bit about my brother of which I was previously unaware,' Percy revealed, hating that he had to sully his own brother's name, but knowing it was vital for Gwen to hear this. 'You were defending yourself, and it was by sheer chance that James hit his head on a rock. Chance, Gwen. You did not want him dead, and it was chance that killed him, *not you*.'

He spoke the final two words with feeling, seeing relief yet disbelief on Gwen's face.

She had never known.

Of course she hadn't, Percy thought bitterly.

A young woman fighting off a titled gentleman in the dark, a struggle, a fall, cries of murder, and she would have been bundled off, away from it all, to the Wallflower Academy, without any explanation.

She was due that explanation now.

'It…it was not my fault?' Gwen whispered.

Percy shook his head. No words were necessary now. He could see that the truth was starting to wipe away some of the pain, the confusion. Gwen's shoulders slackened, all the strength of her hands disappeared and she stood there, as if in shock, as though it had just happened.

'My mother…' Gwen swallowed. 'My mother said I had killed him. That I was a murderess—no one would ever want me.'

Repressing the desire to call the wrath of the heavens down upon Gwen's mother, Percy pulled her close into his welcoming arms.

'Just because your mother thought you least likely to win a man's heart,' he said gently, 'it does not mean you have not done so. Gwen, you are someone who is worthy of love. Worthy of protection. Worthy of a life without scandal.'

Gwen laughed, wiping her eyes. 'I am not so sure…' Then her eyes widened, as though she was surprised at something. 'Did—did you say your mother sent you here? But you would come regardless?'

Percy nodded. Joy was starting to creep into his heart—his bruised and rather battered heart. But it was still whole, and still hers, nonetheless.

He knew what he had to do. It was a surprise it had taken him this long.

Still holding Gwen's hands, Percy lowered himself onto one knee.

'Percy…' said Gwen warningly, an eyebrow raised. 'What are you doing?'

Percy grinned. Everything was going to be perfect. They were even in a rose garden—albeit one that had died away for the winter. He could not have wished for a better moment to propose matrimony to the woman he wanted so much.

'I may have been the one to knock you down when we first met,' Percy said seriously, looking up into Gwen's wondrous face, 'but I am the one who has been bowled over again and again by—by your beauty and your brilliance… Oh, Gwen. All I want is for you to be my wife.'

For a heart-stopping moment, one which Percy certainly did not enjoy, he was not entirely sure what Gwen was going to say. She looked hesitant, passionate emotions flickering across her face, as if each of them was attempting to overwhelm her.

Then she was on her own knees—Gwen, his Gwen—in his arms, her lips on his own, and she was kissing him, clinging to him as though she would never let go.

'Yes,' Gwen murmured, her kisses intertwined with her words. 'Yes, Percy. I will marry you. Yes, with all my heart.'

Percy's arms wrapped around her, pulling her closer.

Least likely to win a duke—that was what she had said. Well, she'd won him, and his heart—though, in truth, he rather thought he was the true victor.

Epilogue

The sunlight that flickered through the large bay window could not be real.

She must be dreaming—must have been dreaming for a long time. Weeks, in fact.

For it could not be her wedding day.

Could it?

The day of her wedding to Percy Devereux, Duke of Knaresby.

A slow smile spread across Gwen's face as she examined her reflection carefully in the tall, full-length looking glass Miss Pike had deigned to have moved into her bedchamber just the day before.

A rather startled and disbelieving woman looked back. She had Gwen's eyes, Gwen's dark hair… Gwen's face, in fact. But it could not be her.

She had never seen herself wearing a gown so elegant. It was of a periwinkle-blue satin, with scalloped edging around the hem, and little embroidered forget-me-nots within the bodice. It was a gown she could never have dreamed of purchasing in all her life.

A tutting sound came from behind her, and Gwen turned with a smile. 'Well?'

Sylvia sighed. 'It is a beautiful gown,'

Gwen glowed. Why shouldn't she, on this day when she was allowed to be the happiest person in the world?

Today she would become Percy's wife. After wanting him so much, and fearing that such a want was wrong… after waiting weeks and weeks, for ever…the day was finally here.

Her wedding day.

'The embroidery is delicately done,' said Rilla quietly. She was holding a matching ribbon in her hand, rubbing her fingers against it slowly. 'I do not believe I have ever felt such small stitching.'

'And the Dowager Duchess purchased it for you herself?' Sylvia said, in amazement.

'Lady Devereux,' corrected Gwen quickly. 'Yes. She said it was both something new and blue.'

Her stomach twisted at those words. She had not yet spoken with her future mother-in-law—at least, not properly. Not alone. She had always been accompanied by Miss Pike, by Percy, or by any number of the wallflowers who had agreed to protect her.

But she could not put it off for ever. After such a generous gift, along with the purchase of gowns for her bridesmaids, Gwen knew she could not ignore Lady Devereux for ever.

Even if she might wish to.

'I never thought this day would come,' Gwen admitted shyly, looking back to the looking glass and marvelling at the transformation one single gown had made. 'But it has.'

And after today she would never need to worry about being apart from Percy. They would be spending the rest of their lives with each other.

'I must thank you,' came Rilla's voice from behind her, 'for including us in your day.'

Gwen's heart contracted painfully. There was no bitterness in her friend's words…no envy. Rilla did not blame her for having found happiness—no more than she blamed anyone for having found joy in the arms of another. But it still hurt her. Gwen could see it in the way Rilla was quieter today than she could ever remember. See it in the way she held herself, shoulders slumped, her usually questing fingers slow and unmoving in her lap.

'I am the one who is grateful to you—and to you, Sylvia,' said Gwen with a bright smile, hoping Rilla would hear it in her words. 'I could not have hoped for two more excellent bridesmaids to steady my nerves in the past few weeks.'

Sylvia grinned as she stepped across the room, a plethora of hairpins in her hands. 'Well, I could not agree more—though it's a shame no other wallflower wished to see the spectacle. Stay still!'

Sylvia was attempting to pin Rilla's hair, one pin now in her mouth, but Rilla twisted away.

'Careful, I may end up scalping you!'

'It doesn't matter,' said Rilla with a sigh. 'No one will be looking at me. They'll be looking at Gwen—quite as they should.'

Gwen swallowed.

She was not going to let this conversation overwhelm her.

'They will look at all three of us.'

'I am just glad of the excuse for a new gown,' said Sylvia with a laugh, pins spilling out of her mouth. 'Blast—sorry, Rilla!'

Rilla shrugged as the hairpins fell to the floor. 'And I am grateful too, even in all my dourness. After all, this might be the closest I get to being a bride myself.'

'Nonsense!' Gwen spoke automatically, hating the defeated tone in Rilla's voice, but there was not much she could say to dissuade her.

After all, she might be right. No gentleman who had ever attended one of Miss Pike's invitations had ever shown a mite of interest in Rilla, despite her beauty and witty conversation. They could not see past her blindness—a sad irony.

Sylvia was chuckling as she helped Rilla put on a pair of earbobs. 'You know, sometimes I think this place is packed to the rafters with rebels, not wallflowers.'

Gwen giggled, sitting on the edge of her bed as she watched her. 'What on earth do you mean?'

'Well, look at us,' said Sylvia, straightening and placing her hands on her hips. 'Me, least likely to actually be a wallflower... Rilla, most likely to become Prime Minister, given half the chance—'

'I still haven't ruled it out,' said Rilla with a wicked laugh.

'And you, managing to bag yourself a duke!' Sylvia finished with a laugh.

The three of them giggled—until a voice cut through their merriment.

'Yes,' said a woman's cold voice. 'Yes, she has.'

Gwen turned in horror, knowing even before her gaze reached the doorway precisely who it would be.

There was something about that family, she told herself miserably, *that made them excellent at standing in doorways and overhearing conversations not intended for them to overhear.*

Lady Devereux was standing there, her arms folded.

Sylvia's laughter stopped abruptly, but Rilla's chuckles continued on for a few heart-stopping moments. Gwen wished she could tell her to be quiet, but her mouth seemed to have frozen and she was unable to say a thing.

Oh, this was it.

Never before had she heard of a wedding being cancelled merely an hour before it was supposed to take place, but she had done it now!

She had offended her future mother-in-law, right before her eyes.

'We...we are not laughing any more,' said Rilla, her joy subsiding. 'Why?'

'Because,' said Gwen in a strangled voice, 'Lady Devereux is here.'

There was a moment of silence, then Rilla broke it. 'Ah.'

'We will wait for you downstairs,' said Sylvia hurriedly, rising even as Gwen turned around to beseech her with her eyes to stay—not to abandon her to her fate. 'Come on, Rilla.'

Rilla rose without a word, and Gwen knew that if she was not to be abandoned by them both she would have to speak.

'I am sure Lady Devereux can have nothing to say to me you cannot hear,' Gwen said desperately, looking at Sylvia with wide eyes.

'I would not be so sure,' said Lady Devereux in clipped tones as Sylvia and Rilla passed her.

Gwen swallowed as the door shut behind her two friends, leaving her alone with her future mother-in-law who had once described her as a flower unremarkable compared to a rose.

It would not be a pleasant meeting, but then, it had had to come. She could not avoid her future mother-in-law for ever. Perhaps it was better to have it out now, here, on her own terms. She was in her own bedchamber, at least.

Still, somehow Gwen wished it had been after the wedding, not before. There was a strange sense of foreboding in her stomach telling her that if she was not careful there would not be a wedding at all.

Oh, if only they had not been laughing about her 'bagging' Percy!

'Miss Knox,' said Lady Devereux in clipped tones.

Gwen smiled weakly. All she had to do was get through this conversation without embarrassing herself. How difficult could it be, really?

Lady Devereux stared at her without smiling. 'A pleasant day.'

Gwen waited, sure the older woman would say something else, but no more words seemed forthcoming.

It was down to her, then, to provide the rest of the conversation. Easier said than done.

'Yes. Very pleasant.'

Very pleasant? Were they talking about the weather?

Gwen had laughed at Miss Pike once when she had tried to teach them about small talk, had considered it ridiculous that resorting to talking about the weather would be a reasonable response in a conversation with someone in Society. But now she could see just how desperately those topics of conversation might be needed in discomforting situations.

Speak. She needed to speak—needed to say something… anything! This was her chance, Gwen knew, to say something to her before the wedding and without an audience.

It was not as though they were going to have any other mother in attendance, after all. Gwen could still remember the sickening sensation that had settled in her lungs as she had read the letter from her mother that had come in response to hers about her impending marriage.

She was to marry Percy Devereux, Duke of Knaresby. Gwen had foolishly believed her mother would be happy—

would be pleased that her daughter had managed to find such a wonderful match.

She should not have been so naïve.

What had that paragraph said?

I think it absolutely disgraceful that a daughter of mine should have decided not only to marry above her station, but above the rank of her own mother's husband. You can forget any hopes of us hosting your wedding reception, let Miss Pike do so if you are so ready to take her advice. How dare you show me up? How dare you?

Gwen had burnt the letter. There was no point keeping anything that dripped such hatred.

Lady Devereux cleared her throat. 'So. You are marrying my son.'

Gwen nodded, and felt a little spark of the boldness she had always been told to force down rising within her. 'Yes. And I am glad to be. And grateful.'

Was that too sycophantic? Gwen could hardly tell. But she knew it was important that Percy's mother knew just how much she loved her son—how grateful she was to have him.

After such confusion, after discovering a tangled past which neither of them had known about until it was too late, Gwen was certainly grateful that they had managed to make their way here, to happiness.

Happiness that, Lady Devereux permitting, would last for ever.

'You are grateful?' Lady Devereux raised an eyebrow. 'I am afraid I do not approve.'

Tension bubbled in Gwen's stomach, bitter bile threatening to rise up her throat, but she managed to swallow it. 'Really?'

'Yes, really,' said Lady Devereux calmly. 'I do not know why you are so grateful. 'Tis my son whom I believe is the lucky one.'

It took Gwen a few moments to realise she had not misheard the woman. Percy the lucky one? Percy, fortunate to be marrying her?

There was some mistake, surely. Perhaps Percy had informed his mother that Gwen had a large dowry, or a connection to an impressive family—which she certainly did not. It made no sense! Why, after such harsh words only a month ago, was Lady Devereux so taken with her now?

But despite Gwen's silence a slow smile had crept over Lady Devereux's face. 'I did not raise him to be a duke, you know. My brother-in-law was married, had two sons… Even when they died it never crossed my mind that Percy would inherit the title. In a way, I think that has made him a better man.'

Gwen swallowed, forced herself to speak. 'I would agree, my lady.'

'And now he can continue to be a better man by marrying someone who is not interested in his title, but in him. In Percy. The man,' said Lady Devereux with a small twinkle in her eye. 'You have endeared yourself to me, Miss Knox, for that. You have won his heart. That wins my loyalty.'

It was all Gwen could do not to sink weakly to her knees onto the floor. Only now did she recognise the tension in her bones for what it was: fear. Fear that Lady Devereux, Percy's mother, the only other important woman in Percy's life, would reject her—as she so nearly had done at that terrible afternoon tea.

'And I believe I owe you an apology.'

Gwen blinked.

Had those words truly come from Lady Devereux's mouth?

The older woman looked uncomfortable, her hands twisting. 'I… I should not have spoken to you so that day, nor the other wallflowers. It was wrong of me. I beg your forgiveness.'

If anyone else had said those words Gwen would have been hard pressed to believe them. No one apologised to a wallflower without significant cause, and Lady Devereux certainly had not been put under pressure by anyone.

Save perhaps Percy, Gwen thought hastily. But even then she could not imagine Lady Devereux would be easily swayed by her son.

But there was a strange look on the woman's face…one that Gwen could not understand.

Regret?

Fear, perhaps?

Lady Devereux walked towards the large bay window, looking out onto the garden. Her eyes were misted, and there was a strange smile on her face.

'I never liked these curtains,' she said quietly. 'But I liked the window. I liked feeling as though I was close to nature…as though, if I wished to, I could escape and disappear out into the wilderness and not return.'

Gwen stared.

No. It could not be—

'I was surprised when Miss Markham sold the place to Miss Pike,' said Lady Devereux with a sigh. 'I had hoped it would close… But there it is.'

She turned to face Gwen, who spluttered, far more rudely than she had intended, 'Y-You were a wallflower here? You cannot have been!'

Lady Devereux raised an eyebrow. 'Why? Do you think

you are the only woman placed here because she is far more trouble than she's worth?'

Gwen laughed, hardly able to believe what she was hearing. It was wild…it was nonsensical…it was…

Believable.

What was it Sylvia had said? Those words she herself had thought numerous times after coming to the Wallflower Academy?

'You know, sometimes I think this place is packed to the rafters with rebels, not wallflowers.'

Gwen swallowed. 'I… I do not know what to say.'

Lady Devereux took a deep breath. 'Quite right too. You'll have plenty of time to think about it later—and then, Your Grace, I hope we will get to know each other better.'

It took a moment for Gwen to realise what Lady Devereux meant, and this time she really did reach out for the side of her bed to sit down upon.

'Your Grace…' she whispered.

Her future mother-in-law chuckled. 'You'll be the Duchess of Knaresby in just under an hour, so you had better get accustomed to it. Here.'

Lady Devereux stepped across the room and pulled from her reticule a box covered in blue velvet. She placed it in Gwen's hands.

'Open it,' she whispered.

Gwen did as she was bade, her head spinning.

Inside the jewellery box was a sapphire tiara.

'You already have your something new and blue,' said Lady Devereux softly. 'I thought you would appreciate something old and borrowed. Blue as well, I suppose. The Devereux sapphires.'

Gwen stared in wonder at the beautiful tiara. It was more fabulous than anything she had ever seen—and only now did her stomach squirm as she wondered, with a jolt, just how many other jewels might be waiting for her in her new life.

Her new married life…as a Devereux.

'Th-Thank you.'

'Oh, you don't need to thank me,' said Lady Devereux with a crisp smile. 'I never had a daughter, and it's high time I spoiled someone. Now… Haven't we got a wedding to go to?'

The day sped by so quickly Gwen could hardly remember it.

A rush of colour, of laughter, of joy. Solemn music and solemn vows, and then smiles all around her.

She saw Miss Pike seated in the front row on her side of the aisle, with a rapturous look at having married off one of her wallflowers so well.

There was a squeeze of her hand. Gwen looked down to see Percy's hand had taken hers, and he smiled as he squeezed it again.

'Ready?' he whispered.

Gwen took a deep breath and nodded. And as they swept down the aisle hand in hand, husband and wife, she could not understand how her heart could withstand such joy, such eager happiness.

She had everything she wanted.

Almost.

'Percy,' Gwen said suddenly, halting in her steps as soon as they'd stepped outside the church. 'We have forgotten something.'

Percy's beaming face was transformed into one full of panic. 'We have?'

Gwen leaned forward and kissed him delicately on the side of the mouth. 'We have forgotten to make any plans for our honeymoon!'

'Oh, you can leave that to me,' he said with a laugh. 'I have some ideas…'

Gwen was not given a chance to ask what they were—his lips had already captured hers, his hands were tight on her waist, and Gwen lost herself to his kiss, to the tantalising, tingling sensation Percy always sparked in her.

'Well, really!'

Gwen and Percy broke apart with wry smiles as Miss Pike's words reached them.

'You have done that before,' Gwen said in a smiling whisper.

Percy grinned as their wedding guests poured out of the church. 'Yes, and I intend to do it again—and again—with increasing frequency.'

'Your Ladyship!' Miss Pike was bustling past them straight to Lady Devereux, with a respectful yet eager look on her face. 'Now you are in a way indebted to the Wallflower Academy. You have your daughter-in-law, and what a fine woman she is. I wonder whether you could see yourself…?'

Percy groaned, and Gwen could not help but laugh. 'It appears your mother is about to be roped into improving the Wallflower Academy! Or at the very least, heaven help us, hosting more afternoon teas…'

Percy sighed and pulled her closer. Gwen's heart was beating so quickly she was certain the whole congregation could hear it. 'Well, perhaps you and she can do an exchange. You can come and live with me, and we can send Mother to the Wallflower Academy.'

He laughed at his jest, but Gwen merely smiled. It was clear Lady Devereux's son had no idea that she herself had once been a wallflower. Fascinating…the secrets one kept from one's family.

'And now, my Duchess?' said Percy with a grin. 'What shall we do now?'

Gwen took a deep breath and felt all the tension and stress and worry—all the things she had believed would hold her back from happiness—fall away.

'Be happy,' she said simply. 'For the rest of our lives.'

'Miss Pike, what an outrage!'

'And try to keep your mother happy,' said Gwen hastily, with a laugh as Percy groaned.

Lady Devereux was staring at Miss Pike in horror.

'Come on. We had better go back to the Academy. The wedding reception will begin soon, and I do not believe it safe to leave Miss Pike and your mother together.'

Percy shook his head with a smile. 'I love you, Gwen—and you have won my affections so utterly I am afraid I am quite in your power.'

Gwen's heart almost burst with joy.

'Good. Just as you should be.'

* * * * *

Least Likely to Win a Duke
is Emily E K Murdoch's debut
for Harlequin Historical!
Look out for the next book in her
The Wallflower Academy miniseries,
coming soon!

COMING NEXT MONTH FROM

All available in print and ebook via Reader Service and online

A DUKE FOR THE PENNILESS WIDOW (Regency)
The Irresistible Dukes • by Christine Merrill

Selina is startled by the attraction she feels for the Duke of Glenmoor, whom she blames for her husband's death! Forced to accept his marriage proposal, can Selina resist surrendering to their passion?

MISS GEORGINA'S MARRIAGE DILEMMA (Victorian)
Rebellious Young Ladies • by Eva Shepherd

Fun-loving Georgina can find joy and pleasure in anything...even her convenient marriage to frosty Adam, Duke of Ravenswood! But can her good nature and their undeniable chemistry penetrate her new husband's walls?

WEDDED TO HIS ENEMY DEBUTANTE (Regency)
by Samantha Hastings

Frederica is the *last* person Samuel, the new Duke of Pelford, wants to marry! But his beautiful nemesis is the only answer to the problems he's inherited.

THE RETURN OF HIS CARIBBEAN HEIRESS (1900s)
by Lydia San Andres

Five years after Leandro Díaz kissed heiress Lucía Troncoso, she's returned... But Leo, hardened by life, holds Lucía—and their attraction—at a distance until danger forces them closer than ever before...

SPINSTER WITH A SCANDALOUS PAST (Regency)
by Sadie King

When Louisa meets the abrasive Sir Isaac Liddell, she's shocked to discover that they have so much in common. But telling him the truth about her past might cost her *everything*!

CONVENIENT VOWS WITH A VIKING (Viking)
by Lucy Morris and Sarah Rodi

Enjoy these two spicy Viking romances! Orla strikes a deal with enslaved Jarl Hakon—she'll buy his freedom *if* the handsome warrior marries her! And Viking Fiske chooses noblewoman Kassia as his bride to save her from an unhappy fate, but her secrets threaten their newfound desire...

YOU CAN FIND MORE INFORMATION ON UPCOMING HARLEQUIN TITLES, FREE EXCERPTS AND MORE AT HARLEQUIN.COM.

HHCNM1223